CHRISTOPI
DEAD MAN'S MUSIC

CHRISTOPHER BUSH was born Charlie Christmas Bush in Norfolk in 1885. His father was a farm labourer and his mother a milliner. In the early years of his childhood he lived with his aunt and uncle in London before returning to Norfolk aged seven, later winning a scholarship to Thetford Grammar School.

As an adult, Bush worked as a schoolmaster for 27 years, pausing only to fight in World War One, until retiring aged 46 in 1931 to be a full-time novelist. His first novel featuring the eccentric Ludovic Travers was published in 1926, and was followed by 62 additional Travers mysteries. These are all to be republished by Dean Street Press.

Christopher Bush fought again in World War Two, and was elected a member of the prestigious Detection Club. He died in 1973.

By Christopher Bush

The Plumley Inheritance
The Perfect Murder Case
Dead Man Twice
Murder at Fenwold
Dancing Death
Dead Man's Music
Cut Throat
The Case of the Unfortunate Village
The Case of the April Fools
The Case of the Three Strange Faces

CHRISTOPHER BUSH

DEAD MAN'S MUSIC

With an introduction
by Curtis Evans

DEAN STREET PRESS

INTRODUCTION

THAT ONCE vast and mighty legion of bright young (and youngish) British crime writers who began publishing their ingenious tales of mystery and imagination during what is known as the Golden Age of detective fiction (traditionally dated from 1920 to 1939) had greatly diminished by the iconoclastic decade of the Sixties, many of these writers having become casualties of time. Of the 38 authors who during the Golden Age had belonged to the Detection Club, a London-based group which included within its ranks many of the finest writers of detective fiction then plying the craft in the United Kingdom, just over a third remained among the living by the second half of the 1960s, while merely seven—Agatha Christie, Anthony Gilbert, Gladys Mitchell, Margery Allingham, John Dickson Carr, Nicholas Blake and Christopher Bush—were still penning crime fiction.

In 1966--a year that saw the sad demise, at the too young age of 62, of Margery Allingham--an executive with the English book publishing firm Macdonald reflected on the continued popularity of the author who today is the least well known among this tiny but accomplished crime writing cohort: Christopher Bush (1885-1973), whose first of his three score and three series detective novels, *The Plumley Inheritance*, had appeared fully four decades earlier, in 1926. "He has a considerable public, a 'steady Bush public,' a public that has endured through many years," the executive boasted of Bush. "He never presents any problem to his publisher, who knows exactly how many copies of a title may be safely printed for the loyal Bush fans; the number is a healthy one too." Yet in 1968, just a couple of years after the Macdonald editor's affirmation of Bush's notable popular duration as a crime writer, the author, now in his 83rd year, bade farewell to mystery fiction with a final detective novel, *The Case of the Prodigal Daughter*, in which, like in Agatha Christie's *Third Girl* (1966), copious references are made, none too favorably, to youthful sex, drugs and rock and roll. Afterwards, outside of the reprinting in the UK in the early 1970s of a scattering of classic Bush titles from the Golden Age, Bush's books, in contrast with those of Christie, Carr, Allingham and Blake, disappeared from mass circulation in both the UK and the US, becoming fervently sought (and ever more unobtainable) treasures by collectors and connoisseurs of classic crime fiction. Now, in one of the signal developments in vintage mystery publishing, Dean Street Press is reprinting 62 of the 63 Christopher Bush detective novels (the lone omission, for now, being the supremely rare *The Plumley Inheritance*, first in the series). These will be published over a period of months, beginning with the release of books 2 to 10 in the series.

Few Golden Age British mystery writers had backgrounds as humble yet simultaneously mysterious, dotted with omissions and evasions, as Christopher Bush, who was born Charlie Christmas Bush on the day of the Nativity in 1885 in the Norfolk village of Great Hockham, to Charles Walter Bush and his second wife, Eva Margaret Long. While the father of Christopher Bush's Detection Club colleague and near exact contemporary Henry Wade (the pseudonym of Henry Lancelot Aubrey-Fletcher) was a baronet who lived in an elegant Georgian mansion and claimed extensive ownership of fertile English fields, Christopher's father resided in a cramped cottage and toiled in fields as a farm laborer, a term that in the late Victorian and Edwardian era, his son lamented many years afterward, "had in it something of contempt....There was something almost of serfdom about it."

Charles Walter Bush was a canny though mercurial individual, his only learning, his son recalled, having been "acquired at the Sunday school." A man of parts, Charles was a tenant farmer of three acres, a thatcher, bricklayer and carpenter (fittingly for the father of a detective novelist, coffins were his specialty), a village radical and a most adept poacher. After a flight from Great Hockham, possibly on account of his poaching activities, Charles, a widower with a baby son whom he had left in the care of his mother, resided in London, where he worked for a firm of spice importers. At a dance in the city, Charles met Christopher's mother, Eva Long, a lovely and sweet-natured young milliner and bonnet maker, sweeping her off her feet with a combination of "good looks and a certain plausibility." After their marriage the couple left London to live in a tiny rented cottage in Great Hockham, where Eva over the next eighteen years gave birth to three sons and five daughters and perforce learned the challenging ways of rural domestic economy.

Decades later an octogenarian Christopher Bush, in his memoir *Winter Harvest: A Norfolk Boyhood* (1967), characterized Great Hockham as a rustic rural redoubt where many of the words that fell from the tongues of the native inhabitants "were those of Shakespeare, Milton and the Authorised Version....Still in general use were words that were standard in Chaucer's time, but had since lost a certain respectability." Christopher amusingly recalled as a young boy telling his mother that a respectable neighbor woman had used profanity, explaining that in his hearing she had told her husband, "George, wipe you that shit off that pig's arse, do you'll datty your trousers," to which his mother had responded that although that particular usage of a four-letter word had not really been *swearing*, he was not to give vent to such language himself.

Great Hockham, which in Christopher Bush's youth had a population of about four hundred souls, was composed of a score or so of cottages, three public houses, a post-office, five shops, a couple of forges and a pair of churches, All Saint's and the Primitive Methodist Chapel, where the Bush family rather vocally worshipped. "The village lived by farming, and most of its men were labourers," Christopher recollected. "Most of the children left school as soon as the law permitted: boys to be absorbed somehow into the land and the girls to go into domestic service." There were three large farms and four smaller ones, and, in something of an anomaly, not one but two squires--the original squire, dubbed "Finch" by Christopher, having let the shooting rights at Little Hockham Hall to one "Green," a wealthy international banker, making the latter man a squire by courtesy. Finch owned most of the local houses and farms, in traditional form receiving rents for them personally on Michaelmas; and when Christopher's father fell out with Green, "a red-faced, pompous, blustering man," over a political election, he lost all of the banker's business, much to his mother's distress. Yet against all odds and adversities, Christopher's life greatly diverged from settled norms in Great Hockham, incidentally producing one of the most distinguished detective novelists from the Golden Age of detective fiction.

Although Christopher Bush was born in Great Hockham, he spent his earliest years in London living with his mother's much older sister, Elizabeth, and her husband, a fur dealer by the name of James Streeter, the couple having no children of their own. Almost certainly of illegitimate birth, Eva had been raised by the Long family from her infancy. She once told her youngest daughter how she recalled the Longs being visited, when she was a child, by a "fine lady in a carriage," whom she believed was her birth mother. Or is it possible that the "fine lady in a carriage" was simply an imaginary figment, like the aristocratic fantasies of Philippa Palfrey in P.D. James's *Innocent Blood* (1980), and that Eva's "sister" Elizabeth was in fact her mother?

The Streeters were a comfortably circumstanced couple at the time they took custody of Christopher. Their household included two maids and a governess for the young boy, whose doting but dutiful "Aunt Lizzie" devoted much of her time to the performance of "good works among the East End poor." When Christopher was seven years old, however, drastically straightened financial circumstances compelled the Streeters to return the boy to his birth parents in Great Hockham.

Fortunately the cause of the education of Christopher, who was not only a capable village cricketer but a precocious reader and scholar, was taken up both by his determined and devoted mother and an idealistic local elementary school headmaster. In his teens Christopher secured a scholarship to Norfolk's Thetford Grammar School, one of England's oldest educational institutions, where Thomas Paine had studied a century-and-a-half earlier. He left Thetford in 1904 to take a position as a junior schoolmaster, missing a chance to go to Cambridge University on yet another scholarship. (Later he proclaimed himself thankful for this turn of events, sardonically speculating that had he received a Cambridge degree he "might have become an exceedingly minor don or something as staid and static and respectable as a publisher.") Christopher would teach English in schools for the next twenty-seven years, retiring at the age of 46 in 1931, after he had established a successful career as a detective novelist.

Christopher's romantic relationships proved far rockier than his career path, not to mention every bit as murky as his mother's familial antecedents. In 1911, when Christopher was teaching in Wood Green School, a co-educational institution in Oxfordshire, he wed county council schoolteacher Ella Maria Pinner, a daughter of a baker neighbor of the Bushes in Great Hockham. The two appear never actually to have lived together, however, and in 1914, when Christopher at the age of 29 headed to war in the 16th (Public Schools) Battalion of the Middlesex Regiment, he falsely claimed in his attestation papers, under penalty of two years' imprisonment with hard labor, to be unmarried.

After four years of service in the Great War, including a year-long stint in Egypt, Christopher returned in 1919 to his position at Wood Green School, where he became involved in another romantic relationship, from which he soon desired to extricate himself. (A photo of the future author, taken at this time in Egypt, shows a rather dashing, thin-mustached man in uniform and is signed "Chris," suggesting that he had dispensed with "Charlie" and taken in its place a diminutive drawn from his middle name.) The next year Winifred Chart, a mathematics teacher at Wood Green, gave birth to a son, whom she named Geoffrey Bush. Christopher was the father of Geoffrey, who later in life became a noted English composer, though for reasons best known to himself Christopher never acknowledged his son. (A letter Geoffrey once sent him was returned unopened.) Winifred claimed that she and Christopher had married but separated, but she refused to speak of her purported spouse forever after and she destroyed all of his letters and other mementos, with the exception of a book of poetry that he had written for her during what she termed their engagement.

Christopher's true mate in life, though with her he had no children, was Florence Marjorie Barclay, the daughter of a draper from Ballymena, Northern Ireland, and, like Ella Pinner and Winifred Chart, a schoolteacher. Christopher and Marjorie likely had become romantically involved by 1929, when Christopher dedicated to her his second detective novel, *The Perfect Murder Case*; and they lived together as man and wife from the 1930s until her death in 1968 (after which, probably not coincidentally, Christopher stopped publishing novels). Christopher returned with Marjorie to the vicinity of Great Hockham when his writing career took flight, purchasing two adjoining cottages and commissioning his father and a stepbrother to build an extension consisting of a kitchen, two bedrooms and a new staircase. (The now sprawling structure, which Christopher called "Home Cottage," is now a bed and breakfast grandiloquently dubbed "Home Hall.") After a falling-out with his father, presumably over the conduct of Christopher's personal life, he and Marjorie in 1932 moved to Beckley, Sussex, where they purchased Horsepen, a lovely Tudor plaster and timber-framed house. In 1953 the couple settled at their final home, The Great House, a centuries-old structure (now a boutique hotel) in Lavenham, Suffolk.

From these three houses Christopher maintained a lucrative and critically esteemed career as a novelist, publishing both detective novels as Christopher Bush and, commencing in 1933 with the acclaimed book *Return* (in the UK, *God and the Rabbit*, 1934), regional novels purposefully drawing on his own life experience, under the pen name Michael Home. (During the 1940s he also published espionage novels under the Michael Home pseudonym.) Although his first detective novel, *The Plumley Inheritance*, made a limited impact, with his second, *The Perfect Murder Case*, Christopher struck gold. The latter novel, a big seller in both the UK and the US, was published in the former country by the prestigious Heinemann, soon to become the publisher of the detective novels of Margery Allingham and Carter Dickson (John Dickson Carr), and in the latter country by the Crime Club imprint of Doubleday, Doran, one of the most important publishers of mystery fiction in the United States.

Over the decade of the 1930s Christopher Bush published, in both the UK and the US as well as other countries around the world, some of the finest detective fiction of the Golden Age, prompting the brilliant Thirties crime fiction reviewer, author and Oxford University Press editor Charles Williams to avow: "Mr. Bush writes of as thoroughly enjoyable murders as any I know." (More recently, mystery genre authority B.A. Pike dubbed these novels by Bush, whom he praised as "one of the most reliable and resourceful of true detective writers", "Golden Age baroque, rendered remarkable by some extraordinary flights of fancy.") In 1937 Christopher Bush became, along with Nicholas Blake, E.C.R. Lorac and Newton Gayle (the writing team of Muna Lee and Maurice West Guinness), one of the final authors initiated into the Detection Club before the outbreak of the Second World War and with it the demise of the Golden Age. Afterward he continued publishing a detective novel or more a year, with his final book in 1968 reaching a total of 63, all of them detailing the investigative adventures of lanky and bespectacled gentleman amateur detective Ludovic Travers. Concurring as I do with the encomia of Charles Williams and B.A. Pike, I will end this introduction by thanking Avril MacArthur for providing invaluable biographical information on her great uncle, and simply wishing fans of classic crime fiction good times as they discover (or rediscover), with this latest splendid series of Dean Street Press classic crime fiction reissues, Christopher Bush's Ludovic Travers detective novels. May a new "Bush public" yet arise!

Curtis Evans

Dead Man's Music (1931)

DEAR SIRS,

Your firm has a reputation for absolute trustworthiness in its handling of affairs, and an implicitly honourable confidence. Will you therefore send me down here a GENTLEMAN; a most reliable, intelligent, cultured man, to see me about certain urgent matters. I want a man of unusual perception, the sort of man who knows that whereas two and two always make four, two elevens are not necessarily twenty-two.

I would particularly like his opinion on some china, and to hear his appreciation of music. He should be sent AT ONCE. I enclose a preliminary payment against expenses.

Yours sincerely,

CLAUDE ROOK

Durangos Limited,
London

BETWEEN 1928 AND 1933, roughly the years when Christopher Bush (1885-1973) established himself as one of the finest writers of British mystery among that brilliant group of authors who were active during the Golden Age of detective fiction, Christopher's young son Geoffrey at his mother's behest "spent five impressionable years as a chorister at Salisbury Cathedral," a signal experience in the boy's young life that inspired him to take up the composition of music. Geoffrey Bush (1920-1998) would go on after the Second World War to become one of the finest British composers of his generation.

The story of Christopher Bush and his son Geoffrey, both of them prodigiously talented men, makes a powerful case for the theory of heritability. The father and son never knew each other in life (of illegitimate birth and raised by his mother, Winifred Chart, Geoffrey once sent his father a letter, but it was returned to him unopened), yet remarkably they shared not only a partiality for detective fiction, Geoffrey co-authoring the classic mystery short story "Baker Dies" with Edmund Crispin (himself a talented composer and an accomplished mystery writer who, after the Second World War, was a Detection Club colleague of Geoffrey's father), but a love for music. No better illustration of this love can be found in Christopher Bush's writing than in his sixth detective novel, *Dead Man's Music* (1931).

Dead Man's Music brings Christopher Bush's series amateur detective Ludovic Travers into an investigation of unnatural death by means of an automobile mishap on a rural road, something which would similarly draw amateur detectives Lord Peter Wimsey and Desmond Merrion into murder cases in a pair of 1934 detective novels, respectively Dorothy L. Sayers's famed *The Nine Tailors* (1934) and Miles Burton's *To Catch a Thief* (1934). While motoring in his Isotta in Sussex (where Bush the next year would settle with his companion of some four decades, Marjorie Barclay), Travers, along with his manservant (and driver), Palmer, are involved in a near collision with a "large, blue tourer" driven by no less than one of Travers's main partners in prior criminal investigations, Scotland Yard superintendent George "the General" Wharton. Emerging from his car, "tallish, slightly stooping, with keen eyes that would have looked positively fierce but for the modifying effect of the lines at their corners and the monstrous, overhanging moustache that curtained the mouth," "The General," once he recognizes Travers, invites the keen amateur sleuth in on his current case, a common police practice during the Golden Age of mystery, when in a murder investigation there seemingly was always a place held open for an eager gentleman of inquiring disposition.

Wharton's investigation concerns a suspicious suicide by hanging at Frenchman's Rise, a recently let thatched cottage near the village of Pawlton Ferris. Not altogether surprisingly, the supposed suicide at the cottage turns out to be a case of murder. Murders disguised as suicides by hanging came into a certain vogue with prominent mystery writers around this time, with the publication not only of *Dead Man's Music*, but Anthony Berkeley's *The Silk Stocking Murders* (1928) and *Jumping*

Jenny (1933), American Clifford Orr's *The Dartmouth Murders* (1929), John Rhode's *The Hanging Woman* (1931) and Henry Wade's *The Hanging Captain* (1932).

Continuing the novel's series of fortuitous happenstances, as far as bringing Travers into Wharton's murder case is concerned, Travers explains that not only is he familiar with the cottage known as Frenchman's Rise ("Looked it over once—for my sister. She was cottage-hunting for a friend."), but that he also recognizes the corpse, despite attempts having been made to alter the dead man's appearance. The next several chapters in the novel are devoted to detailing the time spent by Travers at Mill House in Steyvenning, Sussex, at the request of a strange letter sent to the consulting and publicity firm Durangos, Limited (of which Travers is now a director), by an eccentric individual named Claude Rook, whom Travers believes has turned up again as the corpse at Frenchman's Rise. During a most bizarre evening at Mill House (rather reminiscent of the Hatter's tea party in *Alice's Adventures in Wonderland*), Rook, looking like "an aged, suburban Paderewski" (a reference to the once world-famous Polish concert pianist-composer and politician), urges Travers to appraise his meretricious collection of china and then plays for him Beethoven's *Moonlight Sonata* on his grand piano, utterly transfixing the amateur sleuth and music lover:

> Travers leaned back, eyes closed, holding his empty pipe between his teeth, still wondering would happen. Then he forgot everything but the music….As the air sang in the room, he began to feel an indescribable sadness and before he knew it, he was losing himself in the image in which the quietude was invoking. Then the slow movement ended and the tripping measure began. The bass rolled and trilled, every note clear as a hammer blow, and peeping through his fingers he saw the most amazing pantomime. The face of the player was a kaleidoscope of emotions. As the music changed he would frown or throw back his head proudly or lean over the keys as if to

caress them or strike viciously as if they were a face to be slapped. Travers, feeling like a man who has blundered into the middle of another's devotions, leaned back again in the chair, listening to the sheer joy of it all.

Although Beethoven's *Piano Sonata No. 14*, completed in 1801, had already become a "standard" in the composer's own day (its disturbing emotional impact is detailed as well in *Poison for One*, a 1934 "John Rhode" detective novel by Bush's Detection Club colleague Cecil John Charles Street), Christopher Bush also mentions more recent works and composers, including not only romantics but "moderns." There is Schumann's *Carnaval* (1834-35), Liszt's *Liebestraum* (1850), Richard Strauss's *Don Juan* (1888), Respighi's *Pines of Rome* (1924), and Honegger's Symphonic Movements No. 1 and No. 2 (*Pacific 231*, 1923, and *Rugby*, 1928, called *Railway Train* and *Football Match* in the novel). Before parting company with Travers, Claude Rook hands his guest an original composition by himself, *The Seven Cypresses*, telling the bemused and mazed gentleman, "It isn't for publication. It's for you—in trust!" (The first sheet of the tone poem, composed by the author himself, is included in the book.)

Travers was understandably baffled by his strange stay at Mill House, but, as he and Superintendent Wharton are drawn further into the investigation of the murder of the man known as Claude Rook, they begin to fit more and more pieces into a weird puzzle, unlocking the strange secret of the dead man's music. Along the way Travers and Wharton are helped by their friend John Franklin, head of the Private Enquiries department at Durangos, who, half-Italian himself, makes a colorful errand to *Il bel paese* (the beautiful country) to disinter some clues to the character of Claude Rook.

Highly praised upon its publication by the astute crime fiction critic Charles Williams, a novelist, editor of the Oxford University Press and member, along with J.R.R. Tolkien and C.S. Lewis, of the informal Oxford literary discussion group known as the Inklings, *Dead Man's Music* surely found no keener admirer in later years than Geoffrey Bush, who in his autobiography, *An Unsentimental Education*, wrote:

It was the joy which I had from my own family life which in the end made me realize that in spite of my mother's best efforts something vital had been missing from my childhood. It was too late to retrieve it, and with the death of both my parents, too late even to investigate it. Or so I thought. And then one day out of the blue I received a letter from a prospective post-graduate student. She was planning a thesis on my father, and required my permission (as the only son) for access to certain archives....The researcher put me in touch with surviving members of his side of the family; from them I learnt that he had been a keen amateur singer (as his father, a Breckland thatcher and poacher, had been before him), an equally enthusiastic violinist, a concert-goer, and even on one occasion a composer. (His detective novel *Dead Man's Music* contains the opening bars of a tone poem written by himself....) So it was from my father that I inherited my musical abilities, and it was because I was my father's son that my mother inferred that I needed a musical education, which in those days only a choir school could provide.

In the event Christopher Bush dedicated *Dead Man's Music* not to his son but "To Basil and Rodney and Desmond Rought-Rought with all Good Wishes." Born in Brandon, Suffolk, about fifteen miles from Great Hockham, Norfolk, where Christopher grew up, the Rought-Rought brothers all played cricket for Norfolk, the youngest of the trio, Desmond, having debuted the same year that *Dead Man's Music* was published, in the Minor Counties Championship against Buckinghamshire. Christopher Bush himself played cricket—both literally, a boy on the field in Great Hockham, and figuratively, as a man writing classic fair play detective fiction, where, as the saying goes, everything was cricket.

Chapter One
WHEN BEGGARS DIE

THE GARMENT of his new directorship of Durangos, Limited, sat so tightly on Ludovic Travers that he was not venturing as yet on week-ends that lasted longer than the Friday afternoon till midday on Monday. On this particular Monday morning he was earlier than usual: it would be about ten-thirty when he passed through the village of Pawlton Ferris. His man Palmer was sitting alongside him and the Isotta was doing no more than a lazy twenty, when the accident nearly happened. Altogether it was incredible—according to Travers himself. Never in his life had he mooned at the wheel. The fault indeed was traceable ultimately to his publishers.

Shirleys—who of course had published *The Economics of a Spendthrift*—had rung him up at his sister's place in Sussex, where he'd been spending the week-end, and had reminded him of that very tentative reply he'd given to their recent suggestion of a species of sequel. As the Isotta sauntered round the bend, he was wondering what he should really call the book—if he actually did it. But the title wouldn't come. Half a dozen attracted, and were discarded—then things happened! There was the furious gurgling of a horn, Palmer's hand wrenched round the wheel; there was the sound of his voice apologising, his own instinctive jamming on of brakes—and he found the Isotta broadside to the road, and a large, blue tourer with her radiator almost in the hedge on the other side.

Travers blinked and looked decidedly foolish. He cut short Palmer's reiterated apologies with a "Damn good job you did!", drew the Isotta to the grass verge, then hopped out to square matters. Out of the other car came a mightily indignant figure; tallish, slightly stooping, with keen eyes that would have looked positively fierce but for the modifying, effect of the lines at their corners and the monstrous, overhanging moustache that curtained the mouth.

"I say, sir! I don't know what the devil you think you're do-ing"—That was Wharton.

"I say! I'm frightfully sorry about this"—Travers had begun at the same time. Then they recognised each other.

"Hallo, George!" Travers became most solicitous. "I say! I'm most awfully sorry about this business. First time I've done such a thing in my life."

Wharton shoved out his hand and smiled—but with reserva-tions. The unkind might have said he was remembering to rep-rimand the nephew of the Chief Commissioner.

"Lucky for you we weren't going very fast!" Then a very obvi-ous sarcasm to relieve his feelings. "Coming from a week-end—or going on one?"

Travers smiled modestly. "Any way you like, George. But don't be angry with me! I couldn't bear it." He fished out a ten-bob note and passed it over to Wharton's chauffeur, with a fur-ther apology, then, "What are you doing down here, George?" He passed over his cigarette case and held the lighter while the General—as the Yard knew him—puffed and pondered.

"Know where Frenchman's Rise is?"

"Frenchman's Rise?" Travers frowned. "Yes. Back to the vil-lage, then the first to the left. About a mile and a half on—or maybe more." No comment forthcoming, he put the question blatantly. "What's on there?"

"Don't know quite. Just going to find out." Wharton hunched his shoulders into the heavy coat as if to indicate the sooner the better.

"The county people wouldn't want you if it weren't serious," Travers told him admonishingly. Then his face brightened and he slipped his arm through the other's. "I'll show you the road. Palmer, run the car into the Dolphin yard and wait for me there!"

Somehow Wharton had seen that coming. Had the approach been made at his room in the Yard, he might have been firm; at the least he might have been hopeful in promises. He might, in fact, have made sufficient of the atmosphere to have hinted a delicate acknowledgment of former favours received, and dep-recated the officialdom that prevented the conferring of more.

But the present situation was vastly different. Almost before he knew it, Travers was steering him into the car. In half a minute they'd backed out and were off again—and Wharton hadn't said a word.

"I'll give your man the tip where to turn," said Travers reassuringly. "Devilishly cold to-day. George; what?"

"What do you expect in November?"

"Oh, I don't know," said Travers mildly. "I've known some damn good days in November, George, and I'm only a kitten compared with you. Er—what are you expecting to find when you get to Frenchman's Rise?"

Wharton had to smile somewhere inside. Travers was so amazingly obvious. In any case, there he was, and there, for the time being, he looked like remaining. His tone became the least bit more friendly.

"Case of suicide—or it isn't suicide. Mazer seems to—"

"Colonel Mazer?"

"That's the fellow. Chief Constable. Know him?"

"Oh, rather! He thinks an awful lot of me."

"Does he!" grunted Wharton. "He'd be thinking a damn sight less if he'd been in my car! However, what was I saying? He's got hold of either a remarkably smart medical man or a damnably romantic one. At any rate he got us on the phone early this morning. From what I can gather it might be a mare's nest—but then again it mightn't."

"Mazer's a bit of a fusser," said Travers. "Awful good chap, mind you. Er—what's the suicide? Shooting? poisoning? or what?"

"Hanging!"

Travers made a face. "Plebeian enough!" He tapped at the window and the car drew into a side road. It was a lane really; crudely metalled, and in summer with the hedges more dense, a death-trap for a reckless driver. "Any other of your people coming?"

"Not unless they're wanted," said Wharton. "They can be along in no time if it's necessary."

"Of course!" Travers smiled. "Rather fatuous remark of mine. Any other news?"

"None—except that it's an old man with grey whiskers, who has an American nephew, and might have been hanging there for weeks if it hadn't been for a cat."

"Really!" Travers wondered if the General was pulling his leg. "Faithful things—cats!"

Wharton didn't rise to it. He peered out of the window.

"Gloomy sort of road, this."

"Pretty enough in the summer, and too much off the track for trippers." The car gave a jolt that nearly tipped them out of their seats. "Nearly there now. The road peters out against the house."

"How do you come to know so much about it?" asked Wharton suspiciously.

"Looked it over once—for my sister. She was cottage hunting for a friend."

The car lurched again in a grass hollow, then stopped. Wharton stepped out and saw Frenchman's Rise for the first time—and didn't think much of it. All he saw was a thatched cottage with, probably, six rooms; an untidy garden, a quaint dormer window, and a low, surrounding brick wall. In the summer with its wall roses aflame and its flagged path edged with flowers, it might have had an appeal which it certainly lacked at the moment. The trees, which almost hemmed it in, looked flaunting enough in their last leaves and yet, somehow severe and oppressive, and the meadow that fronted it damp and ragged. Beyond was nothing—but more trees.

As Travers stepped out, two men emerged from the front door; one an elderly man with trim military moustache and erect bearing, the other a youngish man, black-coated, red-haired, of florid complexion, and wearing horn-rims almost as large as those of Travers himself.

"Hallo, Colonel! This is Superintendent Wharton!"

Mazer forebore to ask questions as he shook hands. He indicated his companion.

"This is Doctor Vallance, whom I mentioned to you, Superintendent."

"Capital!" said Wharton, then cleared his throat. "Better get inside and talk it over. Where is he? In one of those sheds?"

"Attic room upstairs—where that window's in the roof."

They passed the plain-clothes man at the door and entered a tiny paved hall, then through a low door into what looked like the living-room. It was bigger than Travers expected and its furnishings were quiet and in good taste. The diamond-paned windows, the coloured chintz, the genuine, unpretentious furniture were really delightful. Then from somewhere out at the back, a sergeant popped his head inside the far door.

"Oh, just a minute, Ansell!" said Mazer. "Will you see them now? or the body first?"

"Better see them first," said Wharton

"Them" turned out to be a local house-agent—Large by name—and a young labourer of the name of Bent. Wharton had Bent in first. His story was this: Early the previous afternoon he'd come that way looking for some bullocks that had broken bounds, and he'd caught sight of a white kitten at the gable window. He'd known the house was empty, since in that queer way in which things in the country have the habit of getting known, he'd heard that the new owner wasn't in yet. However, he'd knocked and knocked, then had decided to release the fastener of the window by breaking a pane. No ladder being available he'd got on the roof by means of the lean-to shed, then had got astride the gable. When he looked into the room he saw a body swinging from a rope and, scared stiff, had bolted for the police. Wharton asked no questions till he'd gone.

"Sounds pretty fishy. I suppose he wasn't trying to make an entry?"

"We don't think he's that sort," said Mazer. "Still we're making inquiries. Even then it wouldn't affect the case of the—er—man upstairs."

Wharton nodded. "How'd the cat get in? Left in?" The other shook his head. "It wasn't left in. If it had been, I think the evidence will show you it ought to have been emaciated, which it wasn't. It was merely hungry. You'll be able to judge for yourself, but we think it got in through a window with a broken pane, just above that lean-to shed."

Wharton nodded again. "I expect you people are right. And, as you say, it's immaterial. Bring the other fellow in, will you?"

Large's story was not in the least bit interesting. Just under a month previously he'd inserted an advertisement in the Sunday papers for letting furnished the cottage known as Frenchman's Rise. It was his own property and had just been vacated by a tenant. The same week he was approached direct by an American gentleman—name of Strawson—who had taken an option on it for a week. He said he wanted it for an uncle of his, at present in a spa, and when he took possession, this uncle would bring his own servants. Four or five days later, the American had returned and concluded the affair, paying down a quarter's rent. He proposed to live there himself for a few days with his own man to look after him and clean up the house, till the uncle—now down with flu—could take over. Thereupon Strawson had occupied the cottage for some days, till, in fact, about ten days before, when he'd left the district. The letter which he'd sent said that he and his man had to return to America at once, but the uncle had the keys and would take possession at his leisure. Mr. Large wasn't to get alarmed if that wasn't for some weeks.

"You weren't alarmed?" asked Wharton.

"Why should I be?" said Large. "There was nothing unusual about the situation—and I had my money!"

"Exactly! And you think this man upstairs is the uncle?"

"Well, I don't know. From what I've heard it might be—but of course I've never seen him . . . alive that is." Wharton nodded, thought things over for a moment, then turned to Mazer. "Perhaps Mr. Large wouldn't mind waiting for a bit till we've had a look upstairs."

Outside the door the colonel halted.

"Something I'd like you to see in this other room." He opened the door of what appeared to be a small sitting-room—a room as charming in a different way as the one they'd just left. Inside the door, short of the gate-legged table, stood an unopened suitcase.

"If we believe this evidence," said Mazer, "he left his bag here as soon as he entered the house; then went straight upstairs and did himself in. There's no food in the house. There's his hat and things where he'd laid 'em down."

"Finger-prints?"

"Never a one—and we've been over the place for hours."

"Who drove him here?"

"We don't know. We're trying to find out."

"And you've no idea who he is? You don't even know his name?"

"Don't know a thing. He might be anybody." Wharton grunted. "Well, we'll have a look at him!" Mazer led the way up to the back bedroom where a short flight of steps went almost vertically to the attic. Wharton followed and Travers came last. The room itself would have been a perfect wedge but for its scant three foot of wall all round before it caved in to form the steep angle. It was a cleanly room, its rafters polished black and its floor spotless; its furniture a solitary chair that lay where the foot of the dead man probably kicked it after he'd adjusted the noose to his neck.

The dead man himself was swinging from a short length of stout cord attached to a hook in a beam that ran across the narrow top of the wedge. Mazer must have touched him, for the body twirled slowly as if protesting sullenly against such a molestation. His height would be less than five foot six; his age, judging by the hair and general appearance, somewhere about sixty. As Wharton steadied the body and turned the face round, Travers took one look at it—and found it enough. The face was a horrible greyish green with a beard cut in that curious, mutton-chop fashion of fifty years ago. The clothes were navy blue, the shoes black, the collar white and the tie black. So much for the reasonably obvious.

"How long's he been dead?" asked Wharton, sniffing the air.

"I should say exactly in accordance with Large's evidence," said Vallance. "Ten days or perhaps just under. The weather's been very sharp or the atmosphere'd have been worse."

"Quite! Any footprints about, Colonel?"

"None. And not a print of any sort."

"And there's been nobody tramping around except your own people?"

"Most decidedly not! I don't expect they tramped around, as you call it, either!"

"Good!" said Wharton placatingly, and contemplated the body for a moment or two. He nodded to himself, why, heaven knew.

"Now then, doctor! What are *your* ideas about all this?"

Vallance took the centre of the stage at once. You might have said he'd been straining at the leash.

"If you don't mind stepping up close."

Wharton duly went closer. Travers moved over from his retreat by the window. Vallance, like a guide in a museum, began his lecture.

"You notice he's been used to wearing glasses—"

"Just a minute!" interrupted Wharton, and turned to Mazer. "Where are they? In that bag downstairs?"

"Yes. There are two pairs in the bag."

Wharton nodded. "We shall have to see if they're for long or short sight. If he wore 'em all the time you'd have expected him to place 'em somewhere close by, before he put that rope on. Sorry, doctor! Carry on!"

"Look at the chin here. See the abrasion? Before death, as you notice." Travers shuddered as the doctor mauled the face about with his fingers then he suddenly sniffed—and put his handkerchief to his nose and mouth.

"Something else," went on Vallance. "I got on the chair and found a corresponding contusion at the back of the skull, where he fell after the blow. If you don't think I'm taking a liberty in saying so, my opinion is that he was knocked down first and hanged after!"

Wharton frowned slightly. "Perhaps we're getting on a wee bit ahead. What you're implying is, in plain English, that somebody knocked him out by a blow to the point, then hanged him to make it look like suicide."

"Exactly!" Vallance nodded excitedly. "Now have a look here, at the whiskers. See the jagged edge? Look at this incised wound! Look at it with your glass! . . . There isn't a bit of haemorrhage, is there?"

Wharton continued to look, then grunted. "I get you. You think he was shaved after death."

Vallance smiled. "Isn't it obvious, really? And look at the edges again, where the whiskers were trimmed. It looks to me as plain as a pikestaff. He had a full beard. After death it was shaved and cut back to this shape." Wharton opened his mouth but the other was too quick. "And look at his hair! That's been cut, too—by a very crude amateur!"

"Just a minute!" Wharton got out his glass again. Those points about the hair interested him for the merest second, then he got the chair and examined the neck. "Hm! Ligature mark seems all right. No actual facial signs of strangulation, if I may put it like that."

"There wouldn't be!" Vallance told him, with just a touch of impatience, it seemed to Travers. "If the ligature was all right, he'd pop off peacefully . . . I mean if he did hang himself, which he didn't."

But Wharton was scribbling in his notebook. He tore out a leaf and handed it to Mazer. "Don't you think I'm using you as an errand boy, Colonel, but will you see that goes off to the Yard at once. Very urgent. You'll see what it is."

He turned to the doctor. "Anything else?"

Vallance looked rather hurt. "I'm afraid there isn't. I thought that was quite enough to—er—justify a report to Colonel Mazer—and to justify us not cutting him down."

Wharton patted him gently on the back, and gave his most expansive smile. "You did absolutely right! If you'll pardon me saying so, you're a man in a thousand. That reminds me. You'll confer of course with my own man—Menzies. Know him?"

Vallance smiled. "Oh yes! I know Menzies all right!"

"Good!" said Wharton. "I naturally don't want to anticipate what you two'll do, but you'll soon find out if death was due to asphyxia or not."

Travers' voice came almost apologetically from the window. "Oh, doctor! If he's been dead ten days, has the body shrunk appreciably?"

"Shrunk!" Vallance smiled. "That opens an extraordinarily big question. It depends on . . . well, all sorts of things."

"I just wondered," said Travers, still very diffidently. "Don't you think, George, that suit's too big for him?"

Wharton pursed his lips and ran his eye methodically from collar to shoes. "Hm! Might be. Mind you, I saw the sleeves were a bit long but I put that down to the droop of the body."

"Excuse me!" said Travers. "May I?" and with handkerchief well to his nose he undid the waistcoat and folded it back. What else he did Wharton couldn't see, but when he'd finished he removed his glasses and began polishing them nervously. "I don't know if you people will agree with me, but if that theory of the doctor's is as right as it seems, then I'd add that the person who did the hanging was about three inches taller than the dead man"—he smiled—"always assuming he owned that suit."

Vallance seemed to be really aware of Travers for the first time. He and Wharton spoke together. "Why?"

"Well, it looks as if they changed clothes to add to the difficulty of identification. They put on him the trousers with their own braces, but the trouser legs looked too long, so they shortened the braces. If you look at the braces you'll see where they were habitually worn—and you'll see that the place to which they're adjusted now, is a perfectly new one."

They had a look. Wharton made his a thorough inspection, then started turning out pockets. He found nothing but some loose change and a soiled handkerchief—unmarked.

"I think Mr. Travers is right," he said. "You see the implication, doctor?"

"I don't know that I do."

"Well, this fellow's own suit was made in the district, where we might have identified it by means of material. The suit—this suit—that was substituted for it, is of the usual blue serge. Probably also it was made miles away." He gave Travers a shrewd look. "Some people might imply from that that this fellow is a

local inhabitant, and the one who did him in wasn't. However
. . . Cut him down, doctor, will you? I'll give you a hand to get
him downstairs."

Travers stood watching as they got the light burden through
the door and down the steps. Then he moistened his lips and
polished his glasses again. Rather sheepishly and like a hybrid of
stork and sparrow, he moved round the room, craning his neck
to the rafters or peering with head on one side at what turned out
to be nothing in particular. And when he'd gone all round, there
seemed one thing, and one thing only, that he was fairly certain
of. But for obviously recent footprints, the floor of that attic was
so clean that it must have been swept with meticulous care. On
the window sill, where the prints of the kitten's feet were plainly
to be seen, the dust was moderately thick; the floor hardly dirtied
the fingers. All that seemed to have escaped the sweeping were
two tiny pieces of paper which the brush had passed over; faintly
yellow in colour and coarse in texture like wallpaper.

He made his way downstairs, then out by the back door,
where a constable in uniform stood on duty. A few feet across a
roughly cindered path was a shed, bare of everything except coal
dust. In the corner, under the grate of the old-fashioned copper,
lay the ash of the last fire. He squatted down and stirred it gently, then opened the tiny, iron door. Nothing but the last ash—
paper ash—and never a piece of paper, even charred, to be seen.

Outside again, he noticed the wooden garage with its pad-
locked door. Behind that was the garden, soggy and dismal;
with rotting cabbages and bare stalks and scattered fruit trees
like so many gaudy scarecrows. He glanced down at his muddy
boots, then made his way round to the front, where a couple of
plain-clothes men were waiting for something to happen. Ab-
sent-mindedly he found himself at the foot of the stairs, wiping
his feet on a white, goat's-hair rug. Back at the door he used the
fibre mat, then listened as voices came from the living-room. He
tapped at the door and entered. On the table lay the body of the
dead man, stripped to the waist.

"It certainly looks like it," Vallance was saying.

"Looks like what?" smiled Travers.

Wharton explained. "The doc, here, thinks this chap's body's under-nourished. Half-starved if you like."

"Why not?" asked Travers flippantly. "If he's had flu, he wouldn't be so frightfully peckish." Perhaps the smile was to show he wasn't to be taken too seriously.

Wharton grunted. "May be something in that. However . . . we'll know a damn sight more when they've had a look inside him."

Travers winced.

"Er—what's your idea about all this business, Mr. Travers?" broke in Vallance. One imagined that Wharton, behind his back, had given the doctor a perfectly staggering idea of the amateur's virtues and eccentricities.

Travers hesitated. "Well, I don't know that I *have* any ideas . . . practical ones. General, of course . . . and philosophical. . . . Even poetical!"

Wharton gave the doctor a look. "Poetical! What do you mean, 'poetical'?"

Travers smiled. "Sorry to be obscure. To tell you the truth, it was a quotation that came into my head . . . rather apposite in a way . . . I mean, it seemed so to me—

"When beggars die there are no comets seen;
The heavens themselves blaze forth the death of princes."

"And that means what?"

Travers fumbled for his glasses. "If you promise not to laugh at me, I'll tell you. If we want to find a word to describe this murder—assuming it is a murder—we've got to use that fine old veteran 'unusual.' When the rank and file of us are murdered, how's it done? Well, people are discovered with bullets in 'em, or poisoned, or bashed about the skull—where they live or near it. But here's a man who's been killed with extraordinary care. His murder's an attempt at a work of art. His body's been brought into what strikes me as a wholly new atmosphere. His facial appearance has been deliberately altered. Why? Exactly how was it so important that he shouldn't be known? But for chance, his body shouldn't have been discovered for weeks, when it might have been unrecognisable. In spite of that they took no chances. There was all this elaboration of disguise. Why? Who was he? A Cabinet Minister or a bishop? Why all this machinery? This—er—manipulation of place and circumstance?" Wharton felt in his pocket and found his pipe. "That's sensible enough—but we'll soon find out who he is, through the usual channels. As soon as our people get here we're going to reconstruct his face—put on whiskers, glasses and so on—then we'll let the press have photos; plenty of 'em."

Travers nodded. "That's a good idea!" He glanced across at the figure on the table. "I wonder what he did look like." He stood there frowning for some seconds, then suddenly looked up. "Just a moment! I've thought of something!"

When he came back he was holding the goatskin rug—and smiling rather shamefacedly. "Got any scissors, George?"

"Some here!" said Vallance.

Wharton gave the rug a wry look. "What's the idea?"

Travers explained. "This hair's almost the spit of his own—I mean, near enough in colour and so on. Couldn't we reconstruct his face now? Just show the hair on the forehead? Beard and so on?"

Vallance hailed the idea. "Better have some water to make the hair stick."

In less than ten minutes he was drawing back to survey his handiwork. Wharton stood by the body, puffing away at his pipe. Vallance seemed satisfied.

"I should say that is what he was like—near enough. Face wants colouring up. I'll put my glasses on him."

The General gave his usual grunt. "Draw that rug up to his chin so he'll look less of a guy." Vallance pottered around. Wharton nodded away.

"Rather a fine-looking old boy . . . if that's what he really was like." He grunted again. "Nobody *I* know." Then over his shoulder: "Come and have a look at him, Mr. Travers. You've a wider range than I have."

Travers, who having set the work going had retired to the lattice window, sauntered over, feeling for his handkerchief. He gave his glasses a rapid polish, then peered down. . . .

"Oh-h-h-h . . ."

Wharton gripped his arm. "What's up?"

Travers turned his head aside. And he was pretty badly upset. It took him a good few moments to find an answer.

"It's all right . . . the face is. That's what he looked like . . . nearly. I mean . . . I know who he is!"

Wharton's eyes bulged.

"I mean . . . I don't know—er—that is . . ."

Wharton's voice altered. "I say . . . Sit down a bit . . . That's it!"

Vallance, who'd been fluttering round, had a look at him, then slipped out for a glass of water.

"I'm all right," said Travers. "Bit of a shock . . . that's all." He smiled. "So frightfully unexpected!" He moistened his lips again. "I'll tell you just what I know of him."

CHAPTER II
THE HOUSE OF QUESTIONS

IT IS NECESSARY here, to get a working acquaintance with Ludovic Travers himself; divested of his trappings as an author, but standing, as it were, unaided on his two legs: the sort of person one meets, for instance, at the house of a mutual friend; whom one then dismisses from one's mind, or maybe thinks of again at odd moments with pleasure or quiet amusement or even exasperation. That, in a way, was how Claude Rook was to meet Travers, and it is the *man*, Travers himself that must partially account for Rook.

John Franklin—and very few people knew Travers better—once said that Travers was a Greek god run to seed; not too happy a presentation of what might have been a reasonably apt portrait. What Franklin meant was probably not so much running to seed, as tending to emaciation. The fine lines of the face were there; the Grecian nose, the clean mouth, and—more romantic—eyes that were big and alert. But he was thin: there was no doubt about that: six foot three of lamppost leanness, with a most unaesthetic pair of horn-rims in front and an incipient baldness behind.

Still, one forgot all that when in personal contact. Then the things that struck you were the whimsical pucker at the corner of his lips, and the friendliness of his eyes. What you sensed at once was his fine, natural courtesy and his likeableness. The delightful resonance of his voice; the queer little moments when he smiled and said nothing; the quiet humour that lay more in the diffident manner of its presentation than in itself; heaps of things like that, one noticed about him—and found them amazingly attractive.

On a certain morning then, of late autumn, Travers was in his private room at Durango House when the bell happened to ring. Sir Francis Weston himself was speaking.

"That you, Travers? . . . Oh, didn't you tell me you were going down to Sussex this week-end? . . . This evening! . . . Just come along a minute, will you? Something I'd like you to see. Most interesting!"

Travers gave a curious little smile; not a gratified one in that Sir Francis was Durangos Limited, but because if Sir Francis said something was interesting, then it would be interesting. As it happened, too, the managing director was in a remarkably genial mood.

"Come along in! Have some coffee. Just having some myself." He pushed the cigarette box handy, then passed over a letter from his desk. "Have a look at that!" Travers polished his glasses and had a look.

> *Private and strictly confidential.*
> Mill House,
> Steyvenning,
> Sussex.
> Nov.—.

Dear Sirs,

Your firm has a reputation for absolute trustworthiness in its handling of affairs, and an implicitly honourable confidence. Will you therefore send me down here a GENTLEMAN; a most reliable, intelligent, cultured man, to see me about certain urgent matters. I want a man of unusual perception, the sort of man who knows that whereas two and two always make four, two elevens are not necessarily twenty-two.

I would particularly like his opinion on some china, and to hear his appreciation of music. He should be sent AT ONCE. I enclose a preliminary payment against expenses.

Yours sincerely,

CLAUDE ROOK.

Durangos Limited,
London.

He watched while he read it a second time, then, "Well, what do you think of it?"

Travers smiled. "I hardly know. 'Implicitly honourable confidence' is delicious. Sounds like Chinese. Er—what was the enclosure?"

"Two ten-pound notes."

"Whew! Looks as if we'll have to give him back some change!"

"Anything else strike you—other than the fact that he's probably mad?"

"Mad!" Travers smiled. "Oh! you mean the mathematics! Now my experience is, the finer the mathematician the more remote from abnormality. Still, that's neither here nor there. That question of china and music hardly strikes me as urgent. Still you never know. Who's handling this? The Detective Bureau?"

"It came through them, only, Franklin being away, as you know, and the letter so unusual, they submitted it to me direct, asking whether to pass on to the Fine Arts."

He poured out Travers' coffee and struck a match for his cigarette. Travers guessed what was in the wind before the other put the casual question.

"Steyvenning near where you're going?"

"Hm! Yes. About six miles off."

"Know this chap Rook by any chance?"

Travers shook his head. "As a matter of fact I don't know Steyvenning at all. It's rather off the map." He looked up and smiled. "You're suggesting I should call and see this chap to-night!"

Sir Francis chuckled. "Well, aren't you the very fellow?"

Travers joined him. "A couple of ten-pound notes aren't to be sneered at. But—er—what about the music?"

"You've no ear?"

"Oh! I don't know," said Travers. "I like it immensely—good stuff that is. The trouble comes when I try to understand it. Still, I might put up a bluff."

"You'll do it then?"

"Oh, rather! Sounds too good to miss." Then with malice aforethought, "I think I'll push off after an early lunch. I'd rather see things by daylight. Perhaps you'll let me have a copy of that letter."

* * * * * *

As it turned out Travers got away after a very early lunch indeed. Palmer had been ready in any case, and with Travers pushing the Isotta along, they were clear of town before one o'clock. There was very little speculating on the way down—the extraordinary character who'd written that letter could neither be imagined nor anticipated. The only feeling Travers had was one of unusual pleasure, like a boy on the way to his first visit to the Zoo.

The old countryman whom he questioned about the road in Steyvenning, gave him plenty of information. When he was a boy, the mill had been a thriving place. Then it had fallen into disuse and now nothing was left of it but a shell, like a lopped-off lighthouse. Then a few years ago the new road had been made to the coast and the old road past the mill had become a secluded lane. The mill house still stood there, under the shelter of the hill, and he'd heard plenty about the Mr. Rook. A quiet sort of old gentleman he was; pottered about in his garden, and a rare one for music so they said.

Travers let the car go easily along that lane which wound about distractedly and almost seemed to turn at times on its tracks. The country was woody, with stretches of rough pasture that seemed as remote from civilisation as the heart of a moor. Then the woods thickened. The gradient steepened, fell to a shallow, unbridged stream, then rose again as the road curved to the lee of a hill.

Mill House looked a lovely and secluded place for the barest moment as the sun caught it. Then the sun went in and Travers felt an unaccountable shiver. The yellow of the trees became drab and monotonous, the shadows intense and oppressive, and the house itself a place of overwhelming depression. Things which he might not have noticed became only too apparent. The gate sagged on its hinges and its paint had peeled. The tiny drive was covered with weeds and the grass that should have been a lawn lay matted and in clumps. Two or three ancient apple trees had dropped their fruit which lay rotting everywhere. On the low house the creeper straggled untidily. Then the sun looked out again and Travers changed his mind. The house was a curious mixture. It was slovenly rather than ruinous. It was not something fine that had decayed; it was something fine that had ceased to bother with outward appearances.

When the door was opened, his impressions seemed to be confirmed. A smartly dressed young maid took his card, and the entrance hall—from what he could see of it in the uncertain light—seemed spotlessly clean. A wideish flight of stairs led upward to a lofty roof, and the walls were lined with pictures; oils by the look of them. Then his ear caught the sound of a door opening and an old woman appeared, shuffling across the hall towards a door that faced the one she had just closed. Some sort of housekeeper, he thought. Against the black of her dress her hair showed white as snow and her hands seemed to be clutching the shawl she was wearing over her bent shoulders.

Another minute and the maid was showing him into what he took at first for a comfortable living-room. Then the grand piano, the 'cello and the music stand made him wonder if it were a music room. Later he knew it to be both, but even that quick glance round was cut short. From over by the far window a man was coming to meet him; a dapper little man in grey tweeds, with trim grey beard and wearing glasses. A neat mass of grey hair, and an exaggerated imperial which stood embossed over the short beard, gave him the air of an aged, suburban Paderewski. He was smiling effusively as he held out his hand.

"Mr. Travers? I'm very pleased to see you, sir."

His clasp was buoyantly firm and the hand warm and damp.

"The pleasure's mine," smiled Travers.

"Your hat—let me take it! And your coat!" He fussed round as Travers took off the heavy ulster, then carried them off to the entrance hall. Travers gave another quick look round. No particular quality about the furniture; old-fashioned stuff mostly. China apparently in that corner cabinet. Rather charming mirror over the mantelpiece—and that figure of a girl and her swain under a tree; was it Chelsea? Really the light was getting very bad.

Rook came bustling back, rubbing his hands and looking as excited as if the visitor were a nephew arrived for a stay after years abroad.

"And your bag, Mr. Travers? Where did you leave it?"

"Bag?" Travers was rather mystified.

"But you're staying the night, surely!"

"But I hadn't dreamt—" began Travers.

The other cut short his expostulation. "Oh, but you must! You've no idea how much we've got to do! You've got a bag with you?"

His manner was so curiously insistent that Travers felt himself being led into something for which he had not the slightest inclination. You couldn't say he was effusive, yet there was something unreal about his insistence. He gave the impression of a lonely man welcoming a relief from loneliness, and yet his manner was just the least bit too interested and lacked that touch of the pathetic which might have made it real.

Travers shook his head. "Sorry! but much as I'd like to, I fear it's impossible. But if you'd be so good as to give my man a cup of tea I don't mind how long I stay to-night."

The other raised his hand with a gesture that was almost foreign. "Of course! Of course! I'll see to it at once."

Travers followed hard on his heels to the hall. Opposite him a door was closing behind the figure of the housekeeper and he caught a glimpse of a kitchen and an outer window.

"If you don't mind," said Travers, "I'll have the car turned round."

Rook shot off at once, Travers once more on his heels. They watched the car reverse and swing round behind the house, then went back to the hall.

"You'll pardon me a moment," said Rook, taking him by the arm and almost pushing him back to the music-room. "I'll see about your man's tea. Have a look at the china. Tell me what you think about it."

His voice was jerky and nervous, like himself. Somewhere about it was a peculiarity that Travers couldn't identify; some mechanical staccato that was almost foreign. As he re-entered the room, his mind refused to concentrate on china—it was that curious person Rook who was occupying his thoughts. His words were not so many; it was a volubility of manner that was so unusual and disconcerting. He seemed to be all on edge—hopping about like a sparrow in a garden where there are cats. He was the least bit gushing, but not with the gush of, say, a *nouveau riche* or one who was not sure of himself. Unless Travers were wrong, this was the man's natural manner. Some southern Frenchmen whom he'd known had had it—and some Italians; yet this man had nothing un-English about him unless it were a sallowness of skin and eyes black as night and as alert as those of a man thirty years younger. Was he mad? slightly demented? or what? Travers shook his head. Eccentric perhaps; possessed of a strange kink or two—but hardly mad.

So to the china. There was no need to open the cabinet. His first look startled him; his next inclination was to laugh. The contents were worthy of a barrow, or a side-table in a tenth-rate antique shop. He smiled—then whipped round with a start.

"What do you make of them?" Rook was asking at his elbow.

Travers fumbled at his glasses.

"We'd better have a light, I think," went on the other without waiting for an answer. He fussed about with a lamp that stood on a stand by the piano, drew the curtains carefully across the windows, then rubbed his hands like a hungry man who anticipates a meal.

"Sit down, Mr. Travers. Tea will be in in a minute. And make yourself at home. You'll smoke?"

"Not before tea, thanks," smiled Travers.

"And the china. What did you think about it?"

Travers cleared his throat, and looked up to find the other regarding him anxiously. "In your—er—letter to Durangos, Mr. Rook, you were good enough to refer to the absolutely honourable methods we employ. Speaking as a director of the—er—firm, I'd like to say this: If you were a casual friend of mine, and I wanted to give you pleasure, I'd say your china was 'very nice' or 'delightfully quaint.' Were I an unscrupulous person, representing an ephemeral or shoddy firm, I'd say it was worth a lot of money—and then collect a fee for valuation. But what you want, I take it, is something different. You want an opinion that is honest—or even brutal."

Rook nodded. "Exactly! Just your honest opinion." Travers cleared his throat again. "If you wish it, I'll give you a description and a valuation of each piece—but the money'll be thrown away. Frankly, Mr. Rook, from a collector's point of view they're valueless. A dealer might give you a few shillings for the lot."

He looked up apprehensively, but the other seemed amused.

"I'm pleased to hear you say so. I took them over with the house, and of course people would insist they were valuable." He chuckled. "Well, I know now!"

"The trouble is you've gone to an awful lot of bother, and wasted good money."

Rook waved his hand airily. "Not 'wasted.' Information's always worth buying, Mr. Travers!"

There was some double meaning in that remark but as Travers watched the other's face there was a tap at the door and the maid entered with a tray.

"You'll come upstairs for a moment?" Rook asked. "Er—thank you." Travers gathered it was the question of toilet he was referring to. Five minutes later, when he came from the bathroom, Rook was waiting for him outside the door. He took Travers' arm affectionately.

"Something I wanted to explain to you. I hope you won't mind, but my housekeeper always has tea with me and usually sits with me till dinner-time. You'll find her a most superior woman—in reduced circumstances . . . if you know what I mean. She once did me an immense service—and I show my gratitude. She's dumb, by the way; accident which affected the vocal cords." His voice lowered. "But she hears perfectly."

Travers made some incoherent reply as the other ushered him into the room. Seated at the tea-table was an elderly woman; older it seemed than Rook himself. At first glance he thought she was foreign—then that surely she must be some relation; the yellowish-ivory skin, for instance, and eyes of deepest black; then knew he must be wrong. About her face was the intangible stamp of quality. Travers knew many an elderly acquaintance who'd have made a much less delightful hand of greeting a stranger. As she smiled it was hard to believe she was dumb; indeed he forgot it for a moment.

"What a charming old place this is, Mrs. Fletcher!"

She smiled again—and nodded, then gave a humorous shudder and indicated the shawl.

"Mary's always cold," explained Rook.

That was a queer, pantomime sort of meal, and yet Travers rather enjoyed it. Rook appeared to be very well read, and yet his knowledge seemed to stop short, as if he were either afraid of committing himself or ashamed of what reading he possessed. They talked about the Stock Exchange, for instance, and Travers looked up quickly at the aptness of Rook's opening remarks. Then he shrivelled up as if even the elements of finance were as little known to him as to a boy in his teens. There was another exasperating trick he had, too, in addition to that abandoning of his own opinions; he would fire a whole series of questions till Travers felt like a housemaster entertaining a chatty little fourth- former. As for the old housekeeper, Travers puzzled his wits more than once. That she had been what is commonly known as a "lady" was apparent in each movement and gesture. Her voice, had she had one, must have been as full of charm as the placid face with its silver hair. All that one could say of her dumbness was that one could sense her comments and her answers and even her questions; and when Rook cut in with some explanation which Travers felt to be wholly unnecessary, it was as if one had touched the discordant keys of a still lovely but long mute harpsichord.

The maid cleared away and the men lit their cigarettes. Mrs. Fletcher put on her spectacles and got out her embroidery. Travers waited for the rest of the commission—but it didn't come yet.

"You find country people make good servants?" he asked, for the sake of conversation.

Rook nodded. "As a rule—yes. Bertha's a very good girl."

"But she's not local!"

The other gave a look that was almost startled. "How do you know that?"

Travers smiled. "I don't! What I mean is, she may be living in the district—or her people may; but I'd say she was brought up in the eastern counties; Suffolk for choice."

Rook looked as pleased as a boy who's got the pieces of the puzzle apart. "You hear, Mary? Mr. Travers is a shrewd observer!" They smiled at each other as if enjoying a secret.

"You're giving me too much credit," expostulated Travers.

Rook was not to be denied. That small exhibition of observation seemed to set him going. "Oh, but I know! Come now! What did you gather from that letter of mine? The one I sent to your firm."

Travers smiled. "And what kind of answer do you wish this time? Polite . . . or frank?"

"Oh, frank! The franker the better!"

"Then I gathered—correct me by all means if I'm wrong—that your letter was merely a cover for something which it didn't mention; that you wished to make a statement of real importance but preferred not to commit yourself before inspecting the man we sent down. Hence the rather—er—intriguing allusions." He ventured on a smile. "Since I've seen your china, I'm even more of that opinion!"

Rook seemed most impressed, though for once he found nothing to say.

"Please pardon my being so—er—impertinent," Travers went on quickly. The other cut him short. He turned to the housekeeper.

"Mr. Travers *must* stay the night! He simply *must!*" She smiled and nodded. Travers felt uncommonly embarrassed. If only Rook would talk business and get it over, he'd be a very relieved man. But Rook started again.

"Tell me, Mr. Travers! That apparently ridiculous conundrum in my letter. Of course you know the answer!"

"Well—er—I don't know." Travers was taken rather by surprise. "You see, it rather depends on the sort of answer you want!"

"Exactly!" Rook was nonplussed for a moment—but only for a moment. "Say two and two. Do they always make four?"

"Well, I believe so. I can think of no mathematical circumstance where the contrary occurs, though I could prove to you with algebraic symbols, making use of a shrewdly disguised fallacy, that two and two made nothing at all."

"Good! Good! I see you know it!" He laughed again, like a schoolboy, then cocked his head aside as ii the real poser were yet to come. "And what about two elevens, Mr. Travers?"

"I'm afraid I'm wrong there," Travers admitted. "The only case I know of where they don't make twenty-two is the case of cricket elevens at Eton—where they're always twelves."

"Wonderful! Simply wonderful! And what about two twelves?"

"Two twelves? Well, bakers' dozens!" Travers told him. "And some publishers have that way of counting—twelve copies as thirteen—as I once discovered to my cost!"

On Rook's face gratification was mixed with surprise. "Really now! Really!" He nodded to himself as if words wouldn't come, then, "And you're an author, Mr. Travers?"

"Well, in a modest way . . . yes."

Rook waved his hand to the housekeeper and again they smiled at each other. Then he raised his hands with a further gesture of admiration and chuckled away to himself. Travers felt as uncomfortable as could be. That Rook was mad he was beginning to have no possible doubt; not so much from those childish questions of his as from his manner.

"And what about two sixes?" His look was comically earnest.

Travers shook his head. "There you have me—unless you should happen to be referring to those candles known as sixes, which are either four or eight inches long, according to weight." He smiled deprecatingly. "I once had to look that up for a crossword puzzle." Rook shook his head as if it were all too good to be true. As he sat there he seemed to be wrestling with some problem, then came apparently to a sudden decision. He got to his feet.

"You were at Eton, Mr. Travers?"

"No. I'm afraid not. I was at Halstead."

"Hm! I just wondered. Not that it matters." He hesitated again as if trying to find the right words. "You won't think me impertinent—or foolish—if I ask you to take part in a childish little experiment for me? You won't mind humouring an old man?"

Travers was taken clean aback, but he treated the matter with all the seriousness that seemed to be expected of him.

"Of course I don't mind."

"Well, look at me then, as I stand here. I'm going upstairs for a minute—no more. When I come down, tell me if you see any difference!" His face and pose were as set as if he were before a camera, while Travers ran his eye over him from crown to toes, and as he did so his opinions underwent yet another subtle change. Rook for the moment was not an irritant—nor an enigma. Somewhere at the back of that ridiculous and flamboyant mind of his was something that was deeply real—and deeply in earnest.

"Finished?"

"Yes, thanks." Travers watched him leave the room, then polished his glasses thoughtfully. Then, as he reached forward for the cigarette box, behind him, from the housekeeper, came a funny little noise like a moan and there she was, nodding her head and trying inarticulately to call his attention to something. Travers came over and as soon as he got to his feet a change seemed to come over her. The eyes that had struck him as so sad looking and quiet now appeared to be smiling. She held out the embroidery.

"Very charming!" he told her—and nodded cheerfully as he handed it back.

But she didn't take it. She pushed it into his hands again as he half let it fall, and pointed frantically at the design. Travers looked puzzled, then took it closer to the lamp. At the end of the flowered design that surrounded what appeared to be the main pattern, was a final two inches that differed from the rest. Then he saw it was a word—STAY.

As he glanced down quickly, she reached out her hand, and her face had a look of overwhelming anxiety.

No sooner did she get the embroidery back in her fingers than she began picking it out feverishly with the needle. Travers had a sudden idea and felt hastily for pencil and paper—but he was too late. Rook, stiffly dignified as before, came into the room.

Travers examined him almost inch by inch as he posed in the light.

"I'm afraid I can't see much difference. You've brushed your hair . . . and you've changed your tie . . . I think it's the same tie, but you've reversed it. The stripe now goes from right to left . . . and you've got a handkerchief in your breast pocket . . . and you've turned up your trousers!"

The other relaxed, then clapped him on the back with an energy that went beyond effusiveness. "Wonderful! Never heard anything like it!"

Travers felt an awful fool. Rook, too, in this effusive vein was positively unbearable. He retreated towards the fireplace and flicked the end of his cigarette.

"Were you serious, Mr. Rook, when you said you'd like me to stay till the morning?"

"Serious! I was never more serious in my life!" Travers nodded. "Then if you're really in earnest, I will stay. If you don't mind—er—sending for him, I'll speak to my man."

CHAPTER III
THE HOUSE OF MUSIC

TRAVERS SPOKE to Palmer in the hall, indifferent as to whether the conversation were overheard or not, provided Palmer understood precisely what the situation was. Not that Travers was alarmed; vaguely uneasy perhaps, and tremendously intrigued, but no more than that. What could happen to him during a night in that house, he couldn't very well see. Let Rook be mad or sane or merely desperately anxious about something, the fact remained that the quiet, old eyes of that housekeeper looked as clear as the wells of truth itself—and now there'd be Palmer, who knew his whereabouts.

"Take the car straight to Pulvery," he told his man. "Say I've been detained over business. To-morrow, take the major to Arundel as I mentioned. Mr. Rook tells me there's a bus I can get at Steyvenning so I'll be along to lunch. If I'm not back by one, bring the car here to fetch me."

Mrs. Fletcher came out as the door closed behind Palmer and Travers handed her the few necessaries he'd taken from the bag. As she took the small case, she smiled and pointed upstairs. By the time she'd got to the landing, Rook came out. He was beaming.

"Do you know you've given me extraordinary pleasure!" His voice lowered. "You didn't think anything unusual in Mrs. Fletcher being in to tea? It didn't strike you as strange?"

"Good God! More riddles!" flashed through Travers' mind.

"Not at all," he said. "She's a most delightful old lady."

"You really think so!" He stroked his beard and nodded to himself with a queer little laugh. "She's been a godsend to me. I'm not allowed to go out, you see. I get fainting fits sometimes—heart not what it should be." He broke off to wave Travers to a chair. "Now! make yourself comfortable. A spot of whisky? Not yet? Well, don't forget to help yourself the minute you feel like it."

Travers suddenly decided to change his mind, and poured out a modest tot. What was going to happen next he hadn't the least idea. All he hoped was that there'd be no more invitations to make an exhibition of himself. A bit of a strain, too, that continual effort to remain courteous, and comprehensive of what one didn't in the least understand. Then Mrs. Fletcher came in again, resuming her embroidering as if nothing had interrupted—and the whole nightmare chatter began once more.

"So you didn't like the china!" laughed Rook.

Travers found it hard to find an answer. "Well, I don't know if I'd put it exactly like that!"

Rook got up and went over to the mantelpiece. In the sloping mirror Travers saw the eyes of the housekeeper follow him as he did something with his back towards them. When he turned round he was holding that early Staffordshire figure of a pair of lovers under a tree.

"And what about this? Mr. Travers didn't surely include this?" he told the housekeeper.

As a matter of fact, Travers hadn't. He got up, took it from Rook's hands with a "Do you mind?" and examined it carefully. The maker had probably had his mind on Chelsea when he moulded and painted it. There was the large, spreading tree, less delicately modelled but each branch balanced against its fellow on the other side. Beneath the tree, in front of the bulbous trunk that lost itself in the base, a woman sat on a rustic seat with a fan behind which she was simpering—or was it that the comparative crudity of the modelling made the lips merely parted? Leaning over the back of the seat was a swain, with doll-like, insipid face; and the whole posing of the figures was so utterly naive that only the quaint colouring gave it the least claim to any sort of beauty.

The base of the group was sturdy, a couple of inches deep perhaps and bulging with blue knots of flowers and tufts of grass through which ran twin rivulets, indicated by blue and white lines. Underneath could be seen a small blowhole and the marks where the group had rested in the kiln.

Travers nodded as he handed it back.

"Now that's really a delightfully interesting old piece! No great value of course—eight or ten pounds perhaps—but so perfectly English of the eighteenth century."

Rook coloured with pleasure. "I'm glad you like it. I did—as soon as I saw it. And you'd give eight or ten pounds for it!"

"If I were a collector . . . yes!"

Rook nodded and beamed again, then looked at it affectionately. He even stroked the tree and looked all round it, shaking his head in a satisfied way.

"I wouldn't sell it. Mary's going to have it." He raised his voice as if she were deaf. "You're going to have it, aren't you, Mary? She always took a fancy to it," he explained, and altogether you'd have thought there'd been unearthed a rare piece of Ming, worth a couple of thousand. Then came more ecstasies as he touched the girl's cheeks roguishly.

"What would you call her? A wench?"

"Well, I suppose they called them nymphs in those days," Travers told him, still trying to seem interested.

Rook shook his head. "A baggage, that's what I call her! A baggage!" he fairly bellowed the word. "Isn't she a baggage, Mary?" He quietened down a bit. "Flirt I suppose you'd call her nowadays. I don't. She's a rosy cheeked baggage! . . . Look how she's hiding behind her fan! . . . Look at her sweetheart's face! ('Like a rabbit's!' thought Travers.) . . . Talking love to her, and the little baggage pretending not to hear!" He frowned. "What's the expression? Ah! Deaf to all entreaties. That's it! Deaf!" He bellowed again. "Deaf to all entreaties!"

The scene was so utterly ludicrous, and yet so painful, that Travers bent down and buried his face in his hands. The other still went on; each word curiously accented.

"Deaf . . . and dead! Dead as mutton!" The alliteration seemed to amuse him. "Deaf and dead! . . . Dead and deaf!" He gave an exaggerated sigh. "Eighteenth century, you said?"

"That's right!" said Travers, and looked up again. Mrs. Fletcher sat stitching away unconcernedly as if those rhapsodies were a nightly occurrence. Travers shuffled in his seat, sipped his drink, stoked his pipe and found nothing more to say. Rook replaced the figure reverently. As he turned round, Travers caught his eye and saw he was amused about something.

"You think I'm an old fool, Mr. Travers!"

"I! Heavens no! Why should I?"

"For every reason in the world! Still, you must let an old man have his fancies. . . . Would you pour me out the barest drink? No soda."

Travers hopped up, and smiled as he handed it over. Something he'd forgotten!

"You won't think me impertinent, Mr. Rook, but in your letter you mentioned the matter of—er—music. Might we have some, do you think?"

Rook sprang up at once. "My dear sir! Anything you like! What shall it be? You can accompany me?"

"I'm afraid not." Thank heaven something at last looked like being done! "I've hardly touched a piano since I left the nursery!"

"Then we can't have the 'cello." He moved rather slowly across to the piano and twiddled a few notes with his right hand.

"What would you like?"

"Well, what would Mrs. Fletcher like?"

That was the first time he had looked other than anxiously amiable. If anything, the sudden expression that came over his face was one of annoyance.

"Mrs. Fletcher always has the music. She has her favourites, like all of us; but this is for you. What shall it be?"

"That's very good of you," said Travers feebly. "Something not too modern, perhaps."

That pleased him. The piano stool was twirled one way, then another, till he got it to his liking. Then he threw back his mop of hair as if it had been twice as long; wiped his fingers on a silk handkerchief that lay on the piano top, then settled himself majestically. Travers held his breath, fearing an anti-climax, as the fingers crooked over the keys. What would come? A mass of discords? or some hackneyed triviality?

But the other stopped tantalisingly in the very act of striking the keys.

"What would you like particularly? Beethoven? One of the sonatas?"

"If you'll be so good," said Travers. "The *Moonlight* . . . or the *Appassionata*."

"Both if you like." He wiped his fingers again; played a few simple chords, then began the *Moonlight*. Travers leaned back, eyes closed, holding his empty pipe between his teeth, still wondering what would happen. Then he forgot everything but the music. The instrument had seemed a superb one, and now even his own limited knowledge made him aware that he was listening to somebody who was worthy of it. As the air sang in the room, he began to feel an indescribable sadness and before he knew it, he was losing himself in the images which the quietude was invoking. Then the slow movement ended and the tripping measure began. The bass rolled and trilled, every note clear as a hammer blow, and peeping through his fingers he saw the most amazing pantomime. The face of the player was a kaleidoscope of emotions. As the music changed he would frown or throw back his head proudly or lean over the keys as if to caress them or strike viciously as if they were a face to be slapped. Travers, feeling like a man who has blundered into the middle of another's devotions, leaned back again in the chair, listening to the sheer joy of it all. Then when the sonata ended and he looked up without words to express the pleasure he had felt, he saw that he and Rook were alone. Mrs. Fletcher had gone, and her embroidery with her.

From then till just before nine when the evening meal was ready, Rook played and played. Had his playing been passable, or even indifferent, Travers might have urged him on as a relief from those mental antics of the earlier evening. As it was, he knew he was listening under unusual and intimate circumstances to something he was never likely to hear again, even in a concert hall. Those things he thought he knew, Rook's interpretation revealed as delightfully unknown; those he had never heard of seemed to have attractions which he had never suspected himself of being capable of appreciating. Not only had he the technique; he had the memory of a recognised master, and altogether it was amazing. There was Rook, looking a mixture of a retired bank manager and stage musician, becoming a wholly new personality and dominating the room and Travers himself.

It was strange too, how suddenly all that seemed to go during the meal that followed. Rook shed his halo and became again the anxious, nervy host of the earlier evening. His manner was an irritating subservience to the other's opinions and points of view. There was the same string of questions, bald and obvious enough and asking for answers as obvious as themselves. When it was all over, the clock was no more than nine-thirty. Somehow Travers sensed that nothing could be done by demanding, however courteously, the real purpose for which he must have been asked there. And it was far too early to suggest bed. Very well then; there'd have to be more music.

"If it isn't an impertinence to ask," he said, "where did you study?"

"I had excellent masters when I was a boy," Rook told him. "Of course I don't deny that I had a certain aptitude—and it was a pleasure to me. For the rest I'm practically self-taught."

"But you must have had years and years of practice!"

Rook nodded. "Yes . . . perhaps I have. You see, I was financially independent; a competence that is—no more. And my peculiar state of health throws me indoors most of the time. And of course, it's my one hobby."

"If I may say so, you've made a magnificent use of it," said Travers wholeheartedly. "Er—do you compose at all?"

Rook looked surprised for a moment—then actually laughed.

"It's rather remarkable, you know, that you should ask me that, because I was just going to mention it myself." He wandered over to the cupboard below the china cabinet and rummaged about for a minute or two, then came back with almost an armful of manuscript paper which he dumped on the table.

"Here they are. All sorts." He picked them up at random, peered at the titles through his tortoiseshell glasses, and made a running comment. All sorts they seemed to be, as he said; chamber music, sonata for piano and 'cello, an overture, various drawing-room pieces, a pianoforte concerto and a symphony. Travers looked at them with a semblance of wisdom as Rook passed them over, but beyond a mass of most untidy symbols, saw nothing. Rook seemed to gather that. "You don't read music fluently."

"I'm afraid I don't," apologised Travers. "I make no bones about owning up. I daresay I could play an air with simple harmonies, but no more."

"You do play a little then?"

Travers smiled. "You flatter me!"

Rook stood there for some time, pushing the leaves about with his fingers, then gathered up the scattered papers and took them back to the cupboard. Then he produced a cigar box.

"Now, Mr. Travers; you must try one of these—just to please me."

"Thank you, I will," said Travers, whose tastes were occasionally Edwardian. "Let me give you a light." The fire was stirred up and they sat for a few moments doing nothing in particular. Then Rook moved restlessly in his chair. Somehow Travers felt he was at last going to come to the point.

"Mr. Travers!"—he pronounced the name most pontifically—"the time has come when you and I can talk a little further. Perhaps you haven't always understood me to-night."

"You may have thought I was a very curious and talkative old fool. So I am!" He gave a shrewd look. "But that's what you expected—after my letter."

Travers protested. "I'm afraid you're putting into my mouth views and—er"

"Mr. Travers! Let me say something else. I didn't know who your firm would send down here. It might have been a man who'd have left the house half an hour after he arrived. You're not what I expected. You *are* a gentleman." He waved aside Travers' protesting hand. "And you're a man of keen observation and wide intelligence."

Travers smiled. "Exhibitions of superficial knowledge!"

"Oh no! Exhibitions like that must be the consequence of a fine taste and wide reading. I've been a judge of men in my time. Sometimes I've judged wrong—but not often. I've asked you nothing about yourself, but I believe you to be the soul of honour. I'm going to prove it!"

Travers, as modest a soul as you'd meet on a summer's day, blushed, but ventured on no more protests. Rook got up again, put his cigar carefully on the ashtray, then went over to a drawer of the side table. He unlocked it and took out yet more manuscript—music, as Travers saw at once. He glanced up to find Rook watching him, then polished his glasses and had a good look at it.

THE SEVEN CYPRESSES

A TONE POEM (VALCETTO) CLAUDE ROOK

(Printed from Rook's MS.)

"Unusual title!"

"Well, perhaps yes. But you remember Respighi's *Pines of Rome*?"

"I've heard it," said Travers. "I can't say I'd recognise it again if I heard it played."

The music itself, as far as Travers was concerned, was sheer gibberish. A slow movement appeared to open with a theme, which he tried to hum to himself but couldn't. The rest was altogether beyond him. Still, he looked as intelligently interested as he could, turned over page after page of the manuscript— thinking desperately for some comment to make—then handed it back.

"I think it ought to be rather fine."

"It means nothing to you?"

"Beyond me entirely," Travers had to confess. "Er—will you play it over to me?"

"With pleasure!" Rook's face brightened up at once. At the piano the same meticulous preparations were made as at the earlier recital; if anything he was more careful about the exact adjustment of the stool and the wiping of his fingers.

"Pardon me a moment!" broke in Travers. "Is there anything particular I'm to listen for?"

"I was just going to tell you. The introductory theme. It's perfectly simple and you'll hear it introduced straightaway. Then immediately it's repeated. After that the poem becomes merely a series of variations—something of the nature of Strauss's *Don Juan*, for instance. You'll almost certainly be able to recognise the theme—the theme of the Seven Cypresses, that."

It took just over a quarter of an hour to play that tone-poem. Now and again Travers did actually recognise the opening theme but most of the time he was groping about for it in the complexity of unfamiliar sounds. The music was magnificent— he knew that; and it had something of a symphony about it in its deliberate contrasts and overwhelming climaxes. But it was the more solemn passages with their resonant bass that he liked most, and then too, he always seemed to catch again that elusive opening theme. When the end came, with the theme, now easily recognisable, dying away in the furthest register, he was almost unaware of it. A final chord and Rook let his hands fall to his side, though he still sat there motionless.

Travers clapped his hands gently. "Bravo! Bravo!"

Rook got up slowly, took the manuscript and held it out.

"You will keep this. A temporary souvenir of your visit. The only copy in existence."

"Oh! but I could never—"

"Please! Please!" He spoke insistently. "I want you to take it. You *must* take it!"

Travers took it gingerly, as he got to his feet. "It's amazingly good of you, Mr. Rook, and I—er—very much appreciate what the—er—gift means." The words came awkwardly. What he felt like saying was, "What the devil do you expect me to do with it?" The thought translated itself into something more courteous. "You'd like me to get this published."

Rook shook his head. "There isn't a publisher who'd look at it!"

"But surely!—"

He cut short Travers' protest. "It isn't for publication. It's for you—in trust!"

"In trust!" Travers didn't understand. "For whom?"

Rook smiled queerly. "You know for whom!"

"You mean . . . Mrs. Fletcher?"

The other looked annoyed for the second time that evening. "Oh no! Not Mrs. Fletcher! You know whom it's for!"

Travers nodded. Rook had better have it his own way. No point in arguing—and the morning might bring more information. So he put the tiny packet of manuscript into his breast pocket and patted it with exaggerated affection.

"I'll look after it. And I'm very grateful for your confidence."

Rook nodded, then his eyes went towards the clock.

"You retire early—or late?"

"Early, if you please," said Travers. "This has been rather a long day."

"Then come along! Ten o'clock's my hour!"

Ten minutes later, Travers was in his pyjamas, having a last look out of the window that faced the derelict lawn, and seeing nothing but those ancient apple- trees that almost touched his bedroom wall. When he'd felt so mentally exhausted he couldn't remember. That evening had been not only hysterical but incomprehensible. Rook must be quite abnormal—perhaps a genius run mad; a trivial, chattering, inflammatory little fop of a man who played like a master and had stored away in that queer brain of his a repertoire that would stagger most memories.

And yet, in spite of his difference of outlook and background, Travers knew there was something likeable about the man, for all his extravagances, and even—the word only then occurred to him—his furtivenesses. Then he smiled. Perhaps the only likeable thing was that Rook seemed so anxious to be liked!

Then there was that housekeeper, with her sad, old face and quiet gentility. Why had she given that embroidered message? Was she bored with loneliness? or with Rook's company? or was it that she wanted Rook to have company for himself, if only for one night? Or was she as abnormal as he? And was the whole household abnormal?

Travers shook his head perplexedly. Sufficient unto the morrow were the mysteries thereof.

CHAPTER IV
TRAVERS STOPS WONDERING

TRAVERS SLEPT remarkably well that night; indeed it was the maid's tapping on the door that woke him at eight o'clock. Half an hour later he strolled down to breakfast to find the table laid, and in the air the faintest smell of cigar smoke. The maid followed on his heels with coffee and bacon.

"Mr. Rook not coming?" he asked.

"No sir. He has his in bed."

"But he'll be down later?"

"Oh yes, sir! About ten he comes down usually."

"And Mrs. Fletcher?"

"She don't come down till just before lunch, sir." Travers fell to, had his breakfast pipe, then hailed the arrival of the news—and no less than three newspapers at that! Almost with the striking of the clock, Rook appeared, fussy and solicitous and nervy as ever. There was some talk about the weather, and the glass going up. Travers chattered away, turning the conversation towards business and finding his hints ignored. Then over yet another pipe, he put a fairly definite feeler.

"That manuscript you handed to me last night. You're perfectly confident of my ability to—er—recognise the person entitled to it? "

"You may not have to," said Rook. "She—" That was what the word seemed to be, as he made a rapid correction and cleared his throat with unnecessary noise as if the word had been part of the process. "You'll find the person and hand it over—if the necessity arises."

"What necessity?"

Rook hesitated. "You'll know . . . if there is a necessity. " His face cleared. "Of course there may not be any necessity, then you'll do nothing. I may even call and ask you to return it."

"Exactly!" Travers was more in the dark than ever. Rook got to his feet.

"Put it away and forget all about it."

"Yes . . . but the real business you want to consult me about!" said Travers desperately.

Rook made a gesture of dismissal. "All over, Mr. Travers! No more business! Put on your coat and come into the garden. It'll be sunny after the frost." Travers followed resignedly. At the front door, Rook took what might have been a precautionary peep at the road—or the weather—then stepped out to the weedy drive. He waved his hand at the trees.

"Country's very beautiful now. This way—through the side gate!"

Travers took the last step or two in front of the older man and opened the gate for him. Beyond the path that skirted the end of the house he caught a glimpse of colour—late chrysanthemums by the look of them—then turned his back on the garden to close the gate. From somewhere very close came the gurgle of a horn. Instinctively he leaned on the gate and craned his neck round the house corner. A smallish saloon, of a perfectly familiar make, was drawing in at the rickety front gate.

Rook must have heard the noise of its squeaky brakes. He too turned in his tracks, though at the moment Travers was not aware of it. He was looking at the driver of the car, a man in ordinary clothes, who remained at the wheel and didn't even put an arm round to open the door for his passenger to alight. As for the passenger—a tall, sallow-faced, grim-looking person in a heavy coat—he paid no attention to the driver. Once out of the car, he appeared to be stretching his legs and as he turned towards the garden gate, Travers saw his face more clearly; the short, bristled moustache that nestled inside the grooves that ran from nose to chin, the cruel cut of the jaw and the tight lips.

It was as he drew back, and just as the sharp knock sounded at the front door, that Travers was aware of two things—and at the same moment. His own conduct—craning round that gate like a curious vulgarian—might be amusing, but it was perfectly unpardonable. Moreover something was happening to Rook. He was clutching the gate. He was trying to speak. Then he slithered to the ground in a heap.

In a moment Travers had him in his arms and was looking for a place to lay him down. Everywhere seemed damp and dirty, and as by then he was almost at the back, he moved along quickly to the kitchen door. It was open—and the room empty. When the maid came in, it was to find her master in a chair by the fire and Travers bathing his face with cold water.

"Mr. Rook had a fainting fit in the garden. Got any sal-volatile?"

The girl stared.

"Stop here with him a moment!" He darted out of the door and up to the bathroom. When he got back again, there was the stranger, rubbing Rook's hands while the girl looked on.

"He'll be O.K. in a minute," he was saying. "Just threw a faint, that's all."

Travers coughed. The other whipped round. Even at the moment Travers felt it was just the least bit melodramatic—steel-grey eyes boring into one, the slight American accent, the hands deep in the coat pockets, the hat tilted backwards—not unlike a scene from the talkies, in fact; especially the question.

"Who might you be, sir?"

"I! Oh! just a caller."

"Staying here?"

"Well—er—-yes and no! You see," he explained mildly, "I arrived last night and I'm going away almost at once."

The other grunted; looked at Rook, then back at Travers who was now preparing the sal-volatile.

"You're not a relation . . . I suppose?"

"Lord no!" He squinted like a chemist as the liquid clouded, then came across. Rook's eyes fluttered as he bent over him, then opened.

"Drink this!" Travers told him, and tilted the glass. Rook drank, spluttered, then turned round in the chair. He stared at the stranger and his mouth opened He moistened his lips, his breath came quickly, then he flopped back in the chair again. Travers felt his pulse and his forehead.

"I think he'll be all right in a minute." He fumbled for his glasses, blinked as he wiped them, then turned to the other. "If I might ask—er—who *are* you, sir?"

"I'm his brother!" snapped the other. "George Rook's my name. Bit of a shock, I expect—seeing me again."

"Really!" Travers appeared gratified, though incongruity in brothers could have gone no farther. The other must have caught the suggestion of surprise.

"Step-brother, to be exact. I might be here for a day or two." He made a gesture as if to push Travers on one side, then leaned over the chair. "How're you making it, Claude?"

Whether Rook responded or not, Travers couldn't see. The other turned to him.

"Got anything here to take away with you?"

"Oh yes! Just sleeping things."

"Then you'd better get 'em together. He oughtn't to be disturbed." With a sudden movement he stooped and picked up the sick man. "I'll take him into that other room." At the door he turned. "I'd like to see you before you go!"

Travers nodded at his back, stood there for a moment surveying the open door, then made his way upstairs. From the window he could see the car—but no driver. A curious business that—and a fitting end to a nightmare experience generally. That brother—or stepbrother—must have spent some time in America, or Canada; his accent seemed that of an Englishman whose intonation and vocabulary have become Americanised. But he spoke like an educated man, in spite of his slang and his boorishness; and he looked like a man who'd been used to handling big things and handling them well. Then, his few belongings packed, Travers shrugged his shoulders. At some later and more convenient season Rook could be called on again, in a purely private way; if, of course, he didn't again approach Durangos in the meantime.

With the attaché case to hand he sat on a chair in the hall and waited. From the living-room came the drone of voices. Once or twice a voice was sharply raised, but what was taking place heaven alone knew. It must have been a quarter of an hour before George Rook came out, closing the door quickly behind him. His face manipulated itself into a set sort of smile as he held out his hand.

"I want to apologise to you, Mr. Trent." His eyes glanced down at the initials that stood out on the attaché case. "You must have thought me almighty rude, handing you out the frozen mitt like that!"

Travers, taken aback, was on the point of a disclaimer. Then some instinct told him it wasn't expected of him. He took the hand limply.

"Oh—er—not at all!"

"Your name is Trent?"

"Oh yes!" He felt again for his glasses, and why he made that answer, he didn't know. Cussedness perhaps—and a furious dislike. Then, "How's your brother? Better?"

"Much better—but he's still in a mighty bad way." He broke off suddenly. "He's approached you about buying and publishing some of his music, hasn't he?"

"Er—yes!"

"You haven't actually bought any?"

"Oh no!" Travers feared he'd been too emphatic.

The other nodded. "I see. Claude wasn't quite himself and I mayn't have caught his drift—but he says he doesn't want to sell any music now. He's given up the idea . . . and he doesn't want to be bothered about it."

Travers smiled comprehendingly. "That's all right. I shan't bother him. If he cares to communicate with me later—well and good. But the approach'll have to come from him; you understand that!"

"Perfectly!" He seemed remarkably satisfied. Then he gave another awkward look. "You seem rather a superior person, if you'll excuse me saying so, to be here buying up music?"

Travers froze up. "You think so? You regard business as something—er—derogatory to a man?"

"No! No! No! You mistake me!" He gave an effusive pat on the back which Travers took without flinching. "And where're you bound for now? Back to town?"

"That's right!" Travers still retained a certain frigidity.

"Well, there's a train due now. I'll take you down in the car." He felt in his pocket and found a paper and pencil.

"Let me have your address, will you? And the firm?"

"There's no firm," said Travers. "Lawrence Trent is the name—as you may see in the *Musical Times*. 75a, Fleet Street. That'll find me."

The paper was put away with a certain amount of play. "We'd better hurry if we don't want to lose that train!"

From the front door Travers watched him get the car round, with much complicated tacking. And without being aware of it he must have noted the car's number and placed its year as he came across to take the seat which Rook indicated.

"I'm not exactly in grade A as a driver, Mr. Trent," he remarked, after one piece of risky cornering. "Cars over in the States, you know, have a different drive."

"Really!" said Travers. "Still, if we get to the station alive it's the one thing that matters!"

But the interesting thing was the confiding. The car dropped to a bare ten miles and clanked along in top.

"I think there are some things you ought to know, Mr. Trent," the other began. "For instance, perhaps you noticed that Claude's not all he should be . . . in the head."

Travers nodded in agreement. "If you don't mind my saying so, I did notice something. He seemed eccentric. Perfectly sane, I imagine. I mean he struck me that way."

"The very thing!" He began a gesture, then clapped his hand quickly to the wheel again as the car lurched. "He has his sane periods. Every year I come over and see to him and his affairs. This year I was over a few months ago . . . then I got an urgent letter from the doctor. That's why I came over specially this trip . . . and why he was so scared at seeing me. You see we didn't want any scandal about this. Some folks would have put him away in an asylum—but not me! I had a doctor here, living in the house with him, to keep an eye on him and report to me regular. Sometimes he'd go a whole year and nothing'd happen. Then a fortnight ago, what does he do but turn this doctor out of the house. I told the fool he oughtn't to have gone, but he says he was right up against it and acted for the best." He nodded back. "That's who it was with me in the car."

"Really! And he actually left the house?"

"He did. And he took a place in the village here, to keep an eye on him till I could make the trip."

"And what do you propose doing?"

"I don't know. We shall have to confer." He seemed to be thinking the situation over, because it was not till they turned into the main road that he went on again. "I should say we'll get him away at once. Don't know where yet."

"Best thing probably," said Travers. "Were his fits at all dangerous?"

"Oh no! You knew when he was due for one—so the doc. said—because he used to talk a lot of—er—poppycock . . . and he suffered from delusions. He'd be all right, of course, while the doc. was with him, but it'd have been mighty dangerous if he'd started talking to anybody else."

"He's older than you?"

"Not so much. We're step-brothers, as I told you. Same father but different mother."

The car drew in at the station gate and Travers got out.

"Let me take your grip!" said Rook.

Travers laughed. "It's only a featherweight!" He paused indecisively, then held out a dissimulating hand. "I'll say good-bye, Mr. Rook—and thank you very much!"

The other cut him short. "I'll see you off. It's the least thing I can do after kicking you out!" He hailed a porter. "Say you! What time's the next London train?"

"Slow's due in ten minutes, sir!"

"Thought I'd better check up on those times I got from Claude," Rook announced. After that he stuck to Travers like a brother; watched him get his ticket and strolled with him up and down the platform. Travers was taken up with the dexterous avoiding of awkward questions and the fabrication of answers. Rook's cross-examination was so obvious that he felt himself justified. As his old nurse would say, "Ask no questions, Master Ludo, and you'll hear no lies!" Travers, on the whole, enjoyed himself enormously. Then the train drew in and he entered his frowsty third-class compartment, while Rook hung on for the last farewells. And as the train turned the bend, Travers, looking out, saw him still on the platform watching the progress of the train.

"He certainly made sure I was going to London!" Travers told himself. As he leaned back in his comer he began to review the situation. The younger Rook struck him as a poisonous sort of person, for all the ingratiating attitude of the previous half-hour. Still, perhaps he was annoyed, as he had some grounds for being. Rook's madness, occasional or not, was a pretty hefty skeleton to have in the family cupboard. Moreover there might be trouble with the authorities if ever that mild madness should turn to something more dangerous. That was why George Rook had asked so many questions—to find out if Travers were the sort of man likely to make any.

The really curious thing was that even after his fainting fit, Claude Rook should have had sufficient energy—or was it cunning?—to throw his brother off the scent by a false statement as to why the visitor was there. But perhaps it was something else—a solicitude for Travers himself and a desire to exonerate him from responsibility and spare him any bothersome enquiries in the future. That implied, of course, that on recovering from that fainting fit Claude Rook had become normal again—and remembered the events of the last twenty hours in spite of it.

An interesting point, that. If he ran across a fellow who knew all about that sort of thing, Travers thought he'd put it up to him. And there was that question of why he'd never come to the point—the real business about which he'd consulted Durangos. Then Travers smiled. Probably for the very exquisite reason that there wasn't any!

When the train drew in at Pulvery, Travers got out. Half a mile along the road he met Palmer with the car. Five minutes later, he was at Pulvery Manor.

* * * * * * *

The following Monday Palmer, unpacking the bag, came across the manuscript of Rook's tone-poem, and asked for instructions. Travers ran an eye over it again, stuck it in an envelope and locked it in the small safe. Several times during the week he went over the events of that twenty-hour stay at Steyvenning, and without getting any forrader; the problem indeed, of finding the exact amount of method in Rook's madness was somewhat beyond him. John Franklin of the Detective Bureau had, of course, to hear all about it, and with the handicap of utter unfamiliarity with place and persons, could make nothing of it either. As for Sir Francis Weston, he listened to the story and smiled; tried to pull Travers' leg about the whole affair, but suggested nothing. All he did agree to was that no account should be rendered to Rook until such time as he asked for it.

Some days after that strange visit, Travers went down to Pulvery again. On the Saturday morning, Palmer—after the most meticulous of instructions—went to Steyvenning with the major's car and drove along observantly by Mill House. It was shut up, the curtains drawn and the whole place more of a desolation than ever. Travers decided to look it over for himself and went over blatantly enough in the afternoon—to get the satisfaction of an outside view of an empty house.

George Rook apparently had definitely taken his brother away for a bit. He looked like coming back or there'd have been a notice of sale on the gate. That brought an idea. In the village he got hold of an estate agent, and the information that the house was Claude Rook's own property. It had been bought cheaply owing to its comparative isolation, though its upkeep was remarkably small—an odd man, for instance, being sufficient to keep the garden in order during the summer and spring. Rook had been there best part of three years, but where he came from the other didn't know.

In the few days that followed, the curious events of that weekend returned less and less frequently to Travers' mind. All that remained was the not very pressing recollection of an odd sort of experience among unusual people in somewhat strange circumstances. Rook became a kind of unhinged genius whom it was hard to place; and his brother an overbearing, hard-bitten individual who had a strong family pride and some little humanity. As for the manuscript, it lay in the safe, forgotten in the press of everyday affairs and the claims of more normal interests.

CHAPTER V
KILLING, NO MURDER

THAT WAS Travers' story, though the method of telling it was very different. The barest outlines alone were given at the moment; the rest came later at all sorts of times during his new association with Wharton. Some of it came from Wharton's questions or when some stray remark or other came back to the General's mind. Then Travers, answering that particular question, would think of something else in the same context, and so the snowball rolled and rolled till it grew to something reasonably solid.

It is as well, moreover, to mention one thing. Travers, whose modesty has already been overmuch harped upon, could not regard himself with his own eyes. He could say what Rook had done or said at a certain time—but he could not put himself into the picture of the same moment. But Wharton could see everything. He knew that Claude Rook must have been interested as soon as Travers' cultured, diffident and remarkably pleasant voice met his ear. Half an hour of his company and Rook must have known he was entertaining a man of outstanding intellect, though its owner was whimsically careful to disguise the fact. Before the evening had gone, he would have known Travers for a man of keen penetration and catholic tastes, and above all for a delightful personality. There was a man, in fact, to use the terms of his own letter, of implicitly honourable confidence. That was why Wharton was keeping a more open mind. He was not disposed straightaway to set Rook down as a wavering, fantastic sort of lunatic. And as usual, Wharton was careful not to commit himself. It suited him very well—at the moment—to see Travers' point of view, and no other.

"I think I'll have another look at him," Travers said, and went over to the table where the body was lying. He looked down for some moments, then shook his head. "I haven't any doubt about it . . . in my own mind. It'd be too impossible for him to have a double." He looked up. "A visit to Mill House will soon settle that."

Wharton rubbed his hands. "Doctor, I dare say there are one or two things of your own you've got to attend to. As soon as ever Menzies arrives, I'll ring you up—and you two can come back here together. Not a word to a soul, of course."

The next proceeding was an interview with the agent.

"Would you mind telling us, Mr. Large, exactly what you re-member of that American gentleman—the nephew?" he asked.

"Well, he was called Strawson . . . and he spoke with an American accent . . . and he looked like an American!"

Travers noticed the pursing of Wharton's lips at that piece of illogic.

"Tallish, was he?"

"Yes . . . about six foot."

"Hatchet faced?"

"Yes . . . he was. A very shrewd, suspicious sort of face. He looked as if he thought you were trying to do him down—and he'd jolly well see you didn't!" Wharton smiled enigmatically. "Capital! And deep lines down his mouth, each side of a dark, clipped moustache?"

Large hesitated. "Deep lines . . . but there wasn't any mous-tache. He was clean-shaven."

"That's interesting!" said Wharton, and turned to Travers. "Enough to go on, do you think?" Travers nodded. Wharton gave the agent his usual effusive benediction, and he was to keep at his house for a bit in case he were wanted. A most detailed account of everything Large could remember of the whole affair was also suggested. Rough notes would do, provided they were legible.

"The devil of it is," said Wharton, tugging away at his mous-tache, "we ought to be in two places at once. How far is this Steyvenning place?"

"Just over twenty miles. Say twenty-two."

"Hm! Far enough away for safety." He fidgeted about again for a moment or two. "We *must* wait for Menzies and Norris. What about yourself? Free for a day or so?"

"It might be arranged," said Travers. "But I'd better ring up at once."

"Good! And if the Colonel's about, ask him to see me, will you? You needn't come back here. I'll be along at the 'Dolphin' in half an hour."

Thanks to Travers' story, there was little now that was wor-rying Wharton to any considerable extent. He even had a per-fectly satisfactory working hypothesis.

George Rook might have induced his brother to come to Frenchman's Rise, with the idea of solitary confinement—or merely seclusion—as a cure for his mania; a sufficient cure, that is, to enable him to return to America. There might have been a quarrel in which the older man had been struck—and the blow had killed him. Then there'd been panic. The body had been disguised and strung up on the beam, and then the other had bolted. That would explain the greater part of what had seemed inexplicable.

Wharton, indeed, warmed to his own theory. Why had Rook been brought to Frenchman's Rise? Why, because the American brother had been alarmed by Travers. He knew he and the doctor—who, by the way, must be a shady customer—were liable to pretty heavy penalties for allowing a virtual lunatic to be at large. He'd called himself a nephew, and made up that cock-and-bull story of a spa, as part of the covering-up process.

And, to make everything easier, the Colonel came in before Wharton had time to see the holes in his own sieve.

"We might let that man Bent go? Don't you think so?" suggested Wharton, when everything else had been settled up.

"I think so," said Mazer. "He's only cluttering up the place."

"And, do me a favour," said Wharton. "Let me have the use of a couple of your men till mine get here. I'd like to know just where that shaving and hair-cutting were done. I think I'd go about it like this . . ."

Mazer wrote it all down.

"I'm going back to the village now. The 'Dolphin,' if you should happen to want me. By the way, I think you said you got no prints."

"Not a single one!" He gave the reply an air of mystery. "We went through everything. My detective sergeant saw to that as soon as we got in. There wasn't a speck of dust—comparatively speaking—on chair-backs and glasses and things like that, that people would have to handle—and yet there was plenty about, if you see what I mean!"

"Quite! They knew the value of finger-prints. However, I think I'd tell your men to be careful. We just might find something that's been overlooked."

When the colonel had gone, Wharton heaved the fastened suitcase on to the table. He made quite a study of it, but without much result. It was an oldish one, in good quality leather, and therefore probably Claude's own and not his brother's. The contents—except for the pairs of glasses in perfectly plain cases—were even less informative: three sets of under-garments, flannel shirts, linen collars, socks, a couple of ties and some handkerchiefs—and not a laundry mark on a single one of them, though in at least three cases he could see where tabs had been cut off and marks picked out. Wharton grunted as he tumbled the contents back. The glasses he put in his pocket.

His next visit was to the kitchen; then he made his way out by the back door and looked about him. The shed first caught his eye and he, too, noted the signs of a fire beneath the copper. He even grubbed about among the ashes. Outside again, he stood for a moment or two surveying the garage door.

In a couple of minutes his chauffeur was at work with a screwdriver and they had the door open. What Wharton was expecting to find, his man didn't know. All that was to be seen was a bare, concrete floor, with scarcely a tyre or oil mark. Except for the dust on the ledges and the cobwebs that hung from the rafters, the garage was as bare as the day it was put up.

"Hm! Swept as clean as the room!" began Wharton, then glared at his man. "What do you think? There's been a car in here? "

"I should say so, sir. There's a smell of petrol!"

Wharton sniffed—and grunted. "Stop here a minute!" He got down on his haunches, looking for tyre marks on the roughly cindered road, and shuffled along the fifteen yards to the outside gate. He got up looking none too pleased.

"That fine spell we had kept the ground too hard," he told the other. Then, "Put the door back and we'll get going. Pull up at the 'Dolphin.'"

* * * * * * *

That early lunch was the last word in scratch meals. As Wharton told Travers, they'd better feed while they could, since heaven might have to provide the next meal. Travers, knowing Ravens to be scarce, tucked into his bread and cheese and left no heel-taps. Also he had to babble away during mouthfuls, while Wharton thought of questions and made notes.

"You're certain this chap Strawson was George Rook?" he asked.

"I suppose I am," said Travers. "Aren't you?"

"Why two names? and change of relationship? and shaving off his moustache?"

Travers smiled. "What's the idea, George, of asking me such fool questions?"

"Nothing like two points of view!" said Wharton placatingly. "You agree that he didn't want to run the risk of anybody at Steyvenning finding any connection with what he did here."

"Exactly! Twenty miles, in the first place, is the devil of a distance in the country, once you get off main roads. All the same he was taking no chances."

"Hm!" Wharton hopped up and prowled round the room restlessly. Then he sat down again and lugged out his pipe.

"You mustn't be annoyed, but isn't the bottom rather knocked out of that poetical idea of yours? What was it? Something about princes."

"It certainly looks like it," smiled Travers, and repeated the quotation.

"'No comets seen, 'eh?" said Wharton. "That's a clever remark, you know. Common sense wrapped up in Sunday clothes! . . . And all that trouble for nothing. You see what I mean?"

"Damned if I do!"

"Well, all that elaborate disguising for nothing. You know what Rook's face was really like; therefore you've queered the pitch. You'll help to reconstruct for the photographs. To-morrow morning every newspaper will have Rook's face on the front page. In twenty-four hours we'll know who he really was."

"Then you *do* think he wasn't everything that appears?" Wharton dismissed that facer with a shrug.

"And if all these wonderful results, George, what do you want *me* for?"

Wharton grunted. "You needn't put it that way, because you'd stop whether I wanted you or not! And don't you want to go to that house again, to see what's happened?"

"Don't you begin worrying about me, George," said Travers. "You'll have quite enough to worry about when you find you *don't* get your results in twenty-four hours!"

Wharton waved a contemptuous hand.

"Just think for a moment," went on Travers amusedly. "Suppose I *do* reconstruct Rook's face. *Do* I?"

"What's this? A riddle?"

"Not at all! What face do I reconstruct? Merely the one he had at Steyvenning. He's lived there like a recluse. Is that the face that launched—I beg your pardon! I mean, is that his real face? Now you're assuming the very contrary to your arguments. You say that whoever cut his hair and beard did so because they didn't want any connection with Steyvenning. Agreed, but . . . they altered his face in a very peculiar way. They left those absurd little mutton-chop whiskers. If Rook had ever worn whiskers like that, then he'd be recognisable by somebody who'd known him at that time. What I say is that they didn't want his face to be a real one. They wanted to *disguise a disguise!*"

"You mean, the way he wore his hair and beard at Steyvenning was a disguise?"

"I should say so. That can be discovered when we get his past history—if we do. We can also discover why."

"Hm! . . . And if you're right, what do you propose?"

"Well—er—why not three photographs? At some time he was almost certainly clean-shaved—that makes one. Then there's how I knew him at Mill House, and how we found him to-day. Purely a suggestion, of course."

There was the sound of a car—two cars—drawing up in the yard. "That's them!" grunted Wharton and made for the door. Travers sat pat, following events from the sounds that came from outside, till the General came back, Chief-Inspector Norris and Menzies with him. Travers duly shook hands.

"Mr. Travers'll give you the outlines, Norris," said Wharton. "Tell him both ends of the story, Mr. Travers! . . . Got all your saws and carving-knives, Menzies? Then we'll get hold of Vallance . . ." The voices droned away.

Wharton got back in the middle of Travers' story and promptly got out his notebook in case he'd missed anything.

"What do you think of it, Norris?" he asked, when Travers had really finished.

"Sounds fishy to me, sir. You don't shut up mad people nowadays as they used to hundreds of years ago."

"Yes, but this was admittedly an illegal shutting up!"

Norris shook his head. "Bit too early yet, sir, to say anything at all. I'd like to look things over."

"Come along then!" said Wharton. "You come in with me and I'll tell you some more. Mr. Travers'll bring that hell-waggon of his."

Judging by the numbers already on the spot, and the new arrivals there looked like being an overflow meeting at Frenchman's Rise. Norris was left to get things going. The General and Travers looked in to see how Menzies was coming along.

Menzies, a grey, old veteran to whom corpses were as common as carrots, was enjoying some joke with Vallance. He lit a cigarette before he gave them his news, and waved it at the naked body.

"One or two things you didn't mention about this fellow!" He grabbed the left arm and showed something quite invisible to Travers. "Couple of prick marks there!"

Wharton produced his glass. "Given a couple of jolts of dope, you think?"

"He'd hardly have done it himself!"

Wharton nodded. "Well, you'll soon know if it's still inside him. When are you taking him away? At once?"

"In a minute or two. But have a look at this first!" Even Travers saw it this time. Round the ankles were distinct chafe marks. Wharton frowned, then got his glasses to work again; and, knowing Menzies, kept his thoughts to himself.

"What's your idea?"

The other sniffed. "Well, it looks as if he's been tied up, doesn't it? Not unlike handcuffs marks either."

"Handcuffs!" Wharton had another look. "Hm! And round his ankles! Where'd they keep the poor devil fastened, Mr. Travers? Up in that attic?" Travers couldn't find an answer, but he fumbled away at his glasses. "It seems incredible to me."

"Incredible!" Menzies snorted. "If handcuffs go on a man's wrists, why shouldn't they go on his ankles? if you can call spindles like that 'ankles'! Mind you, I'm not saying they were handcuffs. I just suggest it."

Travers smiled apologetically. "I didn't mean that, doctor. Er—I suppose anybody could get hold of a pair of handcuffs?"

"Oh, yes!" said Wharton. "Not official pattern necessarily. Any theatrical costumier'd have 'em."

"Or a slop might have dropped 'em!" suggested Menzies, giving Vallance a wink.

"As you say!" said Wharton imperturbably. "A slop might have dropped 'em. Come along, Mr. Travers. We'll have another look upstairs."

Outside the door, one of the local men was waiting with an envelope.

"What's this?" asked Wharton. "Floor sweepings?"

"That's right, sir! In the attic it was, sir—where he was shaved."

Wharton nodded, put the envelope in his pocket and turned towards the stairs.

"Oh! might somebody fetch Mr. Large along?" Travers asked. "There's something I particularly want to ask him."

Wharton called back the man and gave him instructions. It was not till they were in the attic room that Travers explained.

"This is what I was thinking," he said, pulling out those two pieces of paper he'd found on the floor. "It's probably preposterous, but look at this wall. Don't you think the paper's been carefully stripped off?"

Wharton squatted down and had a look. Then he tried his glass, and shuffled along where the light was best.

"Looks like it. But why's it so clean underneath?"

"Don't know, but—er—I'm hoping Large'll be able to explain. You see, what I thought, when Menzies mentioned those hand-cuffs, was that they'd—by 'they,' of course, I mean George Rook and the doctor—well, they'd kept the poor devil up here, tied so that he couldn't get away. Why they should expect that'd cure him of mania, I can't say; still, that's not the immediate point. If he were tied to that hook up there, he couldn't get to the win-dow to attract attention. If he stood on the chair he couldn't be seen, because the room's too dark. But he could reach this wall. Why then shouldn't he have marked it all over—with a nail or a splinter?"

"What sort of marks?"

"Well, he might have written some music. That strikes me as the sort of thing he'd have been likely to do. When the other two discovered it, they found it wouldn't come out without removing the paper. It'd have been too dangerous to leave it on, because it might have been a valuable clue to his identity." He smiled apol-ogetically. "Er—perfectly absurd, of course, but there we are!"

But Wharton was putting the chair under the hook and try-ing the height above the floor. He explained. "If Rook had been allowed this chair permanently in the room, I thought he might have mounted it and unfastened the rope." He reached up with his hand. "You see! . . . he couldn't have managed it."

"Surely that's a further proof that he didn't commit suicide," said Travers. "If he couldn't reach the hook, how'd he get the rope on it?"

"Easy enough!" said Wharton, and proceeded to demon-strate. "He made a loop in it . . . then threw it over . . . like this!"

"Hm!" said Travers. "So he might! . . . But something else! The rope he was hanged with wouldn't reach to the ground; therefore it wasn't the one he was fastened with!"

Wharton looked really pleased at that. "Now that's what I call a sound deduction! The trouble is, we can't rely on the evidence. They may have changed the rope just before—or he might have been fastened by his wrists—or heaps of other red-herrings we'd think of if we'd time." He shrugged his shoulders. "Still, why worry? Soon as they've got him open, we'll know whether he died from hanging or not. One thing's lucky; we know he wasn't hanged by force!"

Travers shook his head gloomily. "I was a damn fool, you know, George. If I'd seen one of you people and told you what happened that week-end."

"Why should you! You'd be sitting on our doorstep if you reported every time you met a man who acted like a lunatic! . . . This sounds like Large!"

From the way the house-agent looked about him as he entered the room, it was clear that that was his first visit since his extraordinary tenant had taken the house over.

"What's this hook for?" Wharton asked.

"Hanging lamp. If you look carefully you'll see there's an asbestos strip countersunk in the beam." Wharton nodded as if he knew that already. "Any differences here since you handed the house over?" Large looked round again, then spotted the wall. "Why! he's taken off that paper I had put on!"

"Why'd you have it papered?"

"Well, I had it whitewashed first; then I thought the room looked too cold, so I had some thick, oak-grained paper put on. You see I'd advertised this attic as suitable for a bedroom."

Wharton grimaced. "No wonder you fellows ride about in motor-cars! . . . I suppose the paper'd strip off easily?"

"Perfectly easily. It's thin paper that takes some getting off."

"These two scraps likely to be pieces from it?"

Large looked, frowned and hesitated to commit himself; not that it was necessary as the General remarked to Travers when he'd gone.

"You saw the ash under the copper?" Travers asked. "Oh yes! I saw the ash all right!" and he led the way to the steps.

Menzies collared him at the foot of the stairs, looking none too pleased. How long was that damn cinema business going on? Vallance oughtn't to be kept hanging about. Wharton pacified him by an insistence on the possibilities of consultation—

and took them both inside. The next hour was a tedious and distressing business for Travers. Rook's face had to have that horrible stare eliminated from the eyes and the gaping mouth had to be got into shape; and there was Travers, having to look on while the dead man came slowly to life. Worst of all was the shaving, and the final flash of the magnesium in the dim light, with the head propped gruesomely up and the camera people as unconcerned as if the scene were a suburban studio.

Then while Wharton was busy over all sorts of things at the same time, Travers wandered off to the car. Frenchman's Rise was like an ant-heap that had been disturbed. What with the lights in the rooms, the police at the doors, the cars lined up, and the small crowd of curious sight-seers herded off the end of the lane, the whole atmosphere was that of the closing scenes of an auction. Then at last Wharton came along—and a plain-clothes man with him.

"Fit?"

"For what?" asked Travers.

"Steyvenning. Like a cup of tea first?"

"Not particularly . . . if you're in a hurry."

"I am . . . and I'm not!" He hopped in alongside and waved his man behind. "You'll want to see Palmer and arrange for a room, so pull up at the 'Dolphin.'"

At the hotel he imparted a little more information.

"Just going along to arrange inquest preliminaries. Take my advice and get some tea. Lewis has to get a gallon or two of oil," and off he went.

"Oil?" asked Travers, and looked at Lewis.

Lewis nodded at the disappearing figure.

"He said you said there were nothing but oil lamps there, sir; and there mightn't be any." Another nod. "Not much *he* misses!"

Travers smiled. "Perhaps you're right. Let me find you a spare can."

CHAPTER VI
WHARTON LOSES A WITNESS

IT TOOK JUST over half an hour to get to Steyvenning. Wharton called at the police station, expecting to pick up another man.

"You got my phone message?" he asked the station sergeant.

"Yes, sir. The man's waiting. Only it wouldn't have been necessary, sir. We've had a man round there for some days now."

"Really!" Wharton wondered why.

"Yes, sir! Mr. Rook sent a note—his brother brought it—to say the house might be unoccupied all the winter, unless he should happen to call there himself for anything—the brother that is, sir. So naturally we kept an eye on the place. Just a minute, sir. I think I've got the note here."

Wharton had a look at it and passed it over to Travers. Travers made a wry face as he handed it back.

"That's not his writing—unless he didn't write the letter he sent us."

"So I thought!" said Wharton. "There was one yam to keep inquiries away from Frenchman's Rise and another set to keep 'em away from this end." He put the note away in his pocket-book. "I'll keep this, sergeant. What was the brother like? I mean, how'd he strike you?"

"Well—er—quite a pleasant-spoken gentleman, sir. American by the look of him."

Wharton merely nodded. "Well, we'll push along now, sergeant. Probably call in on the way back."

They took the policeman aboard and pushed off again. Travers let the car crawl through the ford and round the bend, with the lights full on. Wharton peered out and saw nothing. Just inside the short drive the car was slewed round, with lights on door and windows, and out they hopped.

"What's your name?" Wharton asked the constable.

"Bone, sir!"

"Right then, Bone. You go round to the back door and stay there!" He tried the front door himself—rather hopefully,

Travers thought—then flashed his torch into the windows, only to get a good view of the curtains.

"Break a pane of glass, Lewis, and get inside. If you can open the front door, do so!"

In five minutes Lewis had it open, thanks to the key being left in the lock.

"Good!" said Wharton. "Now bring along the oil and we'll get this Tutankhamen's Tomb lit up!"

In a couple of shakes they had the living-room lamp going and Wharton was having a look round. Travers felt as if it hadn't been more than a day since he last saw that room. At any moment it seemed as if the door must open, and Rook or his housekeeper come in. Wharton began pottering around, touching this and that and squinting along the backs of chairs or whenever there seemed the likelihood of a fingerprint. Then he tried the drawer of the side-table.

"I thought you said this was locked!"

Travers came over. "Well, I distinctly saw Rook lock it."

"Hm! It's open now—and there's nothing in it." He looked round again. "That cupboard there; wasn't that where he kept his music?"

But there was nothing in the cupboard except a few unimportant oddments. Wharton fussed round again; tried the doors of the small sideboard and opened everything that could be opened, from piano to coal-scuttle.

"Somebody's been over this room." His tone was quite aggrieved. "There wasn't any music in that bag of his. . . . And there's no paper ash in that grate. . . . What about having a look in the kitchen? Get the lamp going, Lewis, if there is one."

The kitchen told them nothing—except that it seemed to have been left in a fairly untidy state. Wharton took a cup from the drying-rack over the sink and showed it to Travers.

"Just swished round and stuck there! A woman wouldn't leave a cup like that."

"Where are the women?" asked Travers. "Surely we ought to be able to get hold of that girl Bertha! She'd tell us a whole lot!"

Wharton took him up a bit short. "Damn it all! How many pairs of hands do you think I've got? We'll get hold of her all right!" He moved across to the back door and stooped down to the bolt. Something appeared to be wrong by the way he looked round. Then he tried the top bolt, then lifted the latch. The door opened! So did Wharton's eyes.

"What do you think of that now! Been open the whole time!"

Travers frowned. "Curious! Which way did they go out?"

"This way. The front door was bolted, wasn't it, Lewis?"

"It was, sir. Top and bottom!"

Wharton had another look at the back door as if he expected it to tell him something. Then he looked startled, grabbed the lamp and had a look through pantry and scullery. Next he tried the cupboards of the kitchen dresser, opened the back door again to make sure Bone was there, then bolted it carefully. Finally he lit a couple of candles.

"You stay there, Lewis, and watch the stairs. Mr. Travers and I'll have a look up above."

Wharton went in front, Travers bringing up the rear and looking like an imitation of the Statue of Liberty. The house struck as cold and damp as a tomb.

"My God! I'm cold!" Travers shivered in the heavy ulster.

Wharton grunted. "Hm! Didn't you see the frost on the ground as we came—Sh! You hear that?"

Travers listened. Somewhere in the middle of the deadly silence of the house was a noise as if a window were being drawn open. Wharton stood with mouth open and eyes staring, then tiptoed across the landing. Travers followed, shielding the lamp.

What happened then he didn't know. He saw Wharton make his spring for the door and heard the rush of his feet inside the room, but by the time he'd got inside the door, the General was leaning out of an open window letting out a yell. "There he goes! ... Bone! ... Bone!!!"

Travers, standing there shivering, still managed to see the incongruity—the burlesque balcony scene; Wharton leaning out of the window and the constable doubtless looking up, mouth agape.

"A man's just run off down that road. See if you can get him!"

"A man, sir?"

"A man!!" roared Wharton, till Travers thought the whole of Steyvenning must have heard. "Down there! Get after him!"

There was the sound of feet padding off, then Wharton drew in his head and pulled down the sash.

"Pretty sort of fool's errand he's gone on! Like looking for a black cat in a coal-mine."

Travers set the lamp down. Since the whole affair had been to him little more than noises off stage, he wasn't any too excited.

"What was it? A burglar?"

"Damned if I know!" said Wharton and looked round. "What's the idea of that?"

"That" was the wardrobe, pulled out a good three feet from the wall.

"Looks as if somebody's been looking for something!" Travers suggested lamely. But Wharton was behind the wardrobe, asking for the lamp. A couple of minutes later, he'd made up his mind.

"We'll leave everything as it is till the print people get here. Hold the lamp and we'll see what's in the drawers."

It wasn't hard to see that everything had been disturbed. Under-linen and garments that should have been neatly folded, were disarranged. As for clothes, not a garment carried a tailor's name.

"That's strange, you know," said Wharton. "It isn't as if the tailor's tabs had been cut off. They never were on! When he had a suit made, he must have given special instructions."

"What about the other things?" asked Travers.

"All got laundry marks. And they all seemed to be marked 'C.R.'"

"Just a moment!" said Travers. "Are there any old ones with the C.R. mark?"

Wharton exhibited a vest. "There you are! That's not a new one. What point are you making?"

"I don't know that I'm making any," said Travers. "It merely shows that he brought some of his personal belongings with him when he came here. What about the other rooms?"

He lifted the lamp and the tour recommenced. This time there was no trace of a soul and every window was securely fastened. But one or two things were informative. The bedrooms that had apparently been occupied by maid and housekeeper were bare of everything in the nature of personal belongings. The furniture too, as one could see from the marks on the varnished floors, had been moved out and put back again. Even the linen cupboard appeared to have been pretty thoroughly searched. Outside on the landing, Wharton shook his head, either with annoyance or perplexity.

"Can't make it out! Everything's been mauled about. What've they been looking for?"

"Heaven knows!" said Travers. "Unless old Rook hid his music and they've been looking for that."

"Music!" sniffed Wharton. "And why weren't his clothes taken away? And leaving linen in a place riddled with damp like this!"

"The thing is, *who's* been doing it? And whoever's done it, couldn't have done it all to-night, surely!"

"There's no reason why he shouldn't have been here all day," retorted Wharton. "If that fool Bone gets hold of him—However"—he led the way downstairs again. "We'll go over this place with a microscope to-morrow. No sign of anybody, Lewis?"

"Not this way sir."

"Right! . . . What's in that room, Mr. Travers?"

"Don't know," said Travers. "Never been in."

One glance round that room was enough. At one time it had doubtless been a drawing-room; now it was empty except for a table and three or four chairs that stood forlornly by the wall. There wasn't even a carpet on the floor. Wharton had a look in the grate.

"No fire here for years! Smells a bit musty, don't you think so?"

Out again in the entrance hall they found Lewis, apparently waiting for them. He collared Wharton at once.

"Would you mind having a look here, sir, in the kitchen? I think I've found some footprints!"

Travers saw nothing but Wharton was remarkably interested. He waved Travers to one side, then got down with his glass and apparently followed the prints to the door. Then he had a good look at the fibre mat. Then he began all over again while Travers held the light down close. He even made pencil markings on the tiled floor, explaining what it was all about.

"Two distinct sets of feet, as you see. This is the man's . . . starts here at the mat and goes straight on through the door. No return. That's our friend who took a chance and dropped out of the window. . . . This is a woman's . . . see the heel-mark? . . . goes to the door, and only the faintest traces of coming back again. That shows she went where there was a carpet or rug. After that—"

He broke off suddenly, took a lighted candle from the dresser and opened the back door. Travers followed with the lamp, in time to see him emerging from the shed.

"Ah! Bring the lamp, Mr. Travers, will you? Lewis! you stay in the hall!"

A whiff of wind sent the light flaring as Travers nipped across. The shed seemed chock-a-block with gardening tools, firewood, coal and rubbish generally. But in the comer to the right was a heap of hay, pressed down as if by the weight of a human body. At its foot was an untidy heap—half a dozen sacks. Wharton began footprint hunting.

"Somebody's slept here!"

Wharton paid no attention to that essay in the obvious.

"Looks as if we'll have to get another man or two along. Let's get back to the house. I'll fasten this door."

Inside, he handed his torch over to Lewis.

"Have a look round the garden and see if you can see her. Not much hope, but still, have a look. If you see any footprints, follow 'em up."

He nodded to Travers and stamped off to the living- room.

"Bit warmer in here. . . . May as well make ourselves comfortable till Lewis and that fool of a policeman get back."

Travers shivered as he got out his pipe.

"Who was the woman, George?"

"Your housekeeper friend by the look of it."

"Yes, but—er—why?"

"Because she must have a key to the back door. And she's the only one who'd come back. The servant wouldn't. The man was probably the one who came here with the American. Two keys go to a lock. He had the other one."

"But who left the back door open?"

"She did. He shut it and went upstairs to work leisurely. She left it open because she went out in a hurry, probably when she heard us arrive."

"Yes, but what I mean is, why can't we get hold of her? She must be somewhere close?"

Wharton shrugged his shoulders. "Good enough! You go out and holler!" Then he snorted. "What good can we do—looking for an old woman! There's only the one torch. If we try the roads, she's probably gone just off 'em, into the woods." He shook his head reprovingly. "Impatience is no good! She'll have to go somewhere to-night. As soon as we're ready we'll get off back and arrange for the roads to be patrolled."

"You're quite right," said Travers. "But it—er—worries me, George. You've no idea what a delightful old soul she was! . . . What did she come back here for?"

"Don't know—unless it was to see what had happened to *him*." Then off at a tangent. "By the way, I'll have to get hold of that fellow who did the garden. He'll have to identify the body—officially."

They sat for some time, drawing away at their pipes and saying nothing. To Travers the whole experience seemed like a disjointed dream; as if the evening he had spent weeks before in that room, and the day's horrors at Frenchman's Rise, were all mixed up in some mad nightmare from which he had just woke up, feeling cold, depressed and empty inside. Then Lewis's voice could be heard outside—and the policeman's in answer. Wharton got up and drew the blinds, then had a last look round.

"I'll take this lamp to the hall. Lewis can stay there till I get back."

Travers pulled the coat collar round his ears and hunched his shoulders. The house struck cold to the marrow; just like a tomb, he thought again, and somehow it seemed to smell like one. Wharton and Lewis came in by the kitchen door.

"Nothing doing!" said Wharton. "She's gone. If she should come back, Lewis, keep her here!" and he moved off to the door.

"Look after her!" added Travers. "She's dumb, by the way!" and again at the door, a final word. "Tell her I shall be along in a minute. She knows me."

He got the engine running while Wharton gave Bone yet more orders, then backed her out to the road. Why he was even hopeful of seeing something along that gloomy lane he didn't know, but he let the car crawl and peered at the grass verges or strained his eyes at the short stretches of road between the bends. Then, all at once, he saw something—something that looked like two dark, detached shadows in the middle of the road. Before he knew it, he pulled the car up dead. Wharton had a look.

"Hallo! What's that?" He opened the door and scrambled out. He was kneeling by the body by the time Travers caught him up. Then he undid the coat she was wearing and put his head down. Travers held his breath as he watched.

"She's alive all right! Get the car up!" His breath, Travers noticed, came out in the frosty air like smoke, against the headlights. Wharton got to his knees and lifted her head from the ground. Travers hesitated.

"Is it—er—Mrs. Fletcher?"

"Damn who it is!" snapped Wharton. "Get that car!"

Travers scurried off back and drew the Isotta to the side of the road. Between them they got her inside.

"Put that bag in!" said Wharton, "and draw up at the first house and find out where a doctor lives!"

Travers shot the car off. Just in the main road a passer-by was questioned, then invited in alongside. A couple of hundred yards and they were outside the house. The pair of them staggered to the door with the body while Travers hammered.

"Tell the doctor he's wanted urgently!"

Wharton backed his way in. The maid gave a startled look, then disappeared down the passage. Almost at once the doctor came bustling out—napkin in hand and chewing away.

"Sorry to trouble you," said Wharton, "but here's a woman we found lying in the road!"

* * * * * * *

An hour later, Travers was sitting in the surgery, alone with what was almost certainly a dying woman. Wharton had rushed off to the police station to do some urgent phoning and set this wheel and that in motion, and the doctor had left the room for a moment. Exposure—and utter exhaustion—had seemed to be the trouble; the heart just going, and no more. As Travers sat by the fire, chafing his hands, he was leaning over almost near enough to touch the wrinkled face. Earlier, when she'd swallowed the warm brandy and water the doctor had coaxed into her mouth, and as he chafed her hands, they'd thought for a moment she was going to rouse herself; but the fluttering of the eyelids stopped as suddenly as it began.

As he looked at her, Travers felt an extraordinary tenderness, of which he wasn't in the least ashamed. Hers was a motherly face, full of quiet sorrow. Years ago she must have been almost beautiful; even now the pallid skin and the white hair and the set of the lips had something pathetically lovely about them. Who was she really? Why had she crept back to that house? and the irony of it—running away from some imaginary fear when, had she known it, it was help that was coming! He rose quietly, and as he leaned down, suddenly held his breath. For a moment he'd thought she had gone—then felt the pulse still moving. . . . The doctor came tip-toeing in.

"What's she like?"

"All right!" whispered Travers, and, "Isn't the room too cold?"

"Mustn't have it too warm!" Travers shook his head and rubbed his hands nervously. Then he stepped back as the other drew a chair up. What he was doing he couldn't see; then came a shake of the head.

"Poor old soul! . . . Fine-looking old lady!"

"Nothing else we can do?" whispered Travers.

He shook his head. "She's going fast. . . . Matter of minutes."

"Any pain?"

He shook his head again, then came over to the fire and chafed his own hands.

"She'd have been dead long ago if you fellows hadn't come along."

"Picking her up and—er—moving her, didn't do any harm?"

The question wasn't answered. There was a quiet moan from the chesterfield . . . the sound of heavy breathing . . . a voice; a quavering, complaining voice, like a person muttering in his sleep. But it wasn't merely noises. These were words—phrases; so quiet and droning that for the life of him Travers—ear almost to her lips—couldn't tell what she was saying. Then he suddenly realised the miracle, as he clutched the other's arm.

"She's talking!"

"Talking!"

"Yes!" The lips were still moving as he peered closer, then the head fell sideways as if querulously. With face tense, he leaned over, staring desperately as if to force some meaning out of these almost inaudible mutterings. Then they stopped; suddenly—as if in the middle of a word. Everything appeared to relax as the lips parted—then pouted open. Travers looked up in alarm. The doctor nodded him away and leaned over.

"She's gone!"

Travers turned away, groped for his glasses, then put them on again. The door bell rang. . . . Wharton's voice was heard, then the maid's as she ushered him in. . . . The General came shuffling over.

"How's she now, doctor?"

"Just gone—half a minute ago. Excuse me a moment. I'd better get the case down before I forget anything." Wharton came over and had a look at her. He shook his head as he drew back the rug again.

"There goes what might have settled up this case in five minutes!"

"Don't you *ever* think of anything but cases?" asked Travers quietly.

Wharton shrugged his shoulders. "What else am I paid for? About the inquest, doctor. Day after tomorrow suit you?"

The doctor thought so.

"You perfectly satisfied about cause of death?"

The other looked thoughtful. "Ultimately . . . yes! But that's not everything, you know."

"Mind if our man, Menzies, comes along to see you about her . . . now?"

"By all means! As a matter of fact I'd be rather glad."

"Good!" He looked round again at the shape on the chesterfield. "You didn't know her, I suppose?"

"No! . . . I don't think they ever had a doctor in."

"It wouldn't have been necessary," said Wharton. "They had a doctor living in the house."

"Relative, you mean."

"Oh no! Professionally."

"What on earth for?"

Wharton stressed the question of confidence, then told him.

"I say! that's most amazing. Are you sure you're right?"

Wharton shrugged his shoulders. "That's the story as we heard it. You say there never was a doctor there!"

"I'm dead certain there wasn't!"

"Well, we'll soon have that settled," said Wharton. "Now then; about you and Menzies. Will you have her here—or at the police station?"

"Oh! police station I think."

"Right! I'll arrange it straight away. Ready, Mr. Travers?"

Travers was remarkably quiet during that short journey. Wharton, on the other hand, was quite chatty.

"So that was his housekeeper! . . . Nice-looking old lady. Rather reminded me of an old aunt of mine. How old would she be, do you think?"

"Sixty-five . . . about."

"Hm! Of course women don't wear so well as men . . . that is to say the majority don't. Just in here, on the right. That's it! . . . Where'd you put that bag?"

"Bag? I thought you had it."

"I! Hm!" He hunted round for a minute or so, throwing things here and there and trying impossible places. Then he exploded.

"Damn the bag! What's happened to it?"

"Somebody's probably taken it."

"Taken it! What'd they want to take a bag for?"

"I don't know," said Travers mildly. "What do people take bags for?"

He followed Wharton, still furious, to the door. Quite a lot of people seemed to be inside, as if waiting for somebody—Wharton himself probably. He stood by as the General registered his complaint and saw a couple of men despatched to make enquiries. Then Travers was motioned on again, to what looked like the waiting-room.

"Make yourself comfortable there for a bit," Wharton told him. "I'll send you in some tea as soon as I've got things going."

"Oh!—er—just a moment!" Travers hooked off his glasses. "Something rather peculiar happened at the surgery . . . while you were away. That—er—housekeeper—Mrs. Fletcher—*spoke*. . . . Just at the very last, it was."

"Spoke! What do you mean 'spoke'?"

"What I say! She began to mutter things."

"Then she *wasn't* dumb!"

Travers shook his head. "That's for you people to say. I'm not sufficient of a medical man to know if paralysed nerves can recover under a shock—if her nerves were paralysed. All I do know is that she was muttering."

"What'd she say?"

"I don't know. . . . She was talking—or muttering—in what I took to be Italian."

"Italian!"

"Yes! That's all I know. One word I thought I could catch—a girl's name . . . Lucia."

"Hm! Italian! And what happened then? Did the organ start playing?"

Travers looked at him. "Perhaps it did, George! That was the last thing she said. She said it twice—Lucia! Lucia! . . . like that. Then she drooped over."

CHAPTER VII
POETRY AND PROSE

WHARTON'S FACE lost its flippancy. Travers, if he had felt in the humour, might have smiled at the sudden way in which he ingratiated himself into the new situation.

"Lucia! Means 'Lucy,' doesn't it?"

Travers nodded.

Wharton came back from the door. "Tell me now; why should that man Rook have had an Italian house-keeper."

"Why shouldn't he?"

Wharton smiled blandly. "Ah! now you're huffed!"

"Not in the least! That is, I hope I'm not. Self- analysis is rather difficult, but I don't think you're looking with my eyes. Why should you? . . . I said there was no reason why he shouldn't have had an Italian housekeeper—and I repeat it. It's merely un-usual, that's all. But if Rook made his money in Italy; if he had Italian connections—as hundreds of people have; if he once kept an Italian chef, and Mrs. Fletcher was his widow; then it all be-comes perfectly natural."

Wharton nodded unctuously. "That would be so, of course! But did she look like an Italian when she was alive?"

Travers pondered. "Well, now I come to think of it, the first time I saw her—she did! Or she might have been French. No! she couldn't have been French! I was forgetting. I thought she wasn't the usual type of house-keeper; that is to say I accepted Rook's version of her as correct. There was something about her . . . some natural distinction. I can't explain it exactly."

"You thought she was a lady!"

"Well, yes! At that one meal, for instance, Rook mouthed his food. She behaved without a false note; with a complete natural assurance; and that in the presence of a stranger—and herself supposed to be merely a housekeeper!"

"Hm! And why did you say she certainly wasn't French?"

"George; when people are dying—in semi-consciousness, even if they're bilingual they talk the one language that's in their bones!" He shook his head. "You see the difficulty is really quite a different one. I don't know a hundred words of Italian. It *sounded* like Italian; that's all I know. And I thought I caught the word 'Lucia.' But I won't—I *can't* guarantee anything. She might have been muttering Slav—or Turkish. All I'll say is, I *sensed* it was Italian—and I believe it was." Wharton nodded heavily once or twice, then moved off to the door.

"I shan't be more than half an hour or so. If you can think things over again, so as to give us a bit more to work on, you'll do us a power of good."

Travers sat there as advised but found his mind singularly disinclined to concentration. It was the romantic contacts—Mill House with its living occupants, and the attic at Frenchman's Rise—that kept luring his thoughts away into unprofitable memories.

Wharton's notorious stand-by—a pot of tea—came in; then a pipe or two passed the time. There was the sound of the arrival of a couple of cars; Menzies' voice; the heavy shuffling of feet as the body was brought into the next room; droning of voices all over the place and the telephone bell ringing. Then, about an hour later, in came a constable with a tray, and Wharton at his heels, taking off his coat and muffler.

"Got a hot meal from the local hotel. Thought we could do with it. Quarter of an hour is all I can spare." He rubbed his hands over the tray. Travers drew up a chair.

"Smells good, George. Looks good too."

Wharton, with a hunch of bread between his teeth, nodded. "Any more news?"

"Not yet. We haven't found who's got that bag. The chap who brought us along doesn't know anything—and he's a most unlikely person, so they tell me."

"Probably a sneak thief who took it."

"Might be. Or what about our friend who got out of the window?"

Travers stopped chewing. "That's an idea! But what could she have had in the bag?"

"I know one thing she had in it," said Wharton. "You know the village you come to if you go straight on past Mill House. Flitterton, it's called. Well, we just got word she was there last night and bought a loaf, some butter and cheese. She had 'em written down on paper and just handed it over the counter at the village shop. That's how they remembered her so well. We're now trying to trace how she got to Flitterton. She didn't stay in the shed before last night because the constable says he was in it, sheltering from the rain, the night before, and there wasn't any hay there then. That was the night he thought he heard somebody in the house."

"The same man we disturbed to-night?"

"Might be. What matters is not who he was but what he wanted."

"You mean he wasn't an ordinary burglar."

"Maybe I do," said Wharton. "Burglars aren't fond of doing the same job two nights running—-and they don't move out furniture and look behind it!"

Travers flashed a look at him but the General was steadily munching away.

"Where'd she get the hay?"

"There's a stack opposite the house. By the way we've got off your description of the maid. The Press'll have it to-night."

That was how the meal went on, with Wharton's quarter of an hour stretching to double, in spite of his mastery in timing larynx and gullet.

"Where'd Rook come from?" he asked.

"I don't follow," said Travers.

"Well, before he came here. His bank manager couldn't give us any information. There wasn't any transferred account. Why did he ever come to Mill House?"

"Purely as a suggestion," said Travers, "may I say that a man who buys a house in a remarkably secluded part, and takes over the furniture—suitable or not—may do so because it will be difficult to trace where he *did* come from. There was an unfurnished room at Mill House, yet he didn't bring any furniture with him to fill that particular gap. I suppose you've enquired. Tell me. Did he bring any furniture with him? "

"Not that we can trace. Apparently he arrived in what he wore and what he had in his luggage. That's the annoying part of it. I was counting on tracing him by that."

"You have one excellent method of tracing," said Travers.

"What's that?"

"The piano! It wasn't a new piano. If he were used to the tone and the touch, he'd hang on to it at all costs. Any firm or railway company would remember transportation of a grand piano—and a Blickdorf at that."

Wharton thought that over, then, "Who *was* Rook?"

Travers smiled. Wharton had put the question so disarmingly, as if to himself.

"I haven't the least idea. For one thing I never probably saw him at all—exactly as he was. The only time he struck me as real was when he was playing the piano; and then, paradoxically, he was transfigured."

"He played well?"

"George!" said Travers patiently. "Do you want me to exhaust the superlatives? He was an expert; that's my last word."

"A mad genius!"

"Genius—true; but not necessarily mad. When he looked most mad was probably the only time he was sane."

"Of course, if you're going to talk in epigrams—" said Wharton and shrugged his shoulders. "However; you still think the story the American told you was truer—"

"Frankly, I don't—at this particular moment. If we can prove that what he said about there being a doctor in the house is quite untrue, then the whole story begins to collapse. Mind you, I still think that even if the man you call 'the American' wasn't Rook's step-brother, he must have been somebody with very real authority over him; otherwise why did Rook flop clean over as soon as he saw him?"

Wharton shook his head as if the problem were beyond him. He finished his platter, with Travers toiling in the rear, then wiped his mouth with that immense handkerchief of his, as a sort of prologue to the next question.

"You're good at riddles. Why was Rook tied? Tell me that!"

Travers glanced at him. The General's face was perfectly serious.

"Well—er—so that he couldn't get away!"

"That depends," said Wharton. "Your answer's the obvious one. He might have been tied, not only so that he couldn't get away, but so that the others *could*!"

"You mean?"

"He was tied up in the house. One man might have remained there, or he might not. But *one* could get away, back to the house yonder—especially at night. He could get back there to search for what he was looking for; for what that fellow we disturbed to-night was looking for!"

Wharton's argument received no further elaboration. There was a tap at the door and in came Menzies, with what looked like a collection of letters.

"Something here might amuse you, chief!" Wharton glared at him. "What's the idea? Been to the talkies?"

"Possibly! This is the sort of thing you hear when you do go there. Dying mother. 'Oh, my poor child! What will become of you?'"

Wharton took the packet and had a look. Travers changed his mind about the letters and thought they were playing-cards. When Wharton passed them over, he saw they were photos; the largest not more than four inches by two. Menzies' voice came from the door.

"Heart failure, due to exposure, seems probable. Give me a knock if you want anything."

"Where'd you get these from?" asked Wharton. "From her vest. Special sort of pocket sewn in." Wharton watched the door close, before he referred to the mote in the eye. "Callous lot—police surgeons! . . . Now then! What do you make of 'em?"

Travers had another look, holding each at arm's length, then almost up to his glasses. He sorted them out and handed them back.

"Eight photos of a girl. First at about four years; last at about fifteen. Quite good-looking. Italian probably . . . May even be Lucia!"

Wharton shuffled the photos quickly; re-shuffled them; took them to the light and tried his glass on them.

"We'll get an expert to run his eye over 'em!"

"Just a minute!" said Travers. "May I have another look? Wondering about backgrounds," he explained. "There might be something we could identify from an enlargement. May I have the glass?"

He went over them carefully, then shook his head.

"Devil a thing! Almost looks as if they'd deliberately avoided it!" Then he whipped them round in sudden alarm . . . then smiled. "And there's nothing whatever on the backs!"

Wharton put them away in his pocket. "Done by an amateur, by the look of 'em . . . Who are they? Her daughter?"

"Why speculate? And if she really was sixty-five, it's rather against the law of averages."

Wharton jerked at his watch, glared at it, then jerked it back.

"You don't mind hanging on?"

"Not if it's necessary!"

The smile was wasted on Wharton's back. Travers settled down to another hour of his own company—pipe after pipe, and the rumination that ended where it began. Then at last Wharton's voice was heard; the door opened and in he came, with a very nervous looking old countryman.

"Come along in, Mr. Bastable! We shan't keep you long. One or two things you could tell us about Mr. Rook, that might explain a good deal . . . Try a fill of this!"

"Mr. Bastable," he explained, "used to do Mr. Rook's garden."

His voice lowered to an impressive sort of confidence, that Travers found it hard not to smile at.

"Mr. Bastable has just identified the body!"

He got out his pipe as Travers nodded gravely. Travers followed suit with the pipe, though his mouth was already like a lime-kiln. Bastable's voice was of the earth, earthy; all burred and homely. "I don't know all that about him, sir, as I was telling you. He was a good master—and he paid well."

"Glad to hear it!" said Wharton. "Mind you—I don't like mentioning it now he's dead—there were some people who said the poor old gentleman wasn't right in his head! He had fits of . . . well, you know!"

"I never saw him like it, sir."

"Just what I thought!" He nodded with self-congratulation. "Just what I was telling Mr. Travers here. People will talk scandal and make up what they can't account for . . . You never had the least idea he wasn't right in his head!"

"He was always all right with me, sir." He paused as if hunting for words. "A bit fidgety, sir; he always was that. But as right in the head as you and me, sir!"

"Exactly! . . . And what did you see him do in the garden?"

"Him, sir? Oh! he just pottered about. Used to do a bit of weeding sometimes, only generally he used to watch me. April I used to start, sir, and knock off in October."

Wharton made an elaborate motion of dragging back something from the past.

"Oh! didn't someone tell me he had a doctor living in the house?"

"Doctor, sir! Not that I know of!"

"You mean there couldn't have been?"

"There never weren't no doctor in that house while *I* was there, sir!"

"And you never heard about one?"

"No, sir! There weren't no doctor!"

Wharton looked at Travers and raised his eyebrows.

"Then I must have heard wrongly, Mr. Bastable. For instance, Mrs. Fletcher never mentioned a doctor to you."

The old man's face slowly crinkled to a smile. "She'd have had a rare job, sir. She was dumb!"

Wharton chuckled and slapped himself on the knee. "Of course she was! Fancy me forgetting that!" Then what might have been a roguish look. "But the maid wasn't! I'll bet you sixpence!"

Bastable nodded sideways. "Ah! she was all right, sir. Pretty young thing."

"Where'd she come from? I mean, she wasn't a native of these parts, was she?"

"Lowestoft she come from, sir. One of them seaside places, so they tell me. We was talking one day about the sea and—"

Wharton was patting him on the back.

"Excuse me a moment, Mr. Bastable!"

He left the room rather hurriedly. "More phoning!" thought Travers, and took the mantle of Wharton on him, without the rest of the theatricals.

"How long have you worked at Mill House, Mr. Bastable?"

"Ever since Mr. Rook come here, sir."

"That'd be about three years ago?"

"Two years last Easter, sir."

"Er—where'd he come from?"

"That I don't know, sir. He did tell me once he'd been up in the north."

"Nothing more definite? Scotland, for instance?"

"Well . . . no, sir. He was sort of vague like." Wharton come bustling in again and Norris with him. He made straight for Bastable with outstretched hand.

"Well, Mr. Bastable, we must wish you good-night!" He fairly hustled the old man to his feet. "We're very much obliged to you. You'll be at your house if we should happen to want you in the morning?" and so on till the door closed on him. Travers looked on amusedly.

"We'll have that girl here to-morrow, or my name's Walker. Norris is getting out a description of the American. He's already got Large's version. Let's sit down and compare notes for a bit."

Norris jotted down Travers' rather spasmodic recitation. Wharton slashed into both editions and made his precis. He seemed quite pleased with it.

"This should do the trick! A bit poetical, your version, Mr. Travers, if you don't mind me saying so. That chap Large is a fool! If he describes those desirable residences of his like he did that American, he'd soon have to earn an honest living. Get this off at once, Norris. Tell 'em to rush the cable."

"Talking of poetry," said Travers; "there's something I'd almost forgotten . . . er—if you'd like to insert it. It's a sort of poetical addendum to the facts . . . You remember I told you he didn't drive the car to the house. Well, if he'd been what we might call the predominant partner, he'd surely have driven the car himself . . . Also he was a rotten driver when he *did* drive it!"

"But you said he'd been used to an American car!" said Wharton, rather impatiently.

"Oh, no! I said *he* said he'd been used to an American car! Left hand drive and right hand controls, of course. But that hardly holds water, George. I'll bet I drive an American car and make a better hand of it than he did, even if I do fumble a bit with the levers!"

If Norris, obviously anxious to get off, hadn't put his spoke in there, something rather ingenious might have emerged; but put his spoke in he did—and to such purpose that Travers forthwith resigned.

"Oh! I don't know, sir! If you're looking about for levers, your eye can't be on the road!"

Travers shrugged his shoulders, smiled—and left it at that. "Just one thing I *would* like to be clear about, and that's the question of accent. Strawson, *alias* Rook, *alias* heaven knows what, wasn't a dyed-in-the-wool American."

"How do you know?"

"I don't. Didn't I tell you it was poetical? I've been sitting here to-night, wondering if he was an American trying to be

English, or an Englishman pretending to be American. All I can think is, he's an Englishman who's been used to the society of Americans of the baser sort."

"Toughs?"

"Well . . . not exactly. Say, users of the more obvious slang."

"I see!" said Wharton, and waited for the rest of the poetry. But there wasn't any.

"Get that off now, Norris. And find out if they're on the way yet."

"A few more men coming," he added for Travers' benefit. "This is a job that's going to need quick work . . . What about getting back to the 'Dolphin'? You'd like to turn in." Travers yawned with pleasure at the prospect, then hoisted himself to his feet.

"You haven't a lot of soul for poetry, George—but there are times when you talk extraordinarily good prose!"

CHAPTER VIII
MADMAN'S MUSIC

TRAVERS WAS UP bright and early the following morning, but to very little purpose; it was well after nine o'clock before Wharton made an appearance, and just when the morning papers had been skimmed. The Press people had made a good job of the Rook photos—three of them, in the plumb centre of the General News Page—but it was with a surprise that was almost repugnance that he saw below them the face of the old housekeeper. Almost as soon as the breath was out of her body, Wharton must have rushed the photographers along.

Now he had had time to think them over, there were one or two things about which Travers was puzzled and as soon as Wharton arrived, he tackled him point blank. Travers had not so many points of contact with Wharton as Franklin had. Sometimes indeed, when the head of Durangos' Detective Bureau was positively infuriated by information being withheld, or doled out in a tuppn'y ladle, Travers had been inclined to smile or assume some subtle superiority.

"You rub him the wrong way!" he'd say; then Franklin would blaspheme.

"The wrong way be damned! He's a hoarder; that's what he is! He secretes information and then expects you to work in the dark. He asks you to put two and two together, and then you find he's only given you two and one!"

"Anything definite about Rook's death?" Travers began.

Wharton was aggravatingly non-committal. "Well—in a way. It probably wasn't due to asphyxia."

That was enough for Travers.

"Then what's happening at his inquest?"

"Rook's inquest? Well, there'll just be formal identification of the body and evidence as to the finding. We may lay stress on the fact that he was found *hanged.* Then we'll leave it at that and adjourn for three weeks—and let 'em think what they like. If they assume it's suicide, all the better."

"I see!" said Travers. "Perhaps I'm a bit dense, George; but if I understand you aright, you'll say nothing about handcuffs and wallpaper and all the rest of the novelette."

"That's right!"

"Then why have you given the Press all this publicity? Why should you make such a tremendous fuss over a matter of suicide? Won't everybody know it's something more?"

"Ah!" said Wharton. "You haven't got it right. You see it's the Press—ostensibly—who're making the mystery! Look at the headlines—'UNKNOWN MAN FOUND DEAD IN EMPTY HOUSE. WHO IS HE?' and so on. That's all news interest. *We're* hardly mentioned!"

"I see!" said Travers—and didn't see at all. Wharton went on with his breakfast.

"Any other news?" Travers asked.

"Chiefly negative. We've got Strawson's movements dated more or less accurately. That reminds me. That car number you gave us doesn't exist!"

"Then the license was forged!"

"Why not? It's an easy enough job if you set your mind to it . . . We didn't find any prints in the house, except the old lady's. Still, we're hopeful. What the devil we shall do with 'em if we get any, is quite another matter."

A few moments' more munching, and the General told some further news.

"Something rather interesting. Those glasses of Rook's. They're dummies!"

"Perfectly plain glass!"

"That's it! Quite good quality rims."

Travers digested that while Wharton went on with his meal like a man in a hurry.

"You won't mind my mentioning it," put in Travers mildly, "but what line of attack are you thinking of? I mean, what theory are you working on?"

Wharton took his second cup of tea almost at a gulp, wiped his mouth prodigiously, then hopped up.

"Bit too early for that, isn't it?" He gave Travers a look which was half affectionate, half anxious, and wholly dissimulating. "I've been thinking you'd like to slip back to town for a bit. Nothing here to interest you at the moment. . . . Routine work mostly. . . . I'll give you a ring. Some time to-night probably."

Travers felt suddenly as if he'd been wiped clean and put back on the shelf.

"I'm to be ready if you want me—in other words."

"That's it!" said Wharton. "It might be at any moment. What we should have done without you, heaven knows! . . . I'll ring you up to-morrow in any case."

* * * * * * *

That was why Travers was at Durango House in time for an early lunch. Over his coffee he marked the entry of Sir Francis, and in due course strolled over. The senior director seemed rather surprised; he was more so by the time he'd heard the whole story. Moreover he forgot, very conveniently, his leg-pulling of the previous occasion. He looked mightily important.

"Can't we do something about it?" Then a sudden idea. "Why! the man was a client of ours! He still *is*! His account's not settled!"

"His account's settled all right!" said Travers. "But I don't see what we can do at the moment. I don't think the police would welcome any attempt to get publicity out of it."

Sir Francis looked down his nose.

"You're seeing Franklin about it—confidentially? Just a suggestion, of course!"

Travers assured him that that would be all right. In any case, though he didn't mention the fact, the meeting had already been arranged for that afternoon. Indeed, if Travers hadn't expostulated, Franklin would have kept him there till evening. As it was he must have been talking for the best part of an hour without the questioner being much the wiser.

"It's a pity—in a way—that *I* wasn't there instead of you," said Franklin, and then apologised for the implication. "Tell me! How exactly did she pronounce that word 'Lucia'?" and he proceeded to a series of variations.

Travers shook his head bewilderingly. "My dear fellow! it's no use your testing me for dialects. I tell you I merely caught a couple of words."

"Just a minute!" went on Franklin. "What *might* she have said? Was it anything like this?" and there came more of what was presumably Italian. Travers listened patiently.

"I tell you I haven't the least idea what she said! All I know is, it sounded like the Italian I've heard. It certainly wasn't French—and it wasn't Spanish."

"Right-ho!" said Franklin. "We'll leave it. One thing did occur to me, though. With regard to that little catch question about the two elevens; do you think Rook had that specialised information because he was at Eton himself?"

"I don't think a public school ever sheltered Rook," said Travers. "He was infinitely remote from the type. Also I don't agree that the information was specialised. Most cricketers know it—and every cross-word puzzle is crammed with snippets of information. Now what I would like you to tell me—you knowing twice as much about Wharton as I do—is what he's up to over that inquest business."

Franklin sniffed. "George was probably a mole, several thousand years ago. He loves grubbing about in the dark. What I should guess is this. There's got to be some publicity for the purpose of tracing Rook and his housekeeper, so he gets the Press to take that off his hands. But he doesn't want to alarm certain people, so he keeps the Yard in the background and suggests suicide. That gives him three clear weeks to get results in."

"Alarm what people? The American and the so-called doctor?"

"Yes—probably. I was thinking of the man you disturbed in the house. George wants to create the impression that Mill House is finished with. That's why he rushed extra men to do the place over. I should say it's all nicely shut up again now—like a mole-trap. The next fellow who comes along by night, he'll collar. That might clear up the case."

"Then he's wrong!" said Travers decisively. "If he thinks that chap we disturbed the other night is going to walk into an obvious trap like that, he'll find himself mistaken."

"You never know!" said Franklin oracularly. "You going now? What about dinner in my place to-night?"

"I'd love it! . . . But wait a moment. There's a film I simply must see to-night . . . No! I'll go after an early tea. Seven-thirty suit you?"

"Splendidly!" said Franklin. "And what's the idea of the film?"

"Oh! just the first effort of a company we're financially interested in . . . Seven-thirty then!"

An hour or so's work in his private room; a very early tea, and Travers set off for Shaftesbury Avenue and the Resplendent.

"Big picture on?" he asked the cloakroom attendant, who looked out from his counter round to the illuminated timeboard. "All shown on the board, sir! Travelogue just going on, sir. Big picture, fifteen minutes!"

Travers groped his way to his stall, polished his glasses while the lights were on, then wriggled comfortably to his seat as they dimmed.

PICTURESQUE TUSCANY
COLOGNE COLOUR FILM

Travers was interested. After all that talk about Italian, the mere sight of an organ-grinder would have suggested possibilities. The interest was also a personal one—all those set scenes one knew so well; the little perched villages, the torrents, the winding, dusty roads, the women in clothes of those hectic colours the camera loved; all very jolly and like seeing old friends again. Then something came that was different from the recalling of his own holidays in Rome and the South . . . a clump of cypresses, backing a vast, ornate garden.

Travers, like the foolish knight, was a fellow of the strangest mind in the world; sometimes the most cautious of individuals; then dashing off at a second's notice into any ludicrous, if merely mental, adventure that suddenly presented itself. This time it was the cypresses . . . then that tone-poem of Rook's—*The Seven Cypresses*, of. . . where was it? Val . . . something. What about hearing it again? Suppose there were in it something he'd missed! Suppose . . . then he found himself on his feet, wandering back to the vestibule.

An attendant directed him to the wings at the back of the screen and almost as soon as he got there, the organ finished playing and into it there merged the raucous stridencies of the canned music. A moment or two and there came along a youngish, bald-headed man in black. Travers approached him.

"Excuse me, but—er—could you spare me a moment?"

The other gave him a look, then took the proffered card.

"I take it you are free now for some time," went on Travers. "I mean while the talkie's—er—on?"

"That's right. I have to stay here, of course, in case there's a breakdown."

"Exactly!" and he waited.

The other gave a second look, then, "Come along to my room, will you?" and led the way.

Travers peered round at the massed photos of what he supposed were celebrities, noticed the grand piano, then took the chair offered him. He passed over his very best case of very best cigarettes.

"I've got a most unusual proposition to put up to you. I take it you don't know my name? . . . I thought not. Still, I'm a most respectable person. The thing is this. I have a manuscript—a tone-poem—left me by somebody who's just died. If I get it, will you be so good as to play it for me?"

The other smiled for the first time.

"I'd be very pleased to. Of course you mustn't expect a masterly rendering at sight! Still, I'll try to reproduce the notes. Got it with you?"

"I haven't," said Travers. "But I can get it in a matter of ten minutes, if you'll be so good as to—er—allow me that time."

In the vestibule he glanced at his programme—

ORGANIST:—Rupert Maine, Mus. Bac., F.R.C.O.

Sounded promising—and the chap looked adequate without being ostentatious. Probably one of those super-organists whom the cinema people were paying like Under-Secretaries—if the papers were correct.

When he got back, Maine was just finishing his tea. He pushed aside the tray at once, adjusted his pince-nez and ran his eye over the front page. The title seemed to attract him.

"I should explain," said Travers, "that the composer told me he had in mind Respighi's *Pines of Rome* when he wrote it."

Maine nodded. "Important, was he? I mean, could he have intended to dedicate it to Respighi?"

"I doubt it," said Travers. "He's dead now—poor fellow—but he was a genius of sorts; at least he struck me that way. An erratic genius, shall we say. Even mad, perhaps."

"You've actually heard it played then?"

"I have. Once only—by the composer; and it impressed me very much. That's why I'd like to have a second opinion on it; one as expert as your own, if you'll pardon my saying so."

Maine smiled as he took his seat at the piano. "I think I'd wait till you heard me, if I were you! . . . Manuscript's wonderfully clear—that's one good thing." He flicked out the light. "I'll just have the reading light on, if you don't mind."

Travers leaned back in his chair as he had done that night at Steyvenning. As he caught the first notes of the theme, a curious feeling of depression seemed suddenly to pervade the room. As the treble took up the melody and things came back to his mind, all the experiences of that strange visit seemed amazingly near again. So vivid were they that for a second he almost feared to open his eyes, to see away on the other side of the room the placid figure of an old woman, quietly embroidering. He smiled at his own foolishness as he opened his eyes . . . then sat up with a jerk! From the piano was coming the most extraordinary series of noises; horrible cacophonies as if a lunatic were pounding the notes with his fist.

"I say! Something seems to have gone wrong!" came Maine's voice from the piano. Travers wondered just what that meant. Then the notes were struck again. Travers shuddered.

"Just have a look here!" said Maine. "Look! The whole thing's gibberish!"

Travers peered over his shoulder at the music. There certainly seemed to be the devil of a lot of notes—about as many as he'd seen in the highest-browed effort he'd ever tried to play for himself—and found beyond him. Maine waved his hand contemptuously.

"It's all rubbish! . . . Look at this! It isn't sense at all! It's just notes stuck down on paper! . . . It's noises!"

"Excuse me!" said Travers, "but would you mind seeing how long these—er—noises continue in the manuscript?"

Maine turned over the sheets, snorting now and again, or jabbing down an accusing finger. When he'd finished he gave a perfectly prodigious grunt.

"Hm! . . . Whole thing's rubbish! . . . There's no sense—musical sense—in it!"

"I say! I'm awfully sorry!" said Travers, and looked it. Then he had an idea. "Would you mind if I suggested something? You mentioned—er—noises. Is there any possibility of connecting up with any definite noises? Is the music in any way onomatopaeic? I mean, like Honegger's *Railway Train* or *Football Match*?"

Maine said nothing for a moment, then made a face. "You mean, is it futurist music? Say an example of programme music as it may be in a hundred years' time?"

"Well, something of the sort. Could you possibly see if any sense at all could be made out of it?"

"Impossible! It's unplayable! The notes are unrelated. It's merely a series of unconnected, indiscriminate sounds!" He gave Travers a droll look. "Somebody was pulling your leg!"

Travers blinked as he took off his glasses.

"Perhaps that is so." He shook his head as if puzzled. "Do you know, it's remarkably queer? The composer put that manuscript on the rack—or desk, or whatever you call it—as you did; and he played it right through!"

"He turned the sheets over?"

"Hm! Now you come to mention it, I don't think he did. I assumed he knew it by heart."

"Yes . . . and then?"

"Well, he just played it! He said it was variations on a theme; the theme it opens with. Every now and again I could recognise the theme reappearing—and I'm no musician. It was simply magnificent. I remember it ended in a plaintive sort of run; something like the ending of the *Liebestraum*. Then he took the manuscript off the piano and handed it to me, and I put it straight in my pocket."

Maine shook his head perplexedly as he handed the sheets back.

"He must have been telling you deliberate untruths. I hope I'm not speaking unkindly of a friend of yours. All I mean is, he had the theme in his head; then he sat down and improvised on it, creating the impression that it was all written down. You say he played well?"

"Superbly!"

"Quite! He found extemporising very easy."

Travers looked rather upset for a moment, then his face cleared again.

"Do you know, I think you must be right! When I asked him if he'd like me to get it published for him, he said *no publisher'd look at it*!"

The other grimaced. "He wasn't far wrong!"

He made a movement as if the interview was over, but Travers seemed loath to leave things like that.

"Please don't let me be a nuisance to you, but I feel this rather keenly. It's something very important for me! . . . Tell me! That opening part which you played. Any genius in that?"

Maine shrugged his shoulders. "Fairly obvious stuff . . . An attractive theme—yes! But so are most folk-songs. The genius would lie in what he made of it. As it stands, the theme isn't sufficiently developed to judge." Travers nodded comprehendingly, shook his head as if at some private decision, then picked up his hat. At the door he stopped again.

"Will you do something for me, Mr. Maine? I'll pay your fee, whatever it is . . . but I *will*! I'm a professional man myself, and I expect payment for services rendered! It's this. I'll retain this front page—the legible part. Will you take the rest of it and see if any sense can be made of it at all? Go into it thoroughly. I don't mind what it costs."

Maine smiled dubiously. "Well, I'll have a shot at it . . . though I know it's waste of time. I ought to tell you that beforehand."

"Don't worry about that!" Travers told him. "I'll come and see you again in a few days. You don't mind my being insistent?—but explore it from every side. And if you don't mind, write me a short report." Another idea. "I suppose there's no chance of any enigma being wrapped up in it?"

Maine shook his head. "I doubt it. Still, I'll have a look at it."

"Splendid!" said Travers and held out his hand. "When it's over, you must come and have dinner with me. A Sunday perhaps would suit you best . . ."

* * * * * * *

When Franklin heard the account of that half-hour in the organist's room at the Resplendent, he seemed to see nothing unusual in it—the contrary rather.

"Well, that settles it!"

"Settles what?"

"That he was mad. Who'd do a thing like that if he wasn't?"

"There's no use rushing to extremes," said Travers. "Maine may find something after all. He struck me as a remarkably clever fellow."

"That's just my point!" retorted Franklin. "He's clever enough to know what makes sense and what doesn't. If you're not careful, you'll find he'll be putting you down in the same category as Rook!"

Travers smiled. "Possibly . . . but tell me this! Doesn't Rook's action strike you as rather *calculated* madness? For instance, I'm positive he *could* have written that tone-poem if he'd been inclined. Why did he play it—and play it, mind you, as if for the hundredth time—and then deliberately hand me a collection of rubbish?"

"And with a nice clean front page to act as wrapper!" laughed Franklin. "He did it because he was mad; in your own words—calculated madness; the sort of queer trick an unbalanced mind *would* play. Your friend Maine was right . . . Got that front page with you?" Travers passed it over. Franklin gazed at it solemnly, scowled at it, nodded his head as if the music were in some way being miraculously transmuted, then passed it back.

"It's a bit beyond me. Hymns and Handel are the limit of my musical intelligence. . . . Going to show it to Wharton?"

"If he asks for it."

"Hm!" said Franklin. "One thing did strike me. Why the *Seven* Cypresses?"

Then the telephone bell rang.

CHAPTER IX
WHARTON SHOWS HIS HAND

HALF AN HOUR later, Travers was being shown into Wharton's room at the Yard. The General looked up to the eyes in work but he smiled genially.

"Couldn't do without you long, you see. Take a seat for a bit till I finish up. Cigarettes are alongside you." Travers made himself comfortable as directed. Wharton sat scribbling away, glasses half-way down his nose, looking benevolent and guileless as a missionary. Every now and then he doled out scraps of information.

"We've got hold of that maid. They're now fetching her from Liverpool Street . . . She should have been here now if the train'd been on time . . . I want you to be here while we talk to her. You'll be reassuring, if you don't mind me saying so."

"A new role for me!" said Travers. "And what do you want the car for?"

"Man down in Devonshire—a doctor—thinks he's recognised both Rook and the housekeeper. I'd like to have you there because you'll have more things to listen for—or identify, shall we say?—than I have. And I thought we'd travel at once and get it over. After a scratch meal, of course. Say about nine-thirty."

"What part of Devon?"

"Tiverton. Know it?"

"Pretty well." He smiled. "I take it you want my car because you want to travel!"

Wharton looked up for the first time. "Well yes . . . reasonably. The doctor's going to wait till we get there."

"You didn't think of having him come here—or half-way?"

Under the circumstances Wharton had to make his reply not too crushing. "A lot of good that'd have done. If he's got anything to tell us, it'll be down *there* we've got to look for it . . . We've got some more news about that housekeeper, by the way. We know where she's been."

Travers waited for the rest while Wharton scribbled on. Then there was a tap at the door.

"Miss Smith is here, sir."

"Show her in!" said Wharton briskly. "Bring a pot of tea and cups for three, in five minutes . . . And ask Miss Foster to be ready to come in as soon as I push the bell."

The keen air had flushed the girl's face and she was looking a fiery red as she stood all flustered just inside the door. Wharton got her at her ease, prattled away about everything but what mattered, dragged Travers in and marked time generally till the tea came in. Travers regarded the brew with resignation and took his cup for the good of the cause. Then Wharton came to the point.

"How did you like being at Steyvenning, Miss Smith?"

Travers was surprised at the freedom with which she talked. At Steyvenning she had struck him as a pleasant-faced, jolly, but rather rustic sort of soul. Possibly she was one who flourished on limelight. Possibly, like more than one of her sex he'd seen under similar circumstances, she was expanding under the influence of Wharton's urbane-cum-paternal manner. Whatever the cause, she prattled away as if in her own family circle. With an accent specially produced for the occasion, she informed them that Steyvenning was very nice.

"Everybody treat you well?"

"Oh, yes! The master was very nice, and Mrs. Fletcher, she was an old dear!"

"You didn't find the household at all peculiar? Mr. Rook wasn't queer in his manner?"

"Oh, no! he was very nice!"

"He never struck you as being—well, not quite right in the head."

Her amusement provided the answer.

"Mr. Rook used to play the piano a lot."

"Oh, yes! he used to play a lot—on the piano. I didn't like it very much, what he played."

"You like something more cheerful!" cut in Travers. "Oh, yes! Dance music . . . and bands."

"What about the 'cello? Did he play that?"

"He and Mrs. Fletcher used to play. I mean she used to play the piano."

"Really! She could play the piano, then!"

"Oh, yes! Mr. Rook told me she wasn't always a housekeeper. She used to be a lady, only her husband lost all his money."

"Really!" Wharton was suitably grieved. "Now, Miss Smith; how'd you first come to Steyvenning? Answer an advertisement?"

"Oh, no! The agency sent it to me—at Lowestoft."

"I see. And what made you go so far from home?"

"It was the money. Mrs. Cross, at the agency, she said I'd be lucky if I got forty—only they said they'd give sixty because the house was a bit lonely; and they'd give more if I stayed on."

"And did they?"

She nodded. "I got five pounds a year extra. Seventy pounds I was getting, when I left."

Wharton gave Travers a look. "A most unusual sum! I expect that Miss Smith must have been a very clever girl in the house, Mr. Travers. Any particular conditions attached to the money? That you weren't to gossip, for instance; or go down the village?"

She seemed very surprised at that. "No! I used to do what I liked. I went to church once on the Sundays—and I went to the socials. Oh! and once a week Mr. Rook used to let me go to the pictures with a girl friend of mine."

"In other words, you were very comfortable there!"

"Oh, I *was*! The only thing I didn't like was not having no holidays—and I couldn't go home. Mr. Rook said that was one of the reasons they paid more."

"I expect it was. And now about Mrs. Fletcher. You didn't find it awkward communicating with her? I mean, on account of her being dumb?"

She smiled. "First I did—then I got used to it. They say you can get used to anything!"

"I suppose you can," said Wharton cheerfully. "I imagine you used to talk by signs."

"*She* did—till we got used to each other." She laughed. "Sometimes we used to get in rare old muddles. She didn't seem to know what I was saying. Then she used to smile—oh! and it was ever so funny!"

"That'd be at first?" suggested Travers. "Till she got used to you."

"Yes, it was all right after a bit; just as if we'd been there for years."

"Exactly! And the work was perfectly normal? You did the usual things?" That puzzled her. Wharton explained. "The housework was just the same as in any other house?"

"Oh, yes!"

"Tradesmen used to call?"

"Yes; the farm used to send the milk—and the butter and eggs. Then the butcher came every other day. Oh! and once a month the barber used to come and trim the master's hair."

Wharton nodded. "Now something to make you laugh! Was Mrs. Fletcher fond of macaroni dishes?"

She didn't laugh; she thought. "We used to have macaroni—sometimes. I used to like it . . . because it was made with eggs!"

"You mean 'pudding,' I expect," smiled Travers. "Did you ever use to have it as a separate dish? With tomato sauce, for instance?"

"Yes—sometimes they did."

Wharton nodded over at Travers. "That's unusual—and rather suggestive!" He made a note on the pad at his elbow. "You were saying, Miss Smith, that the barber used to come and trim Mr. Rook's hair. He didn't go out much himself then?"

"Not to the village, he didn't. He went up to London. Twice he went . . . no! three times. Every summer it was."

"While you were there, you mean?"

"Yes! every summer while I was there."

"How long was he away?"

"Only the day! He went up in the morning and he come back the same day."

"You're certain it was *London* he went to?"

"Oh, yes! I heard him *say* he was going to London." Wharton gave Travers yet another look. "Plenty of letters used to arrive, Miss Smith?"

"Not a lot there weren't. You see, Mr. Rook hadn't anybody living and Mrs. Fletcher hadn't either. They told me so."

"Did Mr. Rook ever tell you, or did you ever hear him say, where he came from when he moved to Steyvenning?"

"Not exactly, he didn't. Somewhere up north I understood it was."

"I see! And were there ever any callers?"

"Not while I was there." Then her face lighted up. "Something funny did happen. About a week it was, before Mr. Rook went away."

"That'd be a week before *I* called!" broke in Travers.

"Yes . . . sir. A week before then it was. There was a man come to the back door and asked if we could—No! Mrs. Fletcher wasn't there; she was having tea. He asked *me* if I'd tell him the way to Steyvenning . . . so I told him. Then he asked all sorts of questions about Mr. Rook and offered me half a crown and when I told Mr. Rook he was absolutely furious!"

"What sort of questions?"

"He said how long had he been there . . . and was he a short man . . . and where did he come from." Another appeal to Travers. "We shall have to get further details of that . . . And Mr. Rook was angry, was he?"

"Yes! he stared at me as if I'd done something wrong!"

Travers cut in again. "You didn't think that Mr. Rook wasn't angry at all? That he was—well, frightened?"

That seemed to strike her for the first time. "He did look a bit frightened. Oh! and next morning Mr. Bastable came in the kitchen all riled and said somebody had been walking all over his bed of asters—the one that was under the front window; and he saw Mr. Rook about it and made him go out and see it. Oh!"—her face positively beamed—"I saw the man again, the one what called at the door. It was him who came to the house with Mr. Rook's brother!" Another beam. "The day *that* gentleman was there!"

It was Travers' turn to get excited. "You mean he was the man who drove the car in which Mr. Rook's—er—brother arrived?"

"I don't know whether he drove the car, but he was along with him."

"Splendid!" said Wharton. "What was he like exactly?"

"Well—he wasn't very big; bigger than Mr. Rook, but not big ... And he had dark hair, going grey, and a beard all going grey too."

"A beard! What shape?"

"It wasn't any shape. It was all short, like Mr. Rook's only darker."

"Cut short like this?" and Wharton stroked his chin.

"Yes! Sort of pointed-like."

"What was his voice like? Would you call him a gentleman—an educated man—or not?"

The reply came without hesitation. "He spoke quite nice. Dressed well he was."

"I suppose," said Travers, "you couldn't tell what part of England he came from? I mean, did he speak like the people do in Suffolk? or like a London man? or a Scotsman? or what?"

She thought it over. "No! I don't know where he come from. He spoke ... sort of different. It was a nice voice."

That was as far as they got over the question of identification and, as Wharton well knew, there'd have been no point in forcing things out of her. All that she would insist on was that he wasn't an American; precisely why, neither could gather, unless the talkies were guide and criterion.

"Now about your leaving," went on Wharton. "Tell us just what happened."

"Well, on the Saturday morning, when this gentleman had gone, and Mr. Rook's brother was there, he sent for me—Mr. Rook's brother did—and I had to go into the dining-room and Mr. Rook told me he had to go away at once and I was to go home. And he paid me up for the month and another month instead of notice—oh! and he paid for a telegram form to send home and tell my mother, and then Mr. Rook's brother he took me to the station as soon as I got my things together."

Then followed ten minutes of patient questioning, without much result. All that could be gathered was, that Rook had recovered from his fainting fit and that he spoke normally; in other words, apparently he wasn't being coerced. He'd paid the wages in cash—as he'd always paid. After that she hadn't seen Rook again; moreover, on the way to the station she'd sat behind, and there hadn't been any conversation. The American had seen her into the train and had given her five shillings as a special tip. Her description of him added nothing to what was already known.

"What about Mrs. Fletcher?" asked Wharton. "Did you see her again?"

"No! she wasn't up—and Mr. Rook told me specially she wasn't to be disturbed. I was going to her room after I'd packed, to say good-bye, but the other man—not Mr. Rook's brother—was up there waiting outside the door, and he said I wasn't to go."

"He sort of hustled you downstairs!"

"Well, he took my trunk and carried it down . . . and he made me go first, and when I wanted to say goodbye to Mrs. Fletcher he wouldn't let me . . . and I cried on the way to the station . . . because I thought she'd think it wasn't right of me going away like that." Wharton nodded sympathetically. "Now a peculiar question. Think back over all the time you lived at Mill House. Did anything ever happen there that struck you as peculiar or strange?"

She didn't think for long.

"I thought it was funny that Mr. Rook should tell me he hadn't any relations and then his brother come to see him."

Wharton was delighted. "Splendid! I wondered if you'd think of that . . . Now—anything else? Take your time . . . There's no hurry!"

There was a much longer pause this time; Wharton indeed, had to put a good few leading questions before he got the only piece of information. After she'd been at Mill House for about a year, she went to Steyvenning as usual on her afternoon off, and called to see her friend as arranged. But the friend had been suddenly taken ill, so after staying with her mother for an hour or so, Bertha had returned home at a very much earlier hour than she'd been expected. For some reason or other she had gone to the kitchen by the far gate, and as she passed the dining-room she distinctly heard voices. The blinds were drawn, as it was about five o'clock. As soon as he heard her enter the kitchen, Rook came in at once in a state of alarm. Then she'd explained—and added, artlessly enough, that she hadn't known there was a visitor. Rook looked taken back.

"He asked what I meant, so I told him, and then he said yes; they had had a visitor and he'd just seen the gentleman off at the front door—and I suppose he did because *I* didn't hear him go out. Only what I thought funny was, only the usual two cups come out!"

Wharton nodded knowingly. "You didn't ask about that?"

"No! I didn't, because I didn't think about it till I got to bed and then I thought how funny it was not having tea . . . and then next morning I forgot all about it."

Wharton made a note or two on his pad, made as if to get up, then sat down again.

"Oh! before I forget it. Did a doctor ever call at the house?"

"Not while I was there."

"Anybody ever stay in the house—except you three?"

"Oh, no! . . . nobody!"

"Quite!" Wharton glanced at the clock, then pushed the bell. "Now, Miss Smith, we've arranged for you to stay in London tonight. You'd like to go to the pictures, perhaps? . . . This lady will look after you." He made a very solemn process of the handing over and even surveyed the closing door with a paternal look. Then he bustled back.

"There'll be a lot more questions—only she won't know it!"

Travers smiled. "You just love being mysterious and—er—manipulatory, George; don't you? What do you mean by 'she won't know it'?"

"Oh; gossip at meals, or the movies, or on buses, for the next day or two. Things we couldn't very well ask her. Any suspicions of—er—other than affection between Rook and his housekeeper?"

Travers felt himself bridling up. "What exactly do you mean by that, George?"

"Well, she might have been his wife, for all we know. However"—he waved all that on one side. "What about a bit of a meal?"

In five minutes they were sitting down to it, and Wharton grew more and more loquacious as it progressed. Whether he were merely setting up theories to be shied at, or casting about for ideas to bob up, Travers didn't know.

"That Rook was a remarkably secretive fellow, don't you think?" he asked. "All the way to Suffolk—silly Suffolk, don't they call it?—for a girl. One of the real country type; good worker and no imagination; one who'd take everything for gospel. And no holidays, mind you! No chattering away from home!" He gave a complacent nod. "Rook thought that out extraordinarily well!"

"She could chatter enough in her letters!" remarked Travers.

"Not the same thing—quite. And that big money, to avoid any change."

Travers smiled. "I'm disposed to agree with you on what you're careful not to mention—that Rook was desperately keen on keeping out of the limelight—but aren't people always anxious to keep their servants once they suit?"

Wharton shook his head. "Not to the tune of seventy pounds a year! . . . And what did he go to London for?"

"Er—did he?"

"Well, why shouldn't he? As I see it, it's a safe place for a day." He waved aside Travers' question. "Do you know what I think he went there for? For those photos! He had a safe port of call. Once a year he got a photo—one of those the old lady had sewn up in her vest."

Travers nodded, chiefly to gain time. "Then why don't you have the photos examined by your experts, to see if the paper's of continental origin?"

Wharton grimaced. "That's being done! The trouble is that most of our people, and the Americans as well, have agencies all over Europe. I take it you were referring to Italy?"

"Yes—perhaps I was. Er—any possibility of tracing where Rook went to in London?"

"I doubt it," said Wharton. "We might ask the Press to get at it." He looked with sudden surprise at Travers' plate, as if only then conscious of the speed at which he'd devoured his own meal, shuffled about uneasily for a bit, then, "Mind if I smoke, while you finish?"

He lugged out his pipe, got it alight with some show of care, then cleared his throat. His voice was what Travers described as soothing. "Look here now! Isn't it time we abandoned all that theory we started with? You don't believe it—and I don't. We know there wasn't a word of truth in that yarn Rook's supposed brother fobbed you off with. Was there now?"

"Perhaps not," said Travers—and waited.

"Let's allude to him as the American. He told you that yarn because it fitted the case, and because there was no reason why a comparative stranger shouldn't believe it. I dare say I should have swallowed it myself! But, shall I tell you the first flaw I found in the story, as related by you? It was this. The American gave you the impression that he'd just landed. Also that was partially confirmed by the fact that Rook hadn't seen him before, or he wouldn't have flopped. Yet he—the American—had approached Large days before he went to Mill House! Isn't that so? You remember the dates?"

Travers nodded.

"Then there was that chap supposed to be a doctor. Why didn't he go into the house *with* the supposed brother? No! the American had his plans ready, long before he saw you. That chap who drove him there—the fellow we'll call Driver—had to be accounted for to you." He gave a contemptuous wave of the hand. "There never was a doctor. We've proved that a lie three times over!"

"A damn clever chap—Strawson, or whatever his name was!" Travers spoke with feeling.

"Agreed!" said Wharton. "But there are just as clever about." He paused to relight his pipe, then shot another question. "You ever see a real old Lyceum melodrama?"

"Yes—I believe I did, when I was a boy. Why?"

"Then you probably saw this case! Take Driver, for instance. He tracks old Rook down, tries to peep through the window, attempts to pump the maid, and scares the old chap stiff when the girl tells him about it. Still, he knows he's found his man. He comes back with the American. They get rid of you—and the women; then set about Rook. They wanted him to do something for them, which he wouldn't do; or to give them something which he wouldn't give. You know the dates as well as I do. If you think it out you'll see that Mill House soon got too risky, and they got him away to Frenchman's Rise. They kept him there, tied up. I dare say they tortured him in all sorts of subtle ways—half-starved him and so on—and still he wouldn't give in. Then there was what we might call a culminating scene, and one of them lost his temper and knocked the old man down. That probably killed him—though Menzies didn't find any cardiac lesion, or whatever they call it . . . Now then! Who *was* Rook? What *was* it they wanted?"

Travers made a queer little noise. "George! I wish you wouldn't fire questions at me as if I were a slot machine . . . Still, I *have* been thinking about it—and you mustn't be annoyed at the puerility of what I can suggest. You say, 'Who was Rook, and what did they want?' I'll give you a choice—Lyceum and otherwise. He was a financier to whom the American and Driver had brought—years before—the invention which he managed to steal from them. Or, he was a foreign spy, who'd sold the pass in some way—they being, of course, members of the same gang. Or he was a sea captain, to whom a dying sailor bequeathed a map of hidden treasure. Or he was a roué—who'd ruined the American's daughter, who once had been betrothed to—or the wife of—Driver. Or he was—"

Wharton cut him short with a chuckle. "You've got too vivid an imagination for me. But what was the mystery of the tea-cups?"

"Mystery? You're pulling my leg!"

"Oh, no! Was it no mystery? Was there really a caller, who'd already had tea?"

Wharton looked so genuinely innocent that Travers took him at his face value. "There wasn't a caller. It was Rook and Mrs. Fletcher talking. That's why the maid was allowed out so much; so that they could be normal while she was out of the house."

He put aside the napkin and felt for his cigarette case. Wharton got to his feet.

"And why was all that arrangement necessary?" Travers gave him a droll look.

"Surely, George, that's precisely what we're just going down to Devonshire to find out!"

Wharton grunted. "Let's hope you're right! ... You ready? ... Then we'll start the adventure. When you're hesitating between forty and seventy, remember you've a mighty important person aboard."

"I'll try to," smiled Travers. "But his name isn't necessarily 'Wharton'!"

CHAPTER X
THE DARK BACKWARD

IT WAS ABOUT two in the morning when Travers drew up outside the police station at Tiverton. Wharton, with a facility for sleep as good as Napoleon's, had been oblivious of most of the journey. Travers, for once, was rather cheered by the General's inquiries as to the possibility of a pot of tea.

The doctor, however, seemed wide enough awake. Wharton sniffed the atmosphere of the smoke-misty room with exaggerated noises.

"If I were a detective, I'd say you two had been yarning for the last hour."

The local superintendent lost his wariness at once. "And you wouldn't be far out, sir! How'd you like the tea?"

"Hot as hell!" said Wharton. "And one shade lighter. Now, doctor; what's all this you've got to tell us? Sorry that phone was kicking up such a devil of a row this morning."

"Well, I think I've recognised the photos in the paper. Both of them."

"Splendid!" said Wharton. "Give us all the details. Mr. Travers, here, is an expert who's giving us certain—er—very valuable assistance."

"Well, some years ago—four to be exact—I was called in to a house along the Bampton Road; standing back some distance from the road as a matter of fact. It was to see a servant who had pretty bad indigestion. It turned out to be appendicitis, but that's nothing to do with it. I saw the housekeeper principally; though, mind you, I don't think I should have recognised her if I hadn't been pretty sure of the man. She seemed to be much older in the photo."

"Her hair wasn't grey?"

"Well, greyish, when I knew her. She was an interesting old soul, really. A bit difficult to understand till I got used—"

"Understand! You mean—Pardon me a moment!" Wharton broke off. "I don't want you to think we're mad, but for the last three years she's supposed to have been dumb!"

"Really!" The doctor raised his eyebrows. "Well, she used to speak to me all right! Strong foreign accent, mind you. French she was, so she told me." He laughed. "After a bit I tried her with my own French and we used to get along quite well."

"Probably the same woman. What about the man?"

"I didn't see him a great deal. I thought at the time he must be a retired music master or something like that; he always seemed to be playing the piano—or he was whenever I called. By the way, he told me his housekeeper was really his old governess who'd come down in the world a bit."

"Really! And what did he look like—face, I mean—when he lived here?"

"Clean-shaved; hair quite dark."

"Dark!" Wharton looked across at Travers. "What was the matter? A shock or something?"

"Hold hard a minute!" said the doctor. "I think I can explain that. He used one of those hair-darkening preparations; not a dye—just something to restore the natural colour. I know that because I saw the bottle! That's why your photo with the white hair didn't put me off!"

"Good for you, doctor!" said Wharton. "And about this house of his. Pretty retired, I take it? And he took it furnished?"

The other two looked surprised. "That's right! It stands back from the road in a little lane of its own. He took it furnished on a three years' lease. He was here just under the three years."

"Did he go about much, or keep himself to himself?"

"He kept himself very quiet. His heart wasn't any too good, so he told me, though of course I never examined him."

"I see!" Wharton turned to Travers. "Anything else we want to ask the doctor at the moment?"

"I don't know that there is—except the piano. He had a grand piano, doctor? A big affair in very dark wood?"

"Yes . . . he did."

"You didn't happen to notice if it was a Blickdorf?"

"I'm afraid I didn't. To tell the truth, I've never even heard the name!"

The tea came in, with cups for four. The superintendent stirred up the fire and things became less formal. Wharton took up Travers' cue of the piano.

"I suppose I can interview the owners of the property that Rook hired?"

"Pardon me a moment," interrupted Travers. "He didn't call himself Rook here, I take it?"

"No, he didn't!" said the super. "Robinson; Charles Robinson, was what he called himself."

"And what about the housekeeper?" Travers asked the doctor.

"Flechier. Madame Flechier. That's the name she gave me."

Travers nodded, then, "Mr. Wharton was asking about the ownership of the property."

"It belongs to two old ladies in the town," the super, told them. "But there's something peculiar happened you might like to know about. In accordance with your phone instructions and the wire, we began making inquiries, and one thing we learnt was that about eighteen months ago a man was in the town asking questions about this Robinson or Rook. He asked at the cottages along the same road, and he also spoke to one of my men who happened to be up that way."

"That's interesting!" said Wharton. "What sort of questions did he ask?"

"Personal questions. What sort of looking man was he; what he did with himself—oh! and one very funny one! What became of his piano!"

"Really! And what *did* become of the piano?"

"Well, there again, sir, it struck me as a bit peculiar—so to speak—asking about a piano, so we started making inquiries ourselves. As a matter of fact we've spent the whole day and most of the evening at it. The Misses Lake didn't have a grand piano, and the one in the house belonged to Rook or Robinson, or whatever his name was; therefore he bought it and had it sent here. That's what we can't trace—where it came from. But we have found something. We know where it went to!"

"Good!" said Wharton—and meant it.

"You see, sir, we asked everybody there was to ask and we couldn't get hold of anything. All we knew was that a van called for it early in the morning. Then one of my men had an idea. If the van called early, then it was either a local one from Exeter, for instance, or it was a London one that had put up somewhere else for the night. We worked on both lines—and ran it down at a little pub just this side of Taunton. A Barridges van it was—so the driver told the landlord. They'd taken some furniture to Taunton and came on here to kill two birds with one stone. On the way back they called up again for a drink—and mentioned the piano. . . . And that's all we know."

"All!" said Wharton. "It's quite enough for us." He helped himself to another cup of tea and Travers watched him as he sat there thinking things over. Then he made up his mind—exactly as Travers thought he would.

"He went to Barridges and asked them to collect his piano and keep it till he sent for it. Then he had it brought down to Sussex. . . . Now why shouldn't he have done that before?"

"Why shouldn't he?" repeated Travers.

Wharton got to his feet. "I suppose the van was a plain one?"

"Yes, sir; or else we should have known what firm it belonged to!"

"Exactly! The point is, a plain van probably meant a special request; and if so, the firm are more likely to remember the order. I'll try and get on to the Yard at once."

They listened while he rang up and gave Exchange his number—with an emphatic statement of urgency. Then he did some scribbling in his note-book.

"Any particular details about the man who was asking questions?"

The super, thought back. "I don't know that there were, sir. I believe there was something about a squint in one eye—but we can verify that in the morning."

Wharton nodded. "We'd better have your man here first thing. Doctor, you might let me have the name of that girl you attended—and I'd like her present whereabouts, if known. And the same about any other maid they happened to have." He looked at his watch. "No need to keep you up any longer, doctor. Needless to say we're exceedingly obliged to you. If ever you're up for murder, let me know and I'll see what I can do . . . . What about a shakedown for Mr. Travers? Just two or three hours. I'll take this easy chair in front of the fire here."

* * * * * * *

Actually it was well after eight o'clock when Travers was roused by the station sergeant. Ten minutes later, after a cold sluice, he was tackling a plate of bacon and eggs.

"Where's Superintendent Wharton?" he asked.

"He's been at it the last couple of hours, sir. Just gone off to see the house."

"He got his trunk call all right?"

"I believe so, sir . . . A very active gentleman, sir!"

"Isn't he!" said Travers, wondering if that were a reproof. When the General did turn up, he didn't seem to have a lot of news. The man who did the questioning certainly had some sort of a squint. According to the constable he was a foreigner—at least "he talked funny."

"Nothing new at all?" asked Travers.

"Nothing—except this growth of whiskers. Coming along? We can't expect to hear from Barridges for an hour or two yet."

Travers rubbed his chin. "I think I will. And I don't mind standing yours as well."

On the way back, Wharton called in at one of the banks—why, Travers didn't ask. An hour after that, Wharton's call came through. Barridges had certainly made things hum, and luckily their records were complete. It was a fact that they had handled a Blickdorf grand. Originally it had been sent for storage by a Mrs. Farrow of Hatch Cottage, Beaconcross. On her instructions it had been delivered to a Charles Robinson of Lane End, Tiverton. Later, the piano had been sent for storage again, and had then been delivered to Mrs. Farrow at Mill House, Steyvenning.

"Beaconcross it is!" said Wharton, who'd repeated the news to Travers sotto voce. He smiled with satisfaction as he replaced the receiver. "Know where it is?"

"Quite near London, on the Oxford road," Travers told him, and in ten minutes they were off again. Wharton took the front seat; principally, as he explained to Travers, to keep him from dozing at the wheel.

"You think things are working out all right?" he asked.

"Looks like it!" said Travers, dodging the feeler. Wharton grunted. "Same old game he played here as at Mill House. Who was he afraid of?"

"Lord knows! The man with the squint probably. By the way, was that constable *sure* he was a foreigner? I mean, was he that sort of cove who'd class as foreigner anybody who didn't speak good honest Devon?"

"He was local enough himself," said Wharton. "Mind you, I thought of that—and that's why I didn't press him. He did say he had a hooked nose."

"A Jew! And a lisp perhaps!"

Wharton made a wry face. "You're arguing from the particular to the universal." He seemed quite pleased with that, for he repeated it. "That's it—-from the particular to the universal!" He shook his head. "There are more important things than that.

For instance, if he was hiding, why did he hang on to those initials—C.R.?"

"Peasant strain in him, perhaps."

"What's this? Anthropology?"

Travers laughed. "Hardly! Let's suppose he lived at Beaconcross, where he'd have clothes and things marked C.R. When he came to Tiverton, he wanted to change his name, but a very parsimonious instinct—typical of a peasant, or even a lower middle, class—informed him that he needn't sacrifice his garments or have them all re-marked, provided he fitted the new name to the C.R. When he left for Sussex he did the same thing. You remember we found some perfectly good garments so marked, which were a few years old. The theory depends, of course, on what he called himself at Beaconcross."

"May be something in that," said Wharton, and snuggled into the corner, apparently to think things over. In a few moments his breathing was steady. It was in the outskirts of Oxford that he roused himself, then blinked at Travers accusingly.

"Feeling better, George?"

The sight of the rug that had been drawn over his knees probably modified his answer.

"Well—not so bad. How far now?"

"About half an hour. Where do you want to go? Police station?"

"That'll do. Know where it is?"

"No!—thank God!" said Travers. "Still, they're usually in the main street."

The police station took very little finding, and Wharton set about hearing all there was to hear about Hatch Cottage. There seemed to be available, however, nobody who knew anything about its occupants of all those years ago. The property had even changed hands during the last year. Still, the agents who'd handled it were only a few doors away, and off Wharton went again.

Prosser, the senior partner, was in. Wharton gave away as little as he could, beyond his own credentials, but hinted that the matter was one of extreme urgency.

"I'll tell you what I can," said Prosser. "Luckily we have all the transactions filed. The solicitors'll give you fuller details if you want them."

He hunted up his records, then gave the history of Hatch Cottage as he knew it, while Wharton jotted down the vital facts.

"The place was let on a three years' lease to a Mr. Clifford Rowlandson—furnished—at a rental of £200 a year, and there was the usual agreement. He left at the expiration of the lease, in the August of 1925, and paid over the sum of £25 for dilapidations."

"He did all this himself?"

"Rowlandson, you mean? No! we didn't see him at all, as a matter of fact. Everything was done by correspondence. The cheque was on a local bank, where he opened an account at the same time."

"August, 1922, that is?"

"That's right. No solicitors acted for him, as far as we know. Of course there wasn't anything really for them to do, provided he was satisfied with the agreement."

"What sort of looking man was he?"

"To tell you the truth, I didn't see him till the following spring. He struck me as a very nervous, quiet sort of old chap— but none too strong. He'd white hair—and a short beard. And he wore glasses. I believe there was something about an illness. Still, that might have been on account of his wife."

"His wife!"

"Yes! She died down here you know. Very much younger woman than he was. French, I believe."

"That's very interesting!" said Travers. "What doctor attended her?"

"Sanderson, I think. His house is about a hundred yards along—on the left."

"We'll see him at once!" said Wharton. "Keep all this to yourself, Mr. Prosser. And we may have to call on you again."

They left the car where it was and walked the short distance to the doctor's house. The air was misty and chill, and in the houses lights were already beginning to appear.

"Think he'll be in?"

"Probably the best time of the day," said Travers cheerfully. "The plot thickens, George; what?"

"Thickens!" He grunted. "It's like pea soup. And the same old Tiverton and Sussex recipe."

The doctor, an elderly man, and almost the oldest inhabitant as he jokingly told Wharton, had just got in from an afternoon round of visits. He seemed suitably impressed by the story of anxious relatives and foreign enquiries.

"I remember them quite well," he said. "Mrs. Rowlandson was French; spoke hardly a word of English beyond the very simplest expressions."

"You're sure she was French? I mean, she wasn't Spanish? or Italian?"

The doctor smiled. "Oh no! She was French all right! At least she managed to understand what I said; you know—the sort of stuff one learns at school. She used to make me understand too, and that takes some doing! Her sister was French too." He laughed. "But of course she would be!"

"Her sister!" said Wharton reflectively. "She'd be much older than Mrs. Rowlandson?"

"Ten years probably. A very charming woman, mind you— and most devoted to the sister."

"Quite! And what happened exactly, doctor? Within the bounds of professional secrecy, of course!"

The doctor waved his hand. "Nothing very secret. They lived very quietly; just one maid, and a man to do the garden. Mrs. Rowlandson was expecting her confinement in the January, and I was called in to keep an eye on things. Everything went perfectly well till a month before the time, when she had a most unfortunate accident—slipped up and fell down some stairs. The child was born dead, and we had a pretty bad time with her. Still, we got her through all right, though she never actually got over it. The heart went wrong. I advised Rowlandson to call in a certain man, and he did so. We had two people in, as a matter of fact. However, nothing could be done at all. She used to lie about in a chair when the weather was all right. One afternoon they found her dead; they'd only left her a minute or two. Went off very peacefully."

"What happened to her husband?"

"He was in a fearful way. I thought he was heading for a bad breakdown. Still, we got him round. Shortly after—about the summer of 'twenty-five, it'd be—he left the district. And that's the last I've heard of him."

"Any other children?"

"Not that I know of."

"The sister—was she known as Mrs. Farrow, by any chance?"

"That's right. I seem to have the impression that she was a widow."

"Know her Christian name?"

"He called her Marie. The wife was Lucy."

"Lucy—or Lucille?" smiled Travers.

"Lucille! That's right! I remember now. That'd be it of course. French for 'Lucy,' isn't it?"

Wharton got to his feet and Travers followed suit. There were the usual thanks, and hints at further inquiries; then off they went again.

"Where this time?" asked Travers as he closed the gate.

"Chap who looks after the graveyard. Sexton, or whatever they call him."

One enquiry and the cottage was found. The sexton himself answered the knock. Wharton asked him to step outside for a moment, then noticed the look of disquietude on his face.

"Nothing very important; Mr. Blake, isn't it? Just a visit to the grave of a relative of mine."

"Indeed, sir! And who might that be?"

"A Mrs. Rowlandson. Buried here in 'twenty-five." The man's eyes opened in astonishment. He looked at Wharton, then at Travers, then back at Wharton again.

"It was you who sent the money, sir?"

Wharton shook his head. "Not I! What money do you mean?"

"Money for the grave, sir!"

Wharton shook his head again. "I know nothing about it." He turned to Travers. "Sounds like Claude!" Travers nodded. "Sent from London, was it? This money. And in the summer?"

"That's right, sir! Least, the letter had the London postmark, and it used to come about July. A ten-pound note it had in it, sir. No writing—only: 'To keep Mrs. Rowlandson's grave in proper order.'"

Wharton nodded, then looked round in the dusk. "Show us the grave, will you?"

The man led the way at once. Under an overhanging willow in the far corner of the churchyard, was a small mound of earth, covered with neatly trimmed grass; its outlines marked by whitened stones, carefully placed. At the head, set in the mould, was a jar with freshly cut chrysanthemums.

"My wife always put the flowers there," explained the man, almost apologetically. "She says there's no tombstone nor nothing, and the grave looks so bare."

"It looks remarkably well cared for," said Travers. "And it does you credit." He fumbled for his pocket, but Wharton was too quick for him. He cut short the man's thanks, and protestations of all he intended to do.

"Afraid we must be going. We may be round again in a day or two. . . . I suppose you've never seen anything of Mr. Rowlandson this way since she died?"

"No, sir! He ain't been this way, sir, or I'd have heard about it."

So much for that visit. Outside in the road again, Travers put the same old question.

"Where to now, George?"

"Town—straightaway. You need a good night's rest, and I've got things to do."

"Such as what?"

"What! Hm! Every possible piece of information has to be collected from Tiverton—and from here. That'll mean another dozen men on the job. Still," he gave a sideway nod, "we're moving along! Soon as we know everything about him from the time he first came here, it ought to be easy to find out what happened before."

There was just one question at the police station.

"I haven't time to see Hatch Cottage," Wharton explained to the sergeant. "It's a pretty secluded house, isn't it?"

"That's right, sir! Right off the main road; all woods and common round it—or there used to be. They're just starting to build there now."

For the rest of the few miles to town, Wharton was wide awake but remarkably quiet. So was Travers, for that matter; irrespective of the cares of driving. At Harrow he drew in to the kerb and bought an evening paper; glanced at the front page, then handed it over.

"Thought you might like to see the inquest reports."

Wharton ran his eye over it quickly, then settled to his corner again.

"What happened exactly?" asked Travers.

"Rook's adjourned. Other—natural causes."

"And what's the next move—after that collection of information you were talking about?"

"Damned if I know!" said Wharton. "There may be news of the so-called American. I'm going down to Steyvenning first thing in the morning."

"Anything special?"

"Well—er" He shrugged his shoulders, then made that ponderous toilet with his handkerchief that always announced that something was coming. "I think there's a lot to be learned at Steyvenning; don't you?"

"I daresay there is."

"We might even set a trap for our friend of the other night!"

Travers smiled. "Surely, George, you don't imagine a man'd be such a fool."

"Wait a minute!" said Wharton. "You were going to say he wouldn't walk into a trap. Perhaps he wouldn't—of the kind you're thinking of. This is a new kind of trap. My own invention. It's such a nice trap that it isn't a trap at all! . . . I'll let you have the details later . . . when I've worked them out."

Travers asked no questions. There was nothing of the malicious moreover in the fact that he withheld something of his own till the very last moment, which was when Wharton was saying a temporary farewell and repeating his thanks.

"Oh! something I'd like to put up to you, George; something I've been thinking about more or less all day. Er—you do like to—er—what we might call, hear every side?"

"Every time, my dear fellow! Every time! Doesn't matter how small—or how irrelevant; every detail counts!"

"This is neither," said Travers. "It's merely preposterous—or you'll probably think so. It's something that happened that night I spent at Mill House. You remember I told you that Rook posed in front of me, and then went upstairs. When he came down again, I was to see if I could notice any difference in his clothing, or himself. You remember that?"

"Yes!"

"Well, why shouldn't there have been two men? *One went up and another came down!*"

"You think so! You thought so at the time!"

Travers stammered slightly. "Er—I'm afraid I—er—didn't . . . at the time. I'm just wondering. I mean, could there have been two men?"

"You mean a twin brother—absolutely the dead spit of the other."

"Well, it'd have to be something of the sort, of course."

"Yes—but why? Why should there have been two Rooks in the house?"

"I don't know. I merely thought I'd mention it."

Wharton seemed to be rather impressed. "There might be something in it. The whole case is a queer one. You see, it isn't a question of *what*. We know Rook was killed. We know who did it—though we don't know their names. The thing is—*why* was everything?" He clicked his tongue. "That's what's annoying *me*!"

"Then don't *let* it worry you!" was Travers' rather fatuous advice. He spotted that himself. "Sorry, George. You're going to say that's what you're paid for!"

That virtually ended the pilgrims' progress—and Travers' tour of the western counties. A bath, tea, and he was off to Durango House to settle arrears of work. That done, he hunted up Franklin—but Franklin was out. An urgent matter had taken him abroad for a day or two; at least, that was all the information he found available.

CHAPTER XI
THE SEVEN CYPRESSES

ON THAT EVENING when Franklin had been deprived of an anticipated meal with Travers, he had treated himself to the service dinner in his own room and had then sat smoking in front of the fire, with a drink at his elbow. That was when the idea occurred to him; an idea so perfectly simple that he wondered how on earth it could have escaped Travers' attention. What he forgot was that in the rush of those two days, Travers had had precious little time to think of anything: what he didn't know was that the thought had been in Travers' mind. He was, in fact, about to bring the matter up at that very moment when the telephone bell had rung.

When Travers saw that picture at the Resplendent, he had thought of Italy because his mind was already in that particular groove. At the back of Franklin's mind was much the same preliminary incentive, but the thoughts followed a far different channel. To some extent, Italy was Franklin's native land. He had learned its language from his mother before he spoke his father's tongue, and he still remembered the gratified wonder of his grandfather when on his first visit to Italy he had chattered away like a young Neapolitan who had never been out of sight of Vesuvius.

The thought was this. The man Rook had written—in his mind, if he had never committed it to paper—a tone-poem inspired by a certain aspect of Italian scenery. Surely the inspiration must have been direct. Rook must have seen those Seven Cypresses of—where was it? Valcetto—and have written on the spot or while the memory could still recall sufficient of their first appeal. That was the problem; was there a 'Valcetto'? or was it merely a city of the soul? The name seemed rational enough, and yet not familiar. Franklin frowned to himself, then fetched a gazetteer from his reference shelf.

He found what he wanted. The book—a post-war, expensive, German affair—gave two places of that name; one apparently so near Turin as to be practically a suburb, the other a village tucked away on the heel in the neighbourhood of Taranto. Which was the one that had attracted Rook? Turin, except for the reaches towards the mountains, was rather like a pea on the edge of a plate; as for the village, why should Rook have gone so far from the beaten track? Overland travellers usually had connections to make, and had little leisure for touring the neighbourhood of Taranto or Brindisi.

As Franklin's thoughts wandered still further, certain subtle attractions presented themselves. Suppose it were necessary for enquiries to be made, didn't it look almost providential that both places were to be found on the direct route? One could drop down into Turin, put in half a day over what would be the necessary rest after the railway journey, then take the *direttissimo* for Taranto. Then he stirred restlessly in his chair as another idea presented itself. That music manuscript had not been given to Travers—it had been merely handed over in trust. Rook had even told Travers—to the latter's politely concealed amazement—that he knew the person for whom it was ultimately intended. Now that manuscript had proved to be rubbish—say, the idiotic scribblings of a disordered mind—with one notable exception—*the title page*. Was the title—and that name Valcetto—to be taken as part of an ordered sanity of purpose? Surely it was not too far-fetched to deduce that somewhere at a place called Valcetto and at a spot or house known as The Seven Cypresses, was somebody who knew Rook, and knew him intimately.

Of course there was much more speculation after that before Franklin finally turned in. The following morning it was the first thing he thought about—but with far less enthusiasm. He was even smiling at his flirtation with the romantic, and judicial of the dangers of too fertile an imagination. Then the pendulum swung the other way as he reviewed the case all over again. In his room at Durango House, he found himself inclining once more to his views of the previous night. Then came a sudden resolution, and almost before he was aware of it he found the receiver in his hand and himself asking to be put through to Sir Francis' room. Had the call been delayed a moment longer, he'd certainly have changed his mind; as it so happened, it came through at once. Sir Francis would be glad to see Mr. Franklin straightaway.

He hung up the receiver almost aghast. Why the devil he'd done such a ridiculous thing, he couldn't imagine! In the lift, he thought desperately for some other excuse for the interview, then decided to bank on the fact that the Head of Durangos was the world's most incurable romantic—at least where the Detective Bureau was concerned. Even then as the voice answered his tap and he entered the room, he was totally unprepared.

Sir Francis was in a good mood. He said some nice things about the Department and wondered if Mr. Franklin knew precisely what Mr. Travers was up to. That played into Franklin's hands, particularly the final self-benediction.

"Of course we're only too delighted for Durangos to be connected with cases of this sort! Publicity is everything; and when it's at the public expense!"—He chuckled the rest, then cleared his throat. "What was it you specially wanted to see me about?"

Franklin told his story, added the necessary embellishments and gave the whole a flavour of mystery that was as captivating as it was elusive. His hearer looked wise, was induced to make suggestions of his own, and, before he knew it, was talking of the matter as settled. Then Franklin began to make his own position secure by raising objections that he knew the other would sweep aside.

"It'll be an expensive business, Sir Francis, if we get no results!"

The other waved his hand. "A couple of paragraphs'll be worth it."

"And, of course, we're working independent of the police!"

"Why not?" He chuckled again as a thought struck him. "We've other considerations in our minds, Mr. Franklin. Durangos are the servants of the public"—and so on to the usual peroration that made an automatic tail-piece for the Annual Report.

* * * * * * *

Franklin made an attempt to get hold of Travers that morning, then felt rather relieved that he hadn't succeeded. After all, if things went wrong, the less said the better. By midday he was in the train; in his pocket a special recommendation for the firm's Turin agents. The following afternoon found him in Turin.

The situation there seemed rather hopeless. Valcetto lay well out into the plain, with no more scenery than the back of your hand; moreover it appeared to be perfectly modern in character; a large dormitory that had suddenly grown up round some ancient and now non-existent nucleus. Still, he wasted some hours over a drive round, then decided to leave it for a return visit, should the other end of the trail be definitely uninformative.

It was early in the morning when he finally arrived in Taranto, and with choice of rail or car, decided on the car. The driver whom he approached seemed rather amazed.

"Valcetto! That is forty kilometres!"

"It is!" said Franklin. "But what does that matter?—if I pay."

"*Certamente!* If the gentleman pays!"

The cost was argued out, half was paid down, then Franklin got in. The car seemed to draw away from the town, skirt the harbour, then cut away south towards level country dotted with vines and olives. In a few moments they came in sight of the sea again, then rarely left it. There was a quarter of an hour of that listless sort of scenery, then the landscape changed and they circled little land-locked bays or nipped between the houses of tiny villages that straggled up towards the hills. Then the car made a sudden descent to the shore. Climbing up what seemed a finger of rock thrust down to the sea, and clinging to every foothold, the small town looked like an immense crab that has left the strip of sand and lumbers awkwardly up the slope.

In the *piazza*, that lay below the hill and fronted the sea, the car stopped. Franklin got out, paid the balance of his fare and watched the car disappear at the top of the rise. Then he picked up his bag and made for what announced itself as the Hotel of the Three Kings—proprietor, Giovanni Curanti. A lantern-jawed, tired-looking waiter was wiping the marble-topped tables, and in five minutes he was bringing along the rolls and coffee. He bowed with exceeding deference at the sight of the special tip.

"I may leave my bag here?" Franklin asked. "I may have to call on somebody in the town."

"Certamente, signore," and the waiter grabbed it at once.

"And if I should want a bed, one will be available?"

The waiter indicated the perfectly stupendous pleasure that would give to everybody. Franklin got to his feet and surveyed the small town, to which he had had his back.

"There is a house here, perhaps, called The Seven Cypresses?"

"I Sette Cipressi!" He shrugged his shoulders. "I have been here only two weeks. But cypresses!"—and his wave of the hand illustrated what Franklin could see for himself, that the countryside was dotted with them.

He made more inquiries by the time he'd mounted to the top of the slope, but a house or property of that name seemed to be unknown. Then he systematically searched the small town, and with mixed results. There were cypresses everywhere but division was difficult. There were seven, for instance, if one took the four in front of the *campanile* and added the three that ran alongside the church itself. But that bell tower gave him an idea. From the woman he got the key and mounted to the top till the town lay spread like a drab counterpane. Then away towards the hills—a bare quarter of a mile perhaps—he saw something really definite; an old, flat-roofed house with green shutters, backed by vines and flanked by a grove of olives; and in front of it, like grey sentries, *seven cypresses!*

Even then, it was with a hopeless sort of hope that he made his way towards that house. Surely it was too impossible that anything should happen—and yet, after all those hundreds of miles, something ought to happen. As the narrow road wound behind the house he saw, for instance, the magnificence of the view: that line of purple-green trees in profile, as it were; the delicate greys of olive trees, and the walls of the house itself; the quaint emerald of its shutters, and above it the warmer line of roofs and the rich blue of the sea. Surely a view like that might have inspired a poet, whether in words or music! Then, as he sat down on a stone that had fallen from the coping of the wall, he heard something—the notes of a piano!

He sat there for an hour altogether, smoking pipe after pipe, and all the time the piano was playing. For the first part of the time, the player seemed to be practising—florid runs and passages repeated again and again. Then came something different; music which he knew to be fine but which he neither recognised nor understood. All he did know was that the player was master of the instrument; a player perhaps of the same quality as the old man who had entertained Travers those illimitable miles and what seemed those enormously distant days back, at a house in Sussex.

When the playing finally stopped he moved further back inland towards a rise of ground which overlooked the back of the villa. All he could see was the shuttered windows and not a soul stirring. But as he got back to the road, a car suddenly emerged from the side gate and swung away to the right towards the village. He watched it till it disappeared behind the houses, then an old man—a gardener by the mattock he was carrying—closed the iron gate and went off among the olives. Franklin made his way back to the square.

At lunch there were a dozen or so guests—regular customers by the look of them—and he lingered over his cigar and *Stregu*, till a chance presented itself of getting into conversation with the proprietor. Over another of the liqueurs, they had quite a long chat before Franklin got things where he wanted them. Even then he had to be uncommonly tactful. There was no reason why he—Signor Francesco, a lawyer of Naples—should be making inquiries which went beyond that general interest in one's fellow citizens which is the prerogative of all the world.

"What is the name of the villa up there? The one in the back road, with the cypresses in front?" he asked.

"That would be the Villa Guardini," the *proprietario* told him. "When I was a boy, old Guardini came there every summer with his children and grandchildren. Then his son had it. Then he died and left it to his daughter—the eldest daughter."

Had Franklin seen Travers before he left for Italy, that information might have conveyed something. As it was he nodded politely.

"The summer is your best season?"

The other said it was, and they talked that over. Signor Francesco explained that the company he was interested in hoped to acquire land cheap. The land behind the Villa Guardini seemed moreover the very kind of thing they were looking for.

"Oh! something else I meant to mention. As I was going up past the villa, I heard a piano playing. On my way back it was still playing—superbly, it seemed to me. I listened for quite a time."

"Ah! that would be the daughter. They say she plays very well. Soon she is going to Rome to study."

"She must be fairly old?"

"Quite a young girl. About fifteen!"

Franklin seemed amazed. "That's curious. A friend of mine has a friend in this neighbourhood who has a daughter who also plays the piano superbly. Her name isn't by any chance Barlazzi? Elenore Barlazzi?"

"Lucia's her name. Lucia Rossi. Her father is Cesare Rossi!" The name was spoken with an air of importance that seemed somehow to include the speaker.

"A well-known man is he?"

"A very rich man. They say he used to live in America. That's where all the money is nowadays!"

"America!" Franklin gave an expressive shrug. "As you say, he undoubtedly is very rich."

"Yes! he has all that fine property. And he has two women to see to the house; then there are the *professori* who come from Taranto for his daughter. And three men work on the estate.

That motor-boat there—the green one—that's his! Often he cruises about in the bay, when the weather is calm." His manner suddenly became more expansively important. "Every afternoon, precisely at four, he comes here to take his *aperitivo*. One *Americano* he has—then a second. Then at five, he goes back to the villa again."

"He is a young man?"

"Well, not so young—but not old." He tapped his chest. "He is like myself—*robusto!*"

"About sixty, then," thought Franklin, and nodded comprehendingly. "I saw that he had a car. It came out by the side gate while I was passing. . . . It went towards the town. It seemed a good car."

"Car? A car, was there?" For a moment his face looked almost repulsively interested, then as suddenly changed. "Ah! that would be the *maestro*—the *maestro di musica*—who comes every week from Taranto. The car would perhaps be taking him to the station. All that, they say, costs a fortune!"

"He would be agreeable to selling some land, do you think?"

Curanti shrugged his shoulders. "Who knows? . . . For myself, I think not."

Franklin looked disappointed.

"If you say so, then no doubt it is so. Still, I rely on you, Signor Curanti, as a man of discretion, to repeat nothing of what we've been saying."

He arranged for his room for the night, then went along to inspect it. In his bones he felt something was going to happen. It was as if he sensed, with barely a cloud in the sky, that very shortly there must be thunder. Those things he had already heard: the daughter called Lucia, the mention of America, the piano music, the man Rossi with the initials C.R.; all perfectly everyday and easily explained, were nevertheless curious in the associations they recalled. At four o'clock he would certainly have to see this Cesare Rossi.

Then, looking out from the bedroom window, he saw that something had happened. The film of grey cloud that had covered the sun all day had suddenly decided to disperse itself, and as his eye caught the glow of colour everywhere on roofs and hills, he made up his mind that the place for a man that afternoon was out of doors. In a couple of minutes he was in the square, looking at the sea and then at the rising slope of country, and wondering which way to take. Then he decided on both; a steady climb up into the hills for a mile or so and then a cut back to the shore, and so home again in time to catch a glimpse of Rossi.

For the time of year the going was amazingly sultry, and by the time he'd passed the Villa Guardini he found himself mopping his forehead and fanning his face with his broad hat. Still, it was good to be alive—and back in Italy. Had he known it, he had rarely felt so friendly. Every now and again he smiled to himself, and smiled at the beauty and warmth of the afternoon, and his own contentment rather than at the smaller things that provoked it—the quick scamper of a tiny lizard or the quaintly distorted branches of an olive tree. Then through a gap in a low, trimmed cypress hedge he caught sight of a tree that had fallen so as to make what looked like a sheltered arbour. He smiled to himself as he took the next gap, then settled himself comfortably in the crook of a branch and lugged out his pipe.

He had sat there for perhaps ten minutes, puffing away steadily and looking away at the sea and the roofs and the tiny bends of the road he'd just climbed, when something caught his eye again: first the movement of something white—a woman's blouse—a woman coming up the gradual slope—or was it a girl? Why he sat there so motionless he didn't know, but he watched her through the fork of the branch as he leaned; the free movement of her young limbs and the little pauses when she looked round her or back again at the road. Then, forty yards away, she passed out of sight behind the line of the hedge, and he turned his head to listen for her footsteps as she should go by. But the footsteps never came. Before he knew it, she must have come right up and through a nearer gap. There was a flash of white, the sound of a voice humming a tune; then, there she was in front of him, pausing as if to speak.

What he saw in that merest second was a girl who had already reached womanhood; not tall but clean and straight and supple as a young larch. From the oval of her face—pale, and yet warm as old ivory—her eyes looked out intensely black and startled, like living and detached things. It was a face so sheerly beautiful, so plaintively haunting, that he found himself staring—as he might have stared at the sudden apparition of a young madonna. Then, in a flash, he realised what she was doing there as he saw the book she held tightly with both hands. He scrambled to his feet, hat still on the ground.

"Pardon, *signorina*! I fear I have your seat." He stammered the rest. "I did not know . . . I am just going."

She smiled, or he thought she smiled. Her eyes regarded him steadily and she kept that quiet poise that seemed more of a natural reserve than anything unfriendly. He wondered what her voice would be like.

"It is not my seat, *signore*! I merely come here sometimes." A faint colour came into her cheeks. "I beg that you will remain."

"No! no! I insist." He smiled, pointed to the hat and suddenly stooped down for it. Then he stepped back again, still holding the hat in his hand.

"I wish you good afternoon, *signorina*."

This time she really smiled. Her eyes lit up with sudden friendliness.

"Thank you, *signore*. It is very good of you." She hesitated. "You are a stranger here?"

"Yes. This is the first time I have been here—in Valcetto. I am from Naples. To-morrow, perhaps, I go away again." She was still gravely regarding him. "You, *signorina*, live here—in the town?"

She gave a quick little nod.

"Yes. I live here. When it is sunny I come here in the afternoon, as you see . . . to read a book."

Franklin stayed there. Somehow her gesture seemed to invite it.

"Won't you sit down? . . . I am just going."

He watched her as she took her favourite corner among the branches and drew the short brown skirt over her knees. He half turned as if to go—then hesitated.

"I was going to say I envy you your afternoon, *signorina*, I mean—the country here, and the view, are so beautiful."

She seemed surprised at that.

"But Naples is so much more beautiful!"

Franklin made a sudden gesture.

"The *signorina* knows Naples!"

Her face lit up as if she were going to speak, then she stopped with a curious hesitation and shook her head. He wondered if she had suddenly realised that in talking to him she was doing something not only unusual but desperately unconventional. He bowed gravely.

"I will go now, *signorina*. I hope the sun keeps shining for you."

He bowed again, backed towards the gap, then turned quickly and made his way to the road again. A quarter of a mile on, where the road forked, he took the narrower lane that appeared to lead back to the coast. Then he slowed up—and found himself fumbling again for his pipe.

The experience had been so unusual that he was still feeling curiously intrigued. Why it was he couldn't for the life of him have explained. It wasn't necessarily the strange, quiet beauty of the girl that made his thoughts go back to those few moments when he had spoken to her. And somehow he could not put into words quite what he felt. All he knew was that in some intangible way he had felt in that brief space of time a wish that he knew her—personally—intimately, as a friend; that he could talk to her as a friend—or was it the other way about? that she should know that he—worlds perhaps older than herself—was waiting to be confided in.

That was it. If Franklin had only known it, that was what had appealed to him. He had seen the forlornness, the sadness of the face. That was what had made him think of her as a young madonna. And what Franklin did not know, Travers, had he been there, could have told him. In her face was the same look, the same quiet appeal, that had been on the face of an old woman who had sat placidly embroidering by the light of an oil lamp in an old house in Sussex.

Then something else happened—the sun all at once went in and Franklin found himself sucking away at a cold pipe. He glanced at his watch; another half-hour and Rossi would be at the hotel. He halted a moment to get his bearings, then decided he could do it comfortably if he mended his pace and thought of nothing but the road. For all that, his thoughts would keep running back. Who was she? Not Rossi's daughter! The coincidence would be too fantastic. And yet she must be somebody of consequence; everything about her seemed fresh and fine and instinctively natural . . . and there he was off again; recalling every one of those few seconds; wondering where precisely she lived; who her parents were; wondering whether it had been his own fancy that had made her face so beautifully and quietly sad . . . then the road dropped almost sheer and in a couple of minutes he found himself down by the shore.

* * * * * * *

Back at the hotel he found himself with ten minutes in hand. A quick run upstairs and then he found Curanti and borrowed a newspaper. Shortly before four he was seated in a comer of the glass-covered verandah, a *Campari* at his elbow, waiting to see what happened. From where he sat, the door and the whole sweep of the verandah were in full view. About a dozen patrons were already in the room and more kept arriving, and Luigi the waiter was bustling about, released from hibernation. Then Curanti himself appeared, in black cloth, white collar and huge cummerbund, and Franklin saw the hour was precisely four. The clock had scarcely finished striking when Signor Rossi entered.

Franklin saw the black felt hat as it passed along the level of the glass, then had the man in full view as he mounted the steps, from the neat, spotted necktie to the white suede shoes. The old-fashioned cape he was wearing made him look broader than he was, and as the waiter took it, Franklin saw he was on the thin side, and short. But it was when the hat was off and Rossi turned full face towards him, that Franklin got his shock. There in front of him, unless those photos in his pocket lied, was Claude Rook! There was the mass of white hair, the trim beard and the imperial, and the mouth with its sensual lips. And yet something seemed to be missing—something that changed the character of the face. The glasses—that was it!

Almost as soon as Luigi had taken the hat and coat and while Curanti was still grimacing like a monkey, another elderly man came over, then another entered, and there was handshaking all round. Then the three moved across to a special table, with Curanti respectfully in the rear. Rossi was certainly a man of importance for the proprietor suddenly darted forward, presented the chair, and wiped the table carefully himself. Then drinks came along, and a pack of cards, and the three commenced playing. Franklin could hear little; his corner was too remote. From the exclamations of the players he knew the game was Scopone—and that was all.

But under cover of the paper he got out that issue of the *Record* that held the three photos of Claude Rook. As far as he could see, there could be no mistake, the man was the living image. Then if Rossi was Rook, who in the name of sanity was the dead man of Frenchman's Rise? Then all sorts of ideas came rushing into his head: Claude Rook and Cesare Rossi—the initials C.R.! The piano—was it Rossi himself who had been playing? Surely no child—unless she were an infant prodigy—could have played like that! And was that why all that elaborate disguising had been done at Frenchman's Rise—so that a dead man should be mistaken for another, while the real man, the living man, got away? But got away for what? And why? some insurance swindle on a large scale—would that be it?

Franklin suddenly caught himself in the act of shaking his head. That was not the time to get lost in all sorts of speculations. Far better keep one's eyes open while Rossi was there on view for his brief hour. So the waiter brought him another *Campari* and he sat there smoking quietly, apparently uninterested, but watching the card players in the far corner as they gesticulated or hammered down their cards or stopped to chatter as if there were no cards there. Then just before five the game stopped and all three seemed to become as quiet as friends who have exhausted their conversation and merely utter a casual thought that occurs.

The clock struck five, and Rossi appeared not to have heard it; but almost at once he got to his feet. Luigi arrived with hat and cape, and Curanti came along rubbing his hands. He bowed the three of them to the door, where a fourth joined them, and the party moved outside. Franklin counted six customers that were left. Curanti came back with a face from which all enthusiasm had gone, and Luigi leaned against the wall, legs crossed and duster in hand.

Franklin picked up his paper—then put it down as if it were red-hot. A thought had come to him—the same thought that had come to Travers. When Rook proposed that test at Mill House, had there been two men? *Had one gone up and another come down?* And if so, which had been Rook, and which Rossi?

The idea came with such suddenness that he found himself incapable of reasoned thought. For a minute or two he sat there, mind whirling, then finished his drink and went up to his bedroom.

CHAPTER XII
FRANKLIN GETS TO GRIPS

IT WAS WITH extreme reluctance that Franklin finally had to abandon his theory as to the identity of the man Rossi. It was a gossip with Curanti, after dinner in the proprietor's own room, that revealed the weak spots in the elaborate romance into which his first impressions had grown.

"So that was your Signor Rossi!" he had said. "Quite a grand gentleman—and one who has seen the world." The other agreed. One could see that he included himself in the compliment.

"And you say he has never missed coming here, at the same time every afternoon!"

"That's right!" said Curanti. "He comes always; for years and years now. At the stroke of the clock, as one might say. I prepare myself. He appears. We salute. Luigi fetches the *America-*

nos. There is a game of cards and more *Americanos.* Then—five o'clock, and he goes."

"Amazing! And he is never ill!"

The other shook his head. "A small man, but very robust. He is never ill."

"And he's been doing that all his life?"

"Oh, no! Only since he came here." He leaned back reflectively. "That would be—yes! the year of the riots; that was it! This is November; that was January; almost nine years ago." He wagged his cigar impressively. "No one knew he had come, for a day or two; or where he had come from. Some said America; some said Paris. He had his daughter with him. Then soon afterwards—a week perhaps—he came in here. I recommended him old Pietro for the garden; and Pietro's sons he took on too. Then the women came; then he settled down, as I said. He is a good customer—and my friend!"

Franklin understood—and offered his congratulations. There he was disposed to leave it, for fear some unnecessary remark should set Curanti wondering. Then he got his surprise. Perhaps Curanti wanted to create an impression; perhaps he felt the opportunity ripe for at last imparting the secret; at any rate he lowered his voice as he replenished the small glasses.

"You, *signore,* are a man of intelligence; one who has seen the world—like myself. When I was young, I have lived at Rome, at Nice, at Buda-Pesth. Very well then; we know things, you and I. But we know when to talk. I say nothing; why should I? But I know where he came from before he arrived here. From England!"

"Really! And you discovered that—how?"

The other made no mystery about it. "Old Pietro, he told me. A few days after they came, the little girl, Lucia, almost a baby she was then—was in the garden, and Pietro heard her crying. He spoke to her and she said she wanted her mother, and to go back to England. Then at the same moment, Signor Rossi came himself. He was furious with Pietro. 'I employ you to work in the garden—not to talk to people,' he says. 'One more such thing, and you go.' Then he took the child to the house. Afterwards,

Pietro told me, no one would speak to him—not even old Maria Storno, the housekeeper. Also, Signor Rossi came to question Pietro again; to find out what they had said—and Pietro told him. Signor Rossi said it was true. Her mother was dead—but not in England. He had been in America with an English family—and the child had been confused." He shrugged his shoulders suggestively. "For all that, I believe it was England!"

Franklin nodded admiringly. "You, *signore*, are a man one cannot easily deceive. And, of course, you said nothing of what you thought."

"That is so," said Curanti. "Even when the Englishman came, I said nothing."

Franklin started involuntarily. "The Englishman!"

Curanti looked round, then lowered his voice to a croak. "The spring of last year it was. An *Inglese* came here from Taranto. A rich man by the look of him; a Jew perhaps—who knows? A fine-looking man with a nose like this; and a dark moustache, and a squint in the eye. He came in here—as you did this morning, *signore*, and had breakfast—only the automobile waited all the time. Then he beckoned me and asked for the house of Signor Cesare Rossi—and I told him. I even went with him part of the way till we could see the house!"

"But," protested Franklin, "how were you to know he was English? He might have been an American!"

Curanti's smile was both crafty and condescending. "I spoke to the driver! He had been in England himself—many years. Also he knew the Americans, how they speak. What I did not tell you was that this Englishman spoke no Italian; it was the driver who interpreted for him. . ." He leaned back in the chair and produced his master-stroke of intuition. "Why did he leave the driver here? Why did he not take him to the villa, to interpret? . . . I will tell you! It was because the Signor Rossi knew the English for himself!"

Franklin left unexposed the flaw in that argument. "As you say, the man certainly was English. But why did he see the Signor Rossi?"

Curanti shook his head. "That I do not know. The Englishman returned in about two hours, and left without lunch. In the afternoon, Signor Rossi came in as usual. I said to him, 'I hope the Englishman found his way to the villa,' and he said, 'He was not an Englishman. He was an American. I knew him in America, and being at Taranto—so close—he came to see me.' But I knew he was not speaking the truth. I look into a man's face and I know when he has something to hide. *Signore!* that man was an Englishman!"

In bed that night, Franklin thought things over again. Claude Rook and Cesare Rossi were almost certainly two different individuals. There was, of course, the possibility that they might have exchanged personalities. One might have come over suddenly from England, and the other have returned; but that accepted a resemblance so remarkable as to deceive Curanti and the habitués of the *Albergo dei Tre Re*. Franklin discarded that straightaway. All that seemed certain then, was that Cesare Rossi had arrived in Valcetto over eight years before and had lived there ever since. He had a daughter called Lucia—and there was the matter of a piano, and who played it—the girl, Rossi himself, or the *maestro di musica* from Taranto? Initials—Lucia—Piano—Seven Cypresses; those seemed a remarkably tenuous chain to join the Villa Guardini with Mill House or Frenchman's Rise.

As for that caller, whom Curanti had taken for an Englishman, there was no more information to be gathered. All Franklin's designedly off-hand questions were able to elicit, was that he looked somewhere about forty, was above the average height, had a Jewish appearance, and a cast in one eye. All that Franklin knew therefore—if Curanti's account were to be relied on—was that a third man had entered the case; a man who was not the tall, saturnine American, or the short, bearded driver of the car that had called at Mill House. And even that was the purest surmise. The squint-eyed caller on Rossi might have been the genuine article, with no connection whatever with Mill House or Frenchman's Rise.

For some time after that, Franklin lay there puzzling his wits. How was he to get more information about the man Rossi? Who could be questioned discreetly—and how? Then the solution arrived of its own accord—a solution so simple that it was bound to succeed. Let Rossi give away his own information, without knowing it! That plausible scoundrel Curanti was the only difficulty, and he could be squared. After all, he himself could be away and gone at a moment's notice, and Curanti and Rossi would be left to fight their own battle. With that complacent assurance Franklin fell asleep.

* * * * * * *

After breakfast the following morning, there were no more allusions to Cesare Rossi. Franklin set off for a long walk and, on the way back, had a stroke of luck. An old fisherman seemed to be having some difficulty in slewing round a boat, and Franklin lent a hand. Then they gossiped.

"You are a native of these parts, *signore*?" the old man asked.

"I? No! I am a Neapolitan. A friend of mine told me about this part of the coast, so I thought I'd like to see it. He came a good deal to Valcetto, before the war. A family he knew very well used to come here in the summer too. What were they called, now? Guardini. That was it—Guardini!"

The old man's face lit up.

"Guardini? That would be old Emilio Guardini! He came from Rome every summer."

"You knew him?"

"I knew him, *signore*. And his son and daughter. When he died, his son, Emilio, came—with his own daughters."

"That's good news!" said Franklin. "My friend, to whom I tell all this, will be sure to ask me questions. . . . The Signor Emilio Guardini—he is also dead?"

"Long before the war. During the war the villa was shut up. Then, after the war—once only—the daughters came back. Their mother was dead too. After that they came no more. Then the Signor Rossi came. He lives there now. They say he is a grandson of old Emilio. Where the daughters, his cousins, are, I do not know."

"And this Signor Rossi; he is an important man, is he not?"

"Incredibly rich, so they say. And of great importance. He is the *Segretario del Fascio*! They say he is a friend of the *Duce* himself!"

Franklin nodded reverently. "And these daughters; how old would they be now?"

The old man pondered for a bit.

"The youngest would be the age of my youngest—over thirty. The other was much older. The Signor Emilio was twice married. She was of the first marriage." That was all he knew, beyond the relating of little trivialities that happened years and years before. Still, Franklin jotted it all down. He even concocted a family tree.

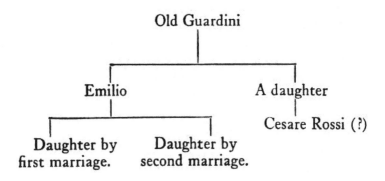

All that, of course, got him no farther, but at least it was something definite. If that scheme of his failed, moreover, the information about Rome and the Guardini family generally was a further line to fall back on. Rome might be a big place, but surely somebody could be found who could fill in the rest of the Guardini details—and the whole of the connection with Rossi.

Franklin made his toilet with particular care that afternoon. His upper lip he had purposely left unshaved, and his blue jowl and dark skin gave him an air that, if not Neapolitan, was certainly not English. There was an air of authority about him too, as he ceremoniously requested an interview with Curanti—alone. The furtive eyes of the proprietor regarded him watchfully as he closed the door.

"You have doubtless been wondering why I stay on here in Valcetto, *signore*," Franklin began. "I have come to regard you as a man of discretion and one who can keep a secret. I am about to entrust to you a matter of extreme confidence—and to ask your help."

"About the Signor Rossi?"

Franklin's eyes narrowed. "Perhaps . . . perhaps not. But why did you ask that?"

Curanti shrugged his shoulders resignedly. "As soon as you arrived, *signore*, you asked Luigi about the house with seven cypresses. At the Villa Guardini there are seven cypresses. This morning, when you took your walk, I counted them for myself."

Franklin smiled graciously. "*Signore*, you are a person whom it is an honour to know. When you take an interest, nothing can be concealed. Still, as I said, it may be he—and it may not. That is where I want your help—for which I will pay . . . well! Also you will not be compromised. This is what I want you to do."

A quarter of an hour's rehearsal, the passing over of earnest money, and Franklin left the room. Whether he had hoodwinked Curanti or not, he neither knew nor cared. Possibly the Italian believed the story of a search, by means of English papers, for an heir to property of fabulous value; in any case, if things went wrong, he and Rossi could console themselves together, and neither a penny the worse.

Five minutes, therefore, before the clock struck, Franklin sat over his *aperitivo* at the table due to be occupied by Rossi and his friends. One of them had already entered, and like a wasp returning to a stopped-up nest, had approached the table, fluttered round, and had then gone away again; possibly to protest to Curanti. But he was out of the way. Not till the actual arrival of Rossi did he make an appearance, and at the same moment Franklin got up as if unaware of the perturbation he was causing. He looked out of the window as if at the weather, then carelessly round the room, eyes resting on nothing, and strolled with a careless indifference in the direction of the stairs. On the table, front page uppermost, lay that copy of the *Record* with its three photos of the dead man.

As Franklin watched from his peephole in the proprietor's room, he saw that Curanti was doing his part well. Chattering with a fluency that had not marked the previous occasion, he adroitly shepherded the three towards the table, now dexterously removing a chair that blocked the way, then placing the chair for Rossi or bustling paternally round the others. The paper seemed to have escaped his notice—but Rossi saw it. He snatched it up, stared, then put it out of sight on his knees. Curanti turned towards him and spoke. Rossi made a careless gesture, produced the paper, tapped it; then as Curanti gave a bow that was more like a scrape, put it away in his pocket. Then the four of them began talking. Curanti joined in. He seemed to be conceding some point; then all of them laughed—and at that moment Luigi appeared with the tray. Curanti bowed his way out.

"What did he say?" Franklin asked quickly.

Curanti thumped himself on the chest, then waved his hand complacently.

"Everything happened as we arranged. I asked if I should take the paper. Then he said it was an American paper, and might he take it to his house and read it, as it recalled old times. So of course I said he might have it, and in any case I could not read American."

"Good!" said Franklin. "Undoubtedly he saw on the front page that photo of the man who so closely resembles himself. If it should be he!" He gesticulated the prospect. "Perhaps there may be a reward for you—who knows? . . . Be ready when he leaves, and say there is no need to bring the paper back."

From his old seat in the corner he watched the card players at their game, till Rossi rose to go. Curanti was at hand at once, and under cover of the mild excitement of the afternoon's farewells, Franklin made his way to the back room. Curanti came in more satisfied than ever.

"I told him not to return the paper, and he asked where it came from. I told him what you said—an Italian gentleman, a lawyer from Naples, had left it that afternoon. He said, 'Is he coming back?' and I said, '*Si, signore!* Certainly he is coming back—because he has booked a room.' Then he nodded his head and went out."

Franklin stripped the balance of the reward from his wad and passed it over.

"You have done well. There may be more; perhaps much more—who knows? But only if nothing is known. Keep this to yourself or it may mean serious trouble. To-night, for instance, I go to see the Signor Rossi—who expects me."

"He expects you, *signore!*"

"Have I not said so?" The look he got was so abrupt that he started back. "That also you will tell no one, or the Signor Rossi may be offended. But if I am offended, that will be much worse!"

He stalked off with such an air that the other watched him with very definite respect. Franklin chuckled to himself as he made his way up to his room. But as he waited for the hour to approach, he left speculation to take care of itself. Above the centre photo—the man with a beard—he had written in English, so plainly that Rossi must have seen it—

'The Villa Guardini, at six o'clock'

In accepting the paper, Rossi had surely accepted the challenge. Very well then; till six o'clock the case could take care of itself.

Just before the hour, he left the hotel and made his way by the lane that skirted the church. Everywhere was dark, and deadly quiet, and as he moved quickly along the road, it was with a sense of foreboding. There was no excitement; everything was too strange for that. The front gateway between the stone pillars looked strange; so did the cypresses themselves. Then from somewhere close, a dog began to bark furiously and tug at its chain. In the distance the bell of the *campanile* struck six. He pushed open the gate and felt his way to the house, which looked like a blue darkness against the sky. Then he stumbled on the step and almost fell against the door. Before he could knock, it opened. An old woman stood there holding a light by her head and peering out to the path.

"The Signor Rossi lives here?" Franklin asked.

There was a long pause, then, "What is it the gentleman wants?"

"I wish to see him. I believe he expects me. Tell him, the gentleman from Naples; the gentleman who had the newspaper."

"The gentleman from Naples . . . who had the newspaper!" She still stood there irresolutely, as if trying to see his face, then drew back grudgingly. "The gentleman will perhaps wait. I will tell the *Signore*."

She gave him a searching look as he took a seat in the cold, stone-flagged hall; turned up the wick of the lamp that stood gloomily on a side table, then waddled away with the candle. Franklin looked round nervously, then listened as a door was opened and voices were heard for the merest moment. He sat there for perhaps a minute, listening for another sound, then raised his eyes to the opposite wall. The only decoration that broke the white-washed monotony of its surface was a picture; a painting of a man—and the very spit of Rossi himself! Or was it Rook? He listened again, then tiptoed across. The man, as he now saw him, was of a different generation; a father perhaps, or a grandfather; probably old Emilio Guardini, the one who seemed to be in the absolute background of every inquiry. But the painting of the clothes was so black that one could guess little else in the gloomy light.

Then, as he shuffled in his chair again, the door in front of him opened, and a girl came out. Her jet-black hair was close cut and down the front of her black frock ran a silver line of chain that ended in a tiny silver cross. But he knew her at once. As he moved to his feet the sound made her stop short in her tracks, then draw back a pace. She stood there for a moment, watching him—then he moved forward. When he came to think of it afterwards he knew why he had done so—why he spoke in English; whispered almost; and his face must have had some intense earnestness about it.

"You are Lucia!"

The little smile checked itself on her lips and her eyes opened wide. He caught the whisper—

"Yes!"

"And it was you who played the piano?"

Her forehead puckered slightly, then she nodded. Franklin nodded too, hesitated, then, still in English—"I would like to talk to you, Lucia . . . Will you be there to-morrow—at the tree?"

Her eyes lowered. Franklin felt for a moment as if in the presence of some strange, remote mystery—the deadly quiet of the house, the quiet of their own voices, and the something that seemed to be hidden in the eyes that were now steadily watching him. Then she smiled gently and gave a little nod.

"Yes . . . to-morrow!"

Almost while she was speaking she turned back to the door and was gone. Franklin stood there for a moment, wondering what had alarmed her, then heard a door open somewhere in the house. In a second or two the shuffling of feet was heard and the old woman reappeared. Just in sight of him she stopped.

"Will the gentleman come this way?"

He followed her along a short, stone-paved passage, which ended in a door which she opened—and then closed after him. In the middle of the room in which he found himself was a stove whose enormous pipe ran back to the outside wall, and before the fire Rossi was sitting, a newspaper on his knees. At the back of him, on the table, was a lamp. The furniture of the room seemed to be merely three or four chairs and a writing- desk. Rossi made no attempt to rise.

"You wish to see me, *signore*?"

Franklin came closer and looked down at him steadily. Then he smiled.

"That is so. But you will not disturb yourself on that account, I beg of you!"

The other let the irony pass—or saw none. He indicated a chair, obviously placed ready.

"Sit down, *signore*, and we will talk . . . May I have the pleasure of your name?"

Franklin took his time before answering. He looked rather effective as he sat there, with all the self-possession in the world, hat drooping lazily from his hand.

"My name is Francesco, but that does not matter . . . for the present. It is *your* name, *signore*, that matters!"

CHAPTER XIII
ROSSI LAUGHS LAST

As ROSSI SHOT a sudden look at him, Franklin saw something that finally blew to the winds that theory of dual identity. It was indeed only the strangeness of the circumstances that gave the discovery its disconcerting effect. Rossi was an Italian of the Italians. He could never have been anything else. How then could the contact with Rook have come about? For years, Rossi had never left the Villa Guardini; for years Rook had lived in Sussex. How then—The other's voice cut across the beginnings of a new series of self-questions.

"That is a strange question! Why do you ask it?"

Franklin kept his eyes steadily on him.

"Shall we speak English? Undoubtedly you know the language—and you have read that paper, and the message I left for you."

"You, too, speak English?"

"To me, either language is the same," said Franklin indifferently. "Still, as you wish. Tell me; why did you admit me—a complete stranger—to your house, on the strength of the photo of a dead man? Who was that man?"

The other shrugged his shoulders. He even looked rather annoyed.

"A coincidence. How should it concern me? There are doubtless in the world a dozen men—a hundred—who look like me! I was not interested, beyond the fact that one is interested in the unusual." He waved his hand with an ornate gesture. "And someone—you say it was yourself—was also interested, and wished to see me. Very well then; that is all . . . unless you have something to tell me, which is—shall we say?—another coincidence?"

Franklin smiled dryly. "All in good time. And you say you have no knowledge of this man. You'll swear to that?"

Rossi's look changed to a sneer; then he leaned forward with a look that was meant undoubtedly to be threatening.

"Who are you? Are you not aware that I have powers to—er—disembarrass myself of people who annoy me? Where are—"

"One moment!" interrupted Franklin. "If you are hinting that you can have me arrested on some charge or other, then all I say is—don't do it! I'm not an Italian—"

"Give me your passport!" Rossi held out his hand.

"Oh, no! My passport has already been seen. You have no authority to demand it—here in your house. I carry no *carta d'identita*! If you want me to leave your house, I will do so—but you have no right to question me."

"And by what right do you question *me*?"

Franklin leaned forward, arms on knees. "Why prevaricate? If you know nothing of this man, you have only to tell me to go! . . . You asked me who I was. Very well, I will tell you—in part. I am an Englishman, and my inquiries are on behalf of the English police. What authority I have does not matter—except that if you refuse to talk to me, I shall return with those who have the power to make even *you* speak. But why talk of that? Here we are; you and I alone; two men who understand each other! If you speak to me in confidence, I will respect that confidence. I swear it!"

The other pondered for a moment or two and Franklin could see that he was hesitating on the edge of some disclosure. As the forehead wrinkled and the lips pouted, Franklin watched like a gambler who waits for the wheel to stop. Rossi waved his hand.

"It is for *you* to speak. Why—beyond the mere resemblance of face—should you connect me with this man? What happens in England—how does it concern me?"

"In this way," said Franklin quietly. "That man—the man of the photos—resembled yourself. He bore the same initials as yourself. He expected some harm to come to him. He killed himself—or he was killed, we do not know which—but before he died he wished to communicate with you. He left something—some papers—in very strict confidence, with a friend of mine; and he left them to the occupant of the house with the seven cypresses, at Valcetto. That is yourself!"

At the first mention of papers he saw the change on Rossi's face—a stare of interest, and a sudden crafty closing-up which merged into the same indifference he had so laboriously shown from the beginning.

"All that, of course, may be. I may have known the man and forgotten him; whereas he remembered me . . . But you say he left papers for me. Where are they? Who has them?"

"A friend of mine has them—as I told you. When you convince him or me that you are the person for whom they were intended, he will certainly hand them over."

Rossi sat quietly for a good minute, then fidgeted nervously with the paper. His first movement of hospitality, when it came, made Franklin more than ever aware that he was dealing with a remarkably devious individual.

"You will take something to drink, *signore*? A glass of wine?" Without waiting for an answer, he tinkled the small handbell that stood at his elbow, then waved his hand apologetically round the room. "A bare room, and not what you English would call 'comfortable'—but I like it. We have other rooms, with modern stoves and things, but I prefer the old ways . . . like my grandfather."

"Pardon me!" said Franklin courteously, "but is that painting—the one by where I was sitting—a portrait of your grandfather?"

Rossi nodded.

"The Signor Emilio Guardini, was he not?"

The arrival of the old woman interrupted the answer, but not before Franklin had seen the lips shaped to make it. He watched the placing of the table and the setting out of wine and glasses, then took the glass of Barolo which Rossi handed him.

"Your very good health, *signore*! Perhaps it was a very lucky day that brought me to Valcetto. Who knows?"

The other finished his wine and set down the glass before answering. "As you say, who knows? And these papers. What is the name of your friend who has them?"

Franklin shook his head. "That I will tell you later, when you have also told me certain things. For instance, with this man in England—this man who so closely resembled yourself, and the Signor Guardini, your grandfather!—was a woman, of the age of the man—or older. She too died, shortly after the man; but before she died she said a good many things—and she spoke the Italian that an Italian speaks. All she said, I am not prepared to tell you at the moment; that will remain—in case there are things you refuse to tell me. But she did mention the name of someone who also lives at this house—Lucia; your daughter Lucia! Also she carried about her pictures of your daughter, whom I have seen. How do you explain that? since you say the man was a stranger to you—and lived in England!"

This time there was no doubt about the surprise. Rossi's voice trembled as he put the question.

"She is dead—this woman?"

Franklin leaned forward again and took the paper.

"This is the woman, as she was when she died . . . There is something, perhaps, you would like to tell me . . . about her?"

The other shook his head abruptly. As he sat there looking at nothing, clean through the room, Franklin could almost see the struggle going on in his mind. Would he speak—or would he not? Then Rossi smiled. He sat up in the chair and as he spoke he gesticulated with a vividness that so veneered his story that at the end the other felt even more mistrust than before. "As you say, I know this man—Rook, as he called himself. He was my cousin, and his father was English. In America I knew him, many years ago, before I came here. He knew my daughter, and the woman, who was his housekeeper, and whose name I have forgotten, she also knew my daughter. Many times she stayed with them. When affairs called me away, she stayed with them always. I helped him with money—and things. He was a relative of mine and I did what I could. Then, after the war, we came back to Rome. There were the troubles then, with the *Comunisti* and evil-minded people who did much harm. Then we others made a discovery—that there was a spy; one who told everything we did, so that the *Comunisti* were prepared. *Signore!* I knew who that man—that *spione* was!" He spat the word out with such venom that Franklin almost ducked away. "It was this man, my cousin! . . . But what could I do? Against my beliefs I helped him to escape—to England. I gave him money, and a passport. Naturally I do not want it to be known that he is a relation of mine. I do not wish it to be known even now; when I am a person of importance among the enemies of Communism. That is why I tell you I do not know him—and that I know nothing . . . That explains everything to you, does it not? I trust you are satisfied."

Franklin nodded reflectively. "Yes . . . almost. But the photos of your daughter. How do you account for those?"

"Ah! That is easy! Every year I sent him money. He had been of service to me, and nobody shall accuse me of ingratitude. Also he was a relative. Very well then; I sent him the money. And at the same time I sent also a photo of my daughter; one each year, because he loved my daughter. And the woman too— she loved my daughter, as if she were her own. As I explained to you, she lived with them as much as she lived with myself. I was so much away!"

Franklin nodded again. "And the men of whom he was afraid; the men who were responsible for his death; who were they? And why did they want to kill him?"

Rossi spread his hands with a gesture of completest ignorance.

"That I do not know. But of course there might have been those who wished to kill him. If he had returned here to Italy, and if what he had done had been known, then he would have been killed here—by those he had betrayed. Or he may have taken with him to England the names of certain other people who were spies like himself, but who still remain here in Italy. Perhaps he threatened them—to betray them. Take myself, for instance. One comes to me and says, 'You were of the *Comunisti*! If you do not pay, then I will speak!' Very well then, I pay. But when the time comes, I disembarrass myself of the man who makes me pay!"

Franklin saw that. As a theory of the reason for the killing of Rook, he even found it attractive. The disquieting thing was the pleasure Rossi seemed to take in the hypothesis he had just advanced. He replenished Franklin's glass and pushed it along the table. Then he smiled.

"As you see, I have been open with you. There was no need for me to have spoken. But I thought it better—as you are a man who will respect the confidences—to speak to you of what I thought would be never known . . . And now those papers that your friend has for me in England. What is his name and address? so that those who represent me may write."

"A moment!" said Franklin. "The reason why this man Rook so resembled you was that he resembled—like you—the man who was also *his* grandfather . . . the Signor Guardini?"

Rossi shrugged indifferently. "That is so—perhaps."

"You sent money, and the photos, to England. To what address did you send them? To Rook direct?"

Rossi shook his head. "That would have been too dangerous. I sent them to . . . a safe person, who could be trusted. He would give them to this Rook, when he called for them."

"Then why did not Rook hand to this intermediary the papers he wished you to have? Why did he give them to my friend?"

Another immense shrug. "Who knows? He was perhaps suspicious. And though I wrote to him, always I impressed on him that he must never write to me—never! It would have been too dangerous."

Franklin frowned. "I see! . . . Well, this is my bargain. If you continue to treat me fairly, I will continue to keep your confidences. Give me the address of that intermediary to whom you sent the letters, and I will give you the name and address of my friend!"

Rossi ruminated—then got to his feet. "Very well! I will write for you what you want—and to show you that I keep back nothing . . . Here is paper on which you may write for me the name and address of your friend."

Franklin printed Travers' name and address in clear letters and folded the sheet of paper. Rossi, at the desk, took much longer, and he handed over the paper with a flourish—and unfolded. Franklin read it—

> P. Naldi,
>   37, Carberry St.,
>   Soho,
>   London,
>   England.

Then he smiled. "So you do know London, *signore*?"

Rossi shrugged his shoulders.

"I'll merely make a copy of an address that has been given me!"

"Yes," persisted Franklin; "but how do you know that your communications reach this address, if you get no letters in return?"

"Ah! you have it wrong! My cousin; it is he who must not answer. But the other—the one who takes the letters—he can answer. He too is my friend. He would let me know if there was a change of address." He rubbed his hands effusively. "And yourself—where do you go to now? Back to this London of yours?"

Franklin hesitated.

"Yes . . . unless you have more to tell me."

Somehow that seemed the very invitation Rossi had been waiting for; at least Franklin had that impression.

"What else should there be?"

"Many things," said Franklin. "Why, for instance, should not this Italian woman—his housekeeper—have come here to Italy, to see your daughter whom she loved so much? She at least had nothing to fear—unless she also was a spy?"

Rossi bit his lip. Then his face lit up.

"*Signore*, you have decided me! There are other things I shall have to tell you." He shook his head slowly. "There is no escaping it. But first I must see certain people. I must consult with others, and have their permission to speak. That will take . . . perhaps three—no, four!—days. Very well then; the fourth night from now, at the same time, you will come here again. That is so—is it not?"

"The fourth night from now. That is, three nights, then I come here again—at six o'clock. Very well, *signore*; I shall be here!"

He took the outstretched hand which felt warm and clammy. Then Rossi rang the bell. In five minutes Franklin was back at the hotel; late for dinner and avoiding the enquiring glances of Curanti, who persisted in hovering in the neighbourhood of his table.

* * * * * * *

Franklin's first resolve when he awoke the following morning was that he would indeed respect implicitly the confidences of the previous night; not that he believed entirely everything that had been told him—far from it. Rossi he regarded as a wholly unscrupulous individual; neither to be trusted in himself nor to be entrusted with much in return. Still, Franklin made up his mind that he would take no immediate advantage of his absence from Valcetto to question those numerous people who might have given him information. One matter only he settled forthwith—the relationship between Rossi and Rook, and a question to Curanti did that. He put it as casually as he could.

"Old Emilio Guardini; he had only the one son—the Emilio who used to come to the Villa in the summer, with his two daughters?"

Curanti said that was so; there was only the one son. His manner was so confident that Franklin took the matter as settled. Rossi then had told one lie at least. If Rossi himself was the son of Guardini's daughter—Rosa her name was, so Curanti said—then where did the cousin-ship with Rook come in?

There was one other question that suggested itself in the course of the same morning, when Franklin caught sight of that really superb motor-boat lying just off shore. When did Rossi first acquire it? Curanti thought it out—then gave a very definite answer. From certain associations which he quoted, he knew it had been bought in the early summer of the previous year.

That, as Franklin saw, was most suggestive. The boat was bought immediately *after* the visit of the man with the squint. Could he have brought Rossi news of some danger that was likely to arrive at any moment? And since the boat was still there, was that danger still likely to arrive? And was it of such a nature that the only way to avoid it was to escape—to get clear *away from Italian territory*?

But the thing that dominated Franklin's mind during that morning was the thought of the afternoon's meeting with the girl Lucia, and what that meeting implied. It was all very confused; indeed he hardly knew his own mind. Wharton would never have understood one point of view—a definite squeamishness about questioning. He would have regarded her as a heaven-sent witness; a woman with a tongue which she could be cajoled into using. Franklin put that part of the problem into the background—and yet knew all the time that it was there. As for the other view, it is curious that for a moment Franklin wished that Travers were there—to have heard it and understood. Paternal instinct, he might have called it; or the desire of the male to protect; and certain it was that Franklin knew one thing—that if he had a daughter he wished she might be like Lucia Rossi.

Before two o'clock he was off; not by the Villa road but the other way. The sun gleamed out fiercely as he leaned back against a curving branch, smoking pipe after pipe and glancing away down to the just-visible roof of her house. Everything was pleasurable anticipation. At the hotel even, things had gone well. Curanti had been put off with hints and circumlocutions—though he mattered little now in any case.

And what was she to be asked when she did come? who her mother was; that would be one thing. English she might have been. If so, that would be really wonderful. Then there was the old housekeeper Travers had seen; the one who kept those photographs. Would Lucia know anything about her? Or about Rook himself? That led his thoughts to England again. How delightful it would be if something happened to Rossi—something that made it necessary for him to take the girl back to England! He imagined his pride as he showed her to Travers. She could live with them—a couple of uncles! And she should go for a year or two to some slap-up school. . . .

He looked at his watch. Well after three. His mood changed to anxiety. Another quarter of an hour and he knew she wasn't coming. Then he began to find excuses.

The father was going away, and there would be heaps of things to do. Perhaps the old woman had been left in charge, and had refused permission to leave the house unaccompanied. Or had he himself alarmed Rossi the previous night by letting him know he had seen his daughter? Still, it could be decided whether Rossi had already gone or not. If he were still in Valcetto he would be at the hotel at his usual hour.

Four o'clock then found Franklin back at the hotel—and, for Curanti, the miracle happening. There was no Rossi! Then, of course, Franklin had to do some explaining. The ever-faithful patron of the hotel was away, making enquiries about those very private matters at which Franklin had hinted. In three days' time he would be back, and then all sorts of wonderful things were going to happen.

After that the time hung heavily on Franklin's hands. Of theories, of course, he had plenty. There was no reason, for instance, why Rook should not have been what Rossi suggested—a blackmailer. Rook, Rossi, and those two men who had yanked Rook out of his shell at Steyvenning, might all have been associated together in Rome at the time, and under the conditions Rossi had stated. If so it was probably to Rome that Rossi had gone. And since he had gone there to confer with a party or parties, he himself still had something to fear. In that context, that theory of the use of the motor-boat seemed more obvious than likely.

The following afternoon he again climbed the hills to the shelter behind the cypress hedge, knowing that nothing would happen and hoping against hope that after all something other than he thought had gone wrong. At four o'clock he was back at the hotel, where Curanti seemed to be hovering more than usual over his patrons, and lingering for some time at the table where two of Rossi's cronies were spending the usual hour.

Then, when the verandah cleared, Franklin was told the news. Curanti was all excitement. And he was certainly aggrieved.

"You were wrong, *signore*, when you told me that Signor Rossi would be back in a day or two. Yesterday, in the afternoon, he went to Taranto, in a car. And his daughter was with him—and very much luggage." Franklin felt a sudden alarm.

"You are sure?"

"I know it, *signore*! Moreover, Signor Prenza called at the Villa just before and Signor Rossi confided to him that he would be away for a long while."

Franklin assumed a complacency that he was far from feeling. "It is you who are wrong. Did I not tell you all this affair was secret? Signor Rossi was making an excuse. You know me, Signor Curanti. I tell you that in two days' time—at four o'clock—you will know that it is I who am right."

In his bedroom Franklin felt more and more alarmed. So that was why the girl had not kept the appointment. Or was she still at the Villa? Had she gone with her father to Taranto merely to see him off, and for the pleasure of the small excursion, as it were? More and more disturbed he prowled round and round the room, then could stand it no longer. With a sudden resolution he seized his hat, and made his way quickly out of the hotel. In five minutes he was knocking at the door of the Villa.

The same dog gave warning of his approach, but this time he had to knock more than once before the door was opened. The old woman spoke first.

"You are the gentleman who came the other night?"

"I am!" said Franklin, and mounted the step towards the light.

She drew back and half closed the door. As she peered out at him, her face looked malevolent and vindictive.

"The master is away. He left word he had finished with you."

"I know he is away. He told me that himself. But when will he be back? "

She gave a sneer of contempt.

"Who knows? For weeks he has gone—or it may be months. He has gone to America!"

Franklin scowled into the darkness. Then he took a step nearer.

"His daughter—the Signorina Lucia; may I speak to *her*?"

The woman closed the door still further till there was nothing to be seen but the white of her hair against the black slit.

"She has gone to America also. If the gentleman annoys the house, I am to inform the police. Tomorrow night the dog will be loose!"

Franklin said nothing. The old woman stood for a moment as if peering out to see how he took that final insult, then as he moved, slammed the door to.

Outside in the road again, Franklin watched the house for some minutes; swearing at himself for the fool he'd been; at that damnable hag of a woman; at the cursed yelping of that dog— and at Rossi himself. As he trudged moodily back to the hotel, the whole bottom seemed to have dropped out of things. What was best to be done? Cut his losses, or get on Rossi's trail? He halted for a moment to think that out, after the first furious outburst had passed. After all, it might take weeks or even months to find Rossi, and when he *was* found, how could he be made to speak? And then a thought! Suppose he had gone to England! If so, he had counted on four days' clear start—and, thanks to the spite of his own housekeeper, he now had barely two. Why not get on his tracks at once?

If he had been capable at that moment of reasonably clear judgment, he might have seen the futility of a plan that depended on nothing but revenge. Still, there it was; his mind was made up. Before returning to the hotel he hunted up a car, arranged terms, and had it drawn up at the door. His things he got together before entering Curanti's office. The proprietor lingered over the bill—over the change—over everything. Franklin lied unblushingly.

"As I told you, I was right. To-night I have been again at the Signor Rossi's house. Tomorrow"—and he gestured the prospect. Curanti followed him to the door but got no more news.

At midnight he was in the express for Paris. All the information he had gathered at the station was that a man and a girl—

resembling Rossi and his daughter—had left for Rome a good many hours before. In the train, Franklin had another pessimistic and infuriating thought. It was perfectly plain that Rossi had kept him hanging about Valcetto so as to gain time to call personally on Travers and get the papers he imagined were waiting for him. Then he smiled. If that were so, Rossi was in a trap. With an imaginary start of four days, he (Rossi) would have no need to hurry on his journey. But the *two* days he really had, could also be made to disappear!

That was why Franklin went to the expense of flying from Lyons to Paris and from there to London. If the expense were questioned, the difference should come out of his own pocket.

And one useful thing he did do, during the train part of the journey; he wrote up every detail of experiences and impressions since he set foot in Valcetto. And yet another idea brought consolation. That address in Soho would be useful. The man who had acted as intermediary between Rossi and Rook could certainly be made to open his mouth, and if Wharton got hold of him, to open it wide!

* * * * * * *

That was why, as soon as he passed the barrier at Victoria, Franklin took a taxi for Carberry Street, Soho. The street he knew merely as a cutting off Poland Street. No. 37, which he had assured himself would be that usual port of call for letters—a tobacconist's, turned out to be a florist's, and a superior one into the bargain. The flat above was a dentist's office. The topmost flat, judging by its general appearance, was the home of the occupants of the shop. Somehow he didn't like the look of it.

Inside the shop a girl was bunching flowers, and behind the counter quite a well-dressed man was reading a paper. Franklin introduced himself and stated his business. The answer he got was courteous but final.

"No, sir. We never take in letters. We've never been asked to!"

"And you have no knowledge of anybody of the name of Rossi—or Rook?"

The man shook his head. "I know a Rossi; I know several. The name's common enough in Soho. But not in the way you mention."

"And you've been here a good many years?"

"I took this business over from my father, and he came here before I was born!"

"That seems to settle it!" smiled Franklin. "And the dentist upstairs; you think he'd be likely?"

The other made a wry face. "He only moved in last week!"

"And who was there before?"

"I was. We had all the top. Then my youngest daughter got married, so I let off the bottom half." Franklin thanked him and left. Outside on the pavement he had another idea—and consulted the paper Rossi had given him. No! there didn't seem any chance of a mistake; 37 it plainly was. Still, it *might* by 57 or 87. But 87 didn't exist, and 57 was a milliner's, with workroom above. The woman whom he attempted to question was offhand and most emphatic.

As Franklin trudged along Poland Street towards Leicester Square, he recognised only too well that Rossi had been one too many for him. All the same, things weren't finished with yet by any manner of means. Travers would have to be seen first—then there'd have to be a report for Sir Francis.

And so on for the rest of the journey; now hopeful, now absurdly pessimistic. Perhaps Rossi had gone to America after all. Perhaps he had seen Travers already—and had gone back to Italy. Then the girl, Lucia, might be in America—or in Rome—or even in London. And in any case, why worry about it all? During all those days he'd been absent, something was bound to have happened. The whole of that visit to Valcetto had been, in all probability, time and money wasted. The Rook Case was most likely over—and Wharton already grubbing his nose into a new one!

CHAPTER XIV
ALL THE LATEST

IT WAS several days before Travers saw anything of Wharton, then one afternoon he rang up and was promptly asked round to dinner. As soon as he'd had time to get his coat off and name his drink, Travers was asking for information. Wharton said there wasn't any; then side-tracked into a request.

"How'd you like to drive me down to Sussex tomorrow?"

"Morning or afternoon?"

"Say after an early lunch—if it suits you."

"Suit me splendidly," said Travers. "What's happening precisely?"

Wharton sipped his drink. "Nothing—yet. We're going to an auction—the quickest event in the county."

Travers didn't see it. "You don't mean one of those affairs that—er—are conducted in the Strand?"

Wharton expanded. "Not that sort of auction. We've had notices in the local Press the last few days, and we've placarded the countryside with bills. Also we've had references in the London papers—though apparently they've been too low-brow for you to notice 'em. The Mill House, Steyvenning, is what's being sold, with contents—as inventoried—at the option of the purchaser."

"Pretty quick work, George! But what's your authority to dispose of the property like that?"

"We haven't any!" said Wharton cheerfully, and during the meal explained the whole business. Rook, it seems, had left with the manager of the local bank an envelope for which he obtained the usual receipt. All that was in private and with a certain amount of mystery. The envelope was to be handed back to nobody but Rook himself; and at his death was to be opened by the manager who was to act in accordance with the instructions contained therein. The manager, it had been, who had approached Wharton at Steyvenning. What the envelope contained was a will—simplicity itself—witnessed by the gardener and the baker's man; stating that everything was to go to the woman known as Mary Fletcher, housekeeper of the deceased. The bank was sole executor.

"What about the deeds of the house?" asked Travers.

"The manager has 'em. Deposited in the usual way. But you see that one point. *'Known as!'* Rook thereby admits it wasn't her name. Neither was Madame Flechier, because that isn't Italian!"

"She might have been Swiss!" said Travers, who had smiled discreetly at Wharton's swift absorption of the theories he had once sniffed at. "Still, that's not the point. The thing is, he was anxious she should get—well, what there was to get. And what was it?—besides the house and contents."

"That's what I was going to tell you," said Wharton reprovingly. "There's wasn't anything to leave, because he hadn't anything—at least we haven't been able to find a trace of anything in the house. He had somewhere about £500 in ordinary current account at the bank. He always had that amount, and on the two occasions when the bank notified him—as he'd requested—that it was getting low, he paid in cash to bring it up to the original sum."

"What sort of cash?"

"Hundred pound notes!" said Wharton, and paused as if expecting some comment. "In the bank, moreover, on *deposit* account, was the sum of £5,000 in the name of Mary Fletcher. This was deposited—also in hundred pound notes, by Rook on his arrival. The book we can't find."

Travers looked surprised. "What was the deposit for? Reward for faithful services—or was it her own money; Rook merely acting as her agent?"

"Don't know," said Wharton. "But listen to this! The same thing happened at Tiverton, but not at Beaconcross. When he left Tiverton the money was withdrawn, and paid in hundred pound notes by request. *But*, some of the notes paid in at Steyvenning differed from those paid out at Tiverton."

Travers opened his eyes. "You mean, Rook must have been in possession of a considerable number of those notes when he arrived in Tiverton. They were his unit of currency, if I may put it that way. Also he should have been in possession of a good few at his death."

"That's right. The trouble is, we haven't been able to trace the original possession. There's no record at Beaconcross, for instance."

"There wouldn't be," said Travers. "And you agree that Rook had a cache, and the American found it."

"Damned if I know!" said Wharton bluntly. "If he and Driver found it, why did they take him away to Frenchman's Rise? And why was a man searching the house?"

"There are other things than money, George!"

"I know that. What I was going to tell you about, was that envelope Rook left at the bank. The man who called himself George Rook, called there with a chit from his supposed brother, asking for the envelope to be handed over. The manager refused—perfectly politely of course—then volunteered to bring it personally to the house. George Rook professed not to know the contents of the chit—except that the manager was supposed to hand over an envelope—and he said he'd tell his brother, and the manager needn't bother to bring it. The very same evening, as far as we've been able to trace, they decamped. That's when they arrived at Frenchman's Rise!"

"Scared stiff!"

"Exactly! But you see the real point. They couldn't bring Rook along to the bank and they daren't admit the manager to the house to see him. Why? Because Rook wasn't in a fit condition to be seen. Probably they'd already been torturing the old chap, or got him to such a state that he'd have appealed to the manager for help. . . . But with regard to your other point, I should say they never got what they wanted. They still want it—and they'll try to get it."

"Hence the auction!"

"Precisely! I've talked it over with those I take my orders from, and they've decided to carry it through. If the heirs—if there are any—do any objecting, that's not my funeral."

Travers nodded. "There's just one point, George—not that you've missed it, because you certainly haven't—and it's that

Rook's two visitors anticipated a certain amount of trouble. They *calculated* that he wouldn't give up what they wanted. That's why they took Frenchman's Rise *before* they came to Steyvenning. Isn't that so?"

"Oh yes! As you imply, they knew their man pretty well. Therefore he wasn't a stranger to them. Therefore they'd probably been in partnership some years before. I'm coming to that later, by the way."

"Oh! and something else," said Travers. "Why didn't Rook do what they wanted? I mean, what is there that a man would hold out for, even to the extent of—say—losing his life?"

"Hundreds of things!" snorted Wharton. "If we took every reason of that kind, it'd mean a new line of research, and my grandson'll be going on with it—if he's fool enough to be a policeman!"

Travers laughed, then suddenly sobered up.

"Do you know, George, I find my sympathies swinging past Rook every time. Rook was more unusual than sympathetic. It's that old woman I can't get off my mind. That's the queerer business. Why, for instance, was she supposed to be dumb?"

Wharton looked at him. "You don't see that! Just think it out! She was Italian—or Swiss—to begin with, and sister of Rook's wife. She was perfectly natural therefore, in posing at Beaconcross and Tiverton as French; and speaking French and some broken English. At Tiverton, she became very definitely French. When she left there, she became dumb, because of the man with the squint."

Travers looked puzzled. Wharton went on patiently. "Rook left Tiverton because he anticipated a visit from the man with the squint. He had been zig-zagging a trail for years, and now things were getting desperate, he thought that trail might after all be followed up through his housekeeper, if it was known that she was a foreigner. That's why she became the English Mary Fletcher—and dumb. If she'd spoken broken English—to the maid, for instance—there'd have been gossip. The trail'd have been easier to follow."

"But it wasn't the man with the squint who came that evening to Mill House, prospecting for Rook! I mean the man who trampled on the flower-bed and asked the maid questions."

"I know it wasn't!" said Wharton, even more patiently. "I'm going to explain that later. Bertha says it was Driver who made the enquiries, and he's quite a different man."

"Then who's the man with the squint?"

"Ah! that's the question!" Wharton spoke with the most exasperating gusto. "If we found him, we'd be somewhere. He's the gentleman who may attend the sale tomorrow!"

"Really! And how's he interested?"

"That'll be our business to find out!" said Wharton enigmatically. He selected a cigar carefully from the box, got it going, settled himself comfortably in the lounge chair—then went off at a tangent.

"As you say, it's that old woman who's the intriguing factor. Did I tell you what happened to her? . . . I didn't. Well, as far as we can trace, she left the same afternoon as the maid. Driver took her to the station, and she had the same case she had the night we found her, and a trunk as well. I should say it's a million to one both were gone over carefully before she was allowed to leave the house. She took a ticket for London, but got out at the junction and stayed the night at the Downs Hotel. She indicated that she was dumb, and wrote down what she wanted. The girl at the desk spotted her for a lady; found out she could hear well enough, and did the rest of the business herself. All the old lady had to do was to nod and smile. Also she planked down a ten-pound note, and had more in her bag. Rook, I should guess, got permission to pay her wages in the presence of the others. She was a model guest and behaved like a dowager duchess. The rest you know. She was away from the hotel on two separate days, on one of which she was seen in the neighbourhood of Mill House. Then she paid her bill, left her trunk in the cloak room at the station, and the same night she spent in the shed. The following night we found her."

"Seems clear enough," said Travers reflectively. "She knew all there was to know—apparently. She and Rook had made all their plans well ahead—that she was to go to the hotel, and so on. Rook probably told her he could look after himself, and she wasn't to worry. She was to stay at the hotel till he could let her know the coast was clear. If anything worse happened, she was sure of the money and could go back to Italy—or Switzerland. Also, as she was presumably dumb, she would escape a considerable deal of awkward enquiry. Things would be pretty easy for her over the will." He hesitated. "But that's all wrong! They *didn't* know anything was going to happen!"

"Why didn't they?"

"Because Rook'd have bolted again! He'd have zig-zagged the trail a bit more! "

"You're wrong!" said Wharton curtly. "Rook was tired of zig-zagging. He got fatalistic. He sat down and waited. The fact that he *didn't* bolt, and that he undoubtedly *did* make arrangements, shows that. So does the fact that he sent to Durangos. And that he made special arrangements with the bank manager."

He put the cigar stump ceremoniously in the ashtray, and blew his nose with ponderous gravity. Travers, knowing that little idiosyncrasy, waited for something to happen. He watched the General replace the silk handkerchief with almost effeminate care, then produce a fistful of papers from his pocket. One—a typewritten copy of a newspaper clipping—he passed over. Travers polished his glasses and had a look.

DAILY RECORD
(Sept. 25th)
PERSONAL COLUMN

JOLLY OLD PALS. C.R. business still for sale, at price suggested. Unless accepted, will be offered elsewhere. UNCLE.

"What's it all mean?" Travers asked. "C.R.'s fairly clear—but what's the rest?"

Wharton took it back and read it again as if he'd never clapped eyes on it before.

"That's what I wanted your opinion on. How we got it was like this. I had every file hunted up—for a purpose which I'll refer to later—and the only thing we ran across was this. It was in five different papers; three insertions each. The C.R.—as you say—is a likely clue. On the other hand it might be hopelessly wrong, though personally I don't think so."

"And who's 'uncle'?"

"The man with the squint! I'll give you a couple of hypotheses—both of which are probably wrong. 'Uncle' was a private detective employed by the American and Driver—who're the Jolly Old Pals—to find Rook's whereabouts. He did so, and withheld the information for a better price; call it, if you like, a mild form of blackmail. He inserted that notice after the first negotiations had fallen through; and as results show they accepted the second offer. Or, 'Uncle' may have been a Jolly Old Pal himself; one of four—Rook completing the party. From there you can go off into any melodrama you like: that Rook stole the usual diamond of fabulous value; that he stole an invention; that he was an informer on the others. But 'Uncle' alone did the searching—most likely as an investment. He got hold of Rook's whereabouts by means of the piano obsession, or something else; and then offered the information. He was too wily a bird to handle it himself. Don't you think that's so?"

Travers gave a sort of affirmatory grunt. Somehow there seemed too much to digest. From beginning to end the case had nothing straightforward in it. From the first day he'd clapped eyes on Rook, everything had been below the surface. It was like gazing at a multitude of objects that lay at the bottom of a river; just discernible for a moment; then invisible; then taking on new shapes as the water changed in its speed or clearness.

"If Driver bought the information," he said, "why did he call at Mill House and ask those questions?"

"As a prelude to paying," said Wharton. "Nobody buys a pig in a poke."

"But they'd already taken Frenchman's Rise!"

"No they hadn't!" corrected Wharton. "They had an option on it, if you remember. They—or rather the American—took it definitely the following Monday. I think you'll find that's correct."

"I expect it is," said Travers. "And what are you going to do about it?"

Wharton looked quite indignant.

"Do about it! What's this auction for?" He lugged out that fistful of papers again, and having found what he wanted, adjusted his old-fashioned glasses. "That's the review of the case. Have a look at the dates." He passed it over. "We'll consider it in terms of years back from now. That'll be simpler."

He went on from memory. "Just over nine years ago, Rook arrived at Beaconcross, with his wife and her sister. He himself is definitely in England but is not seen till the following spring. You might say there is considerable mystery over the whole proceeding; he was, in other words, beginning the same course of conduct he pursued for the next few years."

"One moment!" said Travers. "I forgot to ask you, but I assume therefore you haven't been able to trace a thing before he actually arrived at Beaconcross."

"That's right. The fault may be ours, or it may not, but I admit it. But the inference is that something happened *just before* he arrived at Beaconcross, the consequences of which he wished to avoid. Now what I thought was this. Most of the unusual people in the world come under our notice at some time or other, so I had every record, for as far back as two years previous, hunted up. Every possible avenue has been explored, and we haven't found a combination to fit the case. Other countries have nothing either. All we can assume therefore is that the reason why Rook was hiding, was one that hadn't come under the notice of Scotland Yard. However, to go on with the dates.

"The January after the arrival at Beaconcross, Rook's wife gave birth to a still-born child. Her own health broke down and she developed a kind of pernicious anaemia. Just over two years later, she died. No stone was erected and the record simply states—*Lucy, wife of Clifford Rowlandson*. Then, almost exactly three years after his arrival at Beaconcross, he left for Tiverton, where he takes nothing incriminating away with him, and lives in the same seclusion with his wife's sister. Also I'm definitely convinced there was no question of—er—sex about that proceeding. The maid they had there was also extremely well paid, and she came from Newcastle! He lives there three years, then cuts off in another direction—to Steyvenning. As soon as he leaves, the man with the squint comes, and makes inquiries. Now then; what do you gather from the sequence?" Travers took off his glasses.

"I thought we'd settled that long ago! Obviously he anticipated a visit from the man with the squint!"

"Exactly!" said Wharton triumphantly. "But how did he know it?"

"Well, he might have known it in two ways," said Travers. "The correspondent who sent the photos might have kept him informed."

"Ah!" Wharton wagged his finger. "Assume he got his photo as usual in the July. But it was not till the following *Easter* that he left Tiverton!"

"Yes, I know. But the news he got in July might have been that the danger wasn't to be anticipated before the following Easter—or later. Oh—"

He broke off suddenly. Wharton looked up.

"Well, what is it now?"

"I know how he knew about it! He saw it in the papers. Don't you remember I told you he took in three papers at Steyvenning? What did he want three papers for unless it was because he was afraid he might miss something!"

"Hm!" said Wharton. "Do you know, I think you're right! And if so, the question is, what might he have seen?"

Travers said nothing.

"Of course," went on Wharton ruminatively, "the man with the squint might have been somebody of importance whose arrival was chronicled. Still, that hardly sounds likely. I wonder. Could he have been somebody who was being let out of jail?"

Travers looked up at once. "Why not?"

Wharton shook his head.

"There doesn't seem much to go on. We know nothing about him except this extremely problematic squint. Still, wait till to-morrow's business is over—then we'll go into it."

"One suggestion I would make," said Travers, "and I make it with extreme humility. Begin at the time when Rook arrived at Beaconcross and trace your records for every person with initials C.R., whether that person definitely passed through your hands or was merely inquired for elsewhere."

"To tell you the truth," said Wharton, with that perfectly maddening indifference he could assume on such occasions, "I've had that done already—and pretty thoroughly. And there isn't one who fits the case. Not a potential hermit among 'em! I admit we concentrated on persons convicted."

Travers fell into the trap. "Why only that?"

"Because the men who took Frenchman's Rise were so careful to avoid leaving fingerprints! Those who've never had theirs taken aren't so damn careful as all that."

The French clock tinkled the half-hour and he got up. "No idea it was so late. One o'clock suit you tomorrow? Here?"

"Excellently!" said Travers. "And what time's the auction?"

"About three—at the 'Griffin.' In case your car was noticed when we were down last, we'll park it at a village short and go on in another."

"And what's my job of work?"

"Didn't I tell you! You're the identification department. We chose the hour so as to have artificial light; also it's Saturday, and market day. The bidders will look into the light. You'll be outside in the corridor where there's a door with a glass top. If the American arrives, or Driver, or even the man with the squint, you'll inform Lewis who'll be there with you. Then we'll do the rest." He ran his eyes over Travers from top to toe. "You're lucky! Norris said we'd have to get a giraffe to look over that door!"

Travers smiled modestly. "That's more like you, George. You're getting quite sociable!"

Wharton grunted, thought of something, and stopped short of the door.

"Where's Franklin these days?"

"Well—er—I hear he's abroad on a case. Strictly between ourselves I rather fancy he's in Italy!"

"Italy! What's he doing there?"

"Heaven knows!" said Travers apologetically. "Perhaps he's combining business with pleasure—as we look like doing to-morrow."

Wharton shot a look at him, grunted again—and departed.

CHAPTER XV
WHARTON IS SCARED

"WHAT'S AMUSING YOU, sir?" whispered Lewis.

Travers suddenly realised that he was amused.

"I was thinking," he said, "of one of those peep-show machines that used to flourish at the seaside. I once stole away and had a look through one. This rather reminds me of it."

There certainly was nothing amusing about the scene itself. About twenty persons were present, male—and rural—the whole lot of them, except four gentlemen—presumably the press—who sat at a special table. Some sat stolidly upright, others were having a subdued gossip, and nearly all of them had an air of the uncomfortable.

"What's it now, sir?" asked Lewis.

Travers caught himself in the act of nodding. And he drew back for Lewis to reach up for a book.

"Have you read *The Wreckers*, Lewis?"

"Can't say I have, sir."

" It's about a chap who goes into an auction room and—before he knows it—begins bidding away into thousands of pounds for something that wasn't worth hundreds—apparently."

"Sort of auction room fever, sir; like the women sometimes get!"

"I expect it was," said Travers. "Pretty exciting—wouldn't it be?—if a couple of persons sitting out there were to run that property up to, say, five thousand!"

"You're right there, sir!" said Lewis, and edged up for another look. The room was already hazy with smoke, but the faces could be clearly enough discerned. As far as Travers could make out, there was no sign of the American or Driver; and if one of those potential bidders had a squint, the smoke and the distance concealed it.

Then there was a small commotion. Heads craned round as voices were heard, and in came what turned out to be the auctioneer, and three or four more people at his heels. He was a tall, florid man, ponderous in voice and gesture, and not uninclined to splutter. As he took his seat at the table, his clerk whispered in his ear. One gathered that that was an essential preliminary, since nothing happened. The auctioneer cleared his throat and gazed round the room.

"Well, gentlemen, I presume you all know the conditions of the sale, so I won't go into that. The property is well known to most of you, and those who don't know it have had an opportunity to view," . . . and so on to the general eulogy and the peroration. Another clearing of the throat, then, "Now, gentlemen! what may I say for this really excellent property? Somebody start me at a thousand!"

Travers almost expected some voice to answer like an echo. There was none. Everybody seemed to sit stock-still for a good half-minute, then a hearty voice, with a joviality obviously assumed for the occasion, started the bidding.

"I'll give you a couple of hundred!"

Feet shuffled and there was a murmur of general comment. Travers identified the speaker; a John-Bullish individual who might have stepped out of *Tom Jones*. Hardly a conspirator, that! And he appeared to be a local.

"Two hundred guineas I'm bid! Two hundred guineas, from Mr. James!" Nothing happened for a moment or two, then, "Now, gentlemen! let me have a real bid. Two hundred's a ridiculous price for a property like that! Any advance on two hundred?"

After that things went on leisurely. The bidding came spasmodically and, luckily for Travers, each bidder seemed to be known to the auctioneer.

"Three fifty I'm bid. No, sir! the bidding's against you. Mr. Topp has it. Now it's yours, sir! Three sixty I'm bid. Three sixty from Mr. Clark!" . . . and all the rest of it. Travers found himself looking from side to side of the room, now synchronising with a bidder, now hopelessly behind. At four hundred guineas, Mr. Topp still had it, and what was more, seemed likely to keep it. The bidding held fire, in spite of a recapitulation of the property's virtues, and a sarcastic reminder that the price did not include the furniture.

Travers was more than disappointed. For a few minutes, the whole bottom seemed to have dropped out of things. There was going to be no excitement. The worthy Topp, a heavy-moustached, colourless sort of person who might have been the local baker, was the antithesis of romance. The auctioneer picked up his hammer.

"Well, gentlemen! there's no reserve on the property, as you know." He looked round persuasively. "Any advance on four hundred? Any advance? . . . I'm here to sell this property, gentlemen, not give it away! Four hundred's no price at all. Any advance?"

A last look at the stolid faces and he lifted the hammer.

"For the last time, gentlemen, any advance? Yes, Mr. Topp! the bid's still yours! At four hundred. Any advance?" The hammer wavered. Travers watched it, fascinated.

"Four twenty-five!" came a voice. Travers spotted the owner at once—a quiet, competent-looking man in a grey tweed overcoat. There was a craning of necks to squint at him. The auctioneer lowered the hammer and looked more cheerful.

"Four hundred and twenty-five guineas, I'm bid, gentlemen! Against you, Mr. Topp!"

"Fifty!" said Topp laconically.

The stranger gave no sign. It was all so different from what Travers had so romantically imagined; prosaic, in fact. Nobody, not even the new bidder, seemed at all anxious to become the new owner of Mill House.

"Four fifty I'm bid! It's against you, sir!"

"Five hundred!"

The bid seemed rather reluctant, as if the bidder had realised in the very moment of making it, that he would undoubtedly be ruined by so extravagant an offer. Yet, as Travers sensed, that fifty guineas' rise was meant to be final. And it was. Two minutes later, the auctioneer raised his hammer.

"For the very last time, gentlemen; going at five hundred guineas! Any advance? The last time, gentlemen! Going at five hundred guineas!" The hammer rose, stayed a couple of moments, then fell.

"Sold! at five hundred guineas—to—I didn't catch your name, sir?"

"Edwards! . . . Frederick Edwards!"

The auctioneer nodded. Lewis tiptoed alongside Travers and had a good look.

"Know him, sir?"

Travers shook his head. As Edwards rose, and came forward in the general confusion, he had a good view of him. He was certainly not the American—and far too slender for Driver; and of a different type from both. There was an unassuming, business-like air about him. The hooked nose gave Travers his first flutter of excitement—but the squint wasn't there; there wasn't the faintest sign of it.

"I'll push off now, sir!" whispered Lewis, and was gone before Travers could ask where. Except for the new owner of Mill House, the auctioneer and his clerk, the room was empty. The three sat with backs towards him, heads bent over what might have been the inventory. That went on for twenty minutes perhaps, till Travers got restless; then Edwards got to his feet and the others rose too.

"In the morning then?" Travers thought that was what was said, but he recognised no more. The voices were indistinct and blurred, like a conversation in another room. They droned away towards the door.

He waited for another minute or two, then made his way downstairs to the private room, half expecting to find Wharton. The General was not there. A long wait, then he pushed the bell and ordered tea.

It was an hour after that when Wharton came in. Something had happened as Travers saw by his manner, but it was not till his own tea had come in that the General opened out.

"Edwards left about half an hour ago. Church says."

"Who's Church?"

"The auctioneer. He says Edwards hasn't bought the property in his own name—he's just an agent. They're following up his tracks now."

"Church didn't seem to know him," said Travers. "I take it he isn't a local man?"

"Some sort of relation of the purchaser, I gathered from Church. There may be nothing in it after all." Travers smiled. "You're taking it very philosophically! By the way, you noticed he was Jewish?"

Wharton looked up. "*I* notice! What do you think you're here for? I haven't dared put my foot near the place till I knew he was gone!" He went on munching; then when he'd pushed the tray aside, lugged out his pipe and got to his feet.

"We'll go to the manager's room. There's a telephone there!" and off he stumped. Travers followed, even less romantically minded than ever. Inside the room, Wharton indicated a chair, and made himself comfortable. "Nothing to do but wait."

"Good!" said Travers. He looked round at the glass partition as if to make sure they were really alone. "Something I thought of while I was having tea. What was done about tracing the car that was used at Mill House and Frenchman's Rise?"

"What was done? Oh! the usual things. What's the number of your brother-in-law's car, by the way? The one down here."

Travers looked surprised. "I really can't say, off-hand . . . Something with a nine in it."

"I see! And what's the number of Sir Francis's Rolls?"

Travers looked at him.

"You mean that if I don't know the numbers of cars I've seen scores of times, then why should anybody have remembered the number of the one Driver was using!"

"Got it first time!" said Wharton. "If a car behaves itself— so to speak—there's no reason why it should ever be noticed.

Also it can be used principally at night. And new number plates aren't difficult to get hold of!"

He reached for the newspaper. Travers sat looking into the fire and sucking away at his pipe. When the telephone bell went, it was almost like an explosion. Wharton hopped up like a streak.

"Hallo! . . . Yes! Speaking . . . Really! . . . Yes! . . . A very good idea! . . . Yes! . . . We'll be along right away! What name am I to ask for? . . . Right! Yes! . . . Good-bye!"

"Most illuminating!" said Travers. "Somebody or other, I imagine, has tracked down somebody or other."

"You're improving!" said Wharton and began getting into his greatcoat. "When you're ready, we'll go back and collect your car. We might have to go on to town in a hurry." In the local car, he got more informative.

"Lewis has traced this chap Edwards to Ickenham. He's staying at the 'Green Man'."

"Really!" said Travers politely.

"He followed Edwards in and he went straight to the lounge as if looking for somebody and was hailed by a man who was sitting there with a drink. When Lewis rang me up, they were still sitting in the same corner with their heads together. There wasn't a chance of overhearing."

Half an hour later, Travers drew the Isotta up in the comparative darkness, just short of where the light flooded the open door of the hotel entrance.

"What now?" asked Travers.

"You hop out. I'll take your place at the wheel." He caught the sudden look of amazement. "Dammit! you don't think I'd try to *drive* this hell-waggon! . . . I'll wait here while you have dinner. Get a good look at Edwards's pal—the man with the squint!"

Travers' eyes opened. "I say! you didn't tell me that!"

"I know I didn't! I like to drive with a man who's not worrying about a plan of campaign . . . You get along sharp! Lewis'll be in the lounge, expecting you. Follow his leads!"

Travers thrust his hands nervously into the pockets of his heavy coat and blinked his way in. With a manner that was meant to be self-possessed, he peered into the lounge. Lewis hailed him.

"Hallo, Jack! I was wondering how long you were going to be! What're you going to have?"

He ordered the drinks, and whispered as the waiter left, "They've just gone upstairs! Dinner's ready now. I've ordered for two."

When it came, Travers was taking his short drink at a gulp.

"No need to hurry over it, sir," said Lewis. "Let them get inside first, then we'll know where to sit."

That proved an excellent move. The dining-room was almost empty when they entered; and in the corner furthest from the door sat, as Travers guessed from Lewis's nudge, the two men they wanted. With his back to their own table sat Edwards; opposite him a man of much the same age as himself. Travers, with an indifference which was probably very much overdrawn, had a good look at him.

What he saw was a man clean-shaved and with a head bald as a billiard ball, except for small tufts above his ears. The nose was thin and hooked, and the high forehead, running back to the bald crown, gave him an appearance of cheap guile, which the thin slit of a mouth confirmed. As Edwards made some remark or other and he pursed his lips to a sneer, Travers didn't like the look of him. When he smiled he liked him still less. There was something of the smooth rascal about him. Polished perhaps— or rather veneered. As for the squint, it seemed more like a cast.

"What's his name?" he asked Lewis.

"Lawson. That's how he's registered here."

"Hm!" said Travers. "It's probably near it. He looks quite oriental."

As the meal went on and Travers looked across at the other table, he more than once caught the eyes of the man Lawson; not staring perhaps, but certainly interested. Travers, indeed, grew rather worried. It wasn't the intensity of the other's look that perturbed him so much as the fact that whenever he looked up, those eyes seemed to have been regarding him. Then came the other side of Lewis's time calculation. As their own joint arrived, the meal of the others came to an end and they moved off, in the direction of the lounge. In the room now, except themselves, there remained one diner only—a well set-up, youngish man whose table completed the equilateral triangle.

When the waiter arrived with the rest of the trimmings that went with the joint, a remarkably peculiar thing happened; all pre-arranged seemingly, and yet spontaneous. Lewis picked up the menu card and looked across at the solitary diner; then as the waiter leaned over his plate, back to the table Lawson had left, engaged him in conversation, craning his neck round for the purpose.

"How far's the station from here, waiter?"

"Station, sir! About a quarter of a mile, sir."

"Pretty good service? To London, for instance?" That went on for about half a minute. The interesting thing was the solitary diner. The carpet giving no sound, he slipped across to the other table. Travers thought he must be looking for sugar or mustard or something missing—till he saw him deliberately take the menu card and replace it with his own. Back at the table, he coughed. Lewis's inquiries ceased at once and the waiter moved off.

"Extraordinary thing—" began Travers.

"It's all right, sir," said Lewis. "He's one of our own men. Did he get it all right?"

"If you mean the menu card, I rather think he did."

Lewis nodded. "Their fingerprints are on that. Don't look across but our man's now off. He'll pass it to the General in the car. We've got the waiter's, and the clerk's who wrote it, and a separate one of Edwards'."

"I see." Travers was feeling vaguely the presence of romance after all, and himself a rather useless ally of the forces of detection.

"And what do we do now? Go home?"

"Can't say, sir. You go to the lounge when we've finished. It'll look better. Be ready to come out as soon as I look inside the door."

In the lounge, Travers found romance at closer quarters. A dozen or so people were there, in their little groups, and having located his men he took a seat a couple of yards away and waited till his coffee and liqueur arrived. Then he lit a cigarette and as he snapped the lighter, found Lawson at his elbow. The voice was suave.

"Excuse me, sir, but may I—er—trouble you for a light?"

"Do!" smiled Travers; flicked it on, and held it.

Lawson drew at the cigarette with a certain deliberation, gave a crisp thanks, then sank sort of tentatively into the padded settle alongside him.

"Quite delightful weather!"

"Yes—er—isn't it!" said Travers. "On the cold side, perhaps."

"Yes," said Lawson—and waited. He cleared his throat with a quick cough or two. "Please don't think me rude, but I'm sure I've met you before. Er—tell me! Is your name Trent, by any chance?"

Travers felt himself suddenly stiffen—then wondered if the flushing of his face had been too noticeable. He leaned over and took a sip at his coffee.

"Er—Trent? No! . . . Sorry! but my name's Travers."

"Travers!" The other smiled dryly. "Rather alike, aren't they? in a way . . . This chap was in the music trade." Travers could feel the eyes searching him, and for the life of him daren't look up. "Some sort of a publisher, I think he was."

"Really!" Travers raised his eyebrows, then shook his head regretfully. His hand moved instinctively to his breast pocket and his card case—then stopped. He removed his glasses instead.

"I'm afraid I've never run across him. In any case I'm the world's worst musician!"

Lawson rose. "I'm awfully sorry, really—but . . ."

"Perfectly natural mistake!" smiled Travers. "Only if there's anybody like myself walking about, it's more of a miracle than a coincidence."

A couple of minutes and Lewis, mercifully, put in an appearance. Travers finished his liqueur at a gulp, nodded a friendly goodnight to Lawson, then followed Lewis out. Two minutes later they were off. A mile outside the town and Travers dimmed the headlights and drew gently in to the side of the road.

"Something gone wrong?" asked Wharton nervously.

"Yes!" said Travers. "Only it was ten minutes ago."

He told him all about it. Wharton, with the events at Mill House much less clearly in his mind, didn't quite see the point till Travers made it clear. Then he seemed positively scared.

"You mean to say he recognised you as the man Rook said had called to buy some music!"

"That's right!" said Travers, who was just as flustered. "But it's much worse than that! He wasn't there—Lawson wasn't! Therefore he must have seen the American and Driver and they've told him all about me! That definitely establishes connection between the three of them!"

Wharton grunted, said nothing for a minute, then heaved himself up.

"Anything else they know about you?"

"How can *I* tell?" said Travers. "I *was* going to give Lawson my card, to sort of show my good faith—then I thought better of it."

"Good job you did!" snorted Wharton. "You might have got a knife in your ribs next time you went home!" He leaned out and opened the door. "I'm going back. No! I'd rather walk. It'll do me good!" He passed his small attaché case over to Lewis. "Let the fingerprint people have this tonight!"

"But—er—what's the idea?" stammered Travers. "You're surely having him watched!"

Wharton hunched his shoulders into his greatcoat. "He's being watched all right!"

"Then what are you going back for?"

Wharton hesitated. "To tell the truth, I don't know. It's up to me to find out." He nodded his head and moved away so suddenly that though Travers leaned out at the door, he was doubtful whether his goodnight reached him or not.

* * * * * * *

But as Wharton trudged along m the darkness, his mind was no more made up than it had been when that sudden intuition urged him to get out of the car. But he knew precisely what had been behind the urge—the realisation that back in the hotel they'd just left was a man who had been in intimate contact with every other actor in the tragedy; the man who—if he could be made—could clear up the whole problem in fewer minutes than the days that had elapsed since the body of Claude Rook had swung from the beam at Frenchman's Rise.

For a few moments he had thought of confrontation; but that was all too vague. What he knew was far too indefinite to force a confession, even if the laws of evidence were what they'd been in the good old days when justice was more important than touchiness. Moreover, the man with the squint had done nothing that brought him within the law. To collect evidence of a man's whereabouts and sell it to the highest bidder, was no crime. To buy a dead man's house through a third party was a perfectly legitimate action. No! Wharton shook his head as he discarded that method of attack. To confront Lawson might not only be futile; it might be positively dangerous. Let him know he was under suspicion and he might warn his confederates.

That produced another thought. The man whom he thought of as the American, he had never much concentrated on. The personal description had proved to be too vague; and it was reasonable to assume, moreover, that he had left the country. But the false step Lawson had taken in challenging Travers by the name of Trent, seemed, as Travers said, certain proof that Lawson had recently been in contact with the American, who therefore had not left the country after all. Indeed, why had Lawson bought that house if it were not to hand it over to the American and Driver? He was their agent—and probably whether they liked it or not. In that case, all that was needed was patience. Sooner or later Lawson would lead the way to the others. Then Wharton shook his head again. Patience was all very well, but he himself daren't wait much longer. Too much time had already been spent on the case, and even that auction had been in the nature of a gamble.

It was not till he was back in the main street that he determined on one thing that he certainly would do. He would have a look at Lawson. Though he had had no hand in the affair of Frenchman's Rise, he must have been concerned in the original business that brought the four of them together. Years before—twenty years perhaps—a crime may have been committed, the harvest of which was only then being reaped. And if there was one thing Wharton was sure of, it was his memory for faces. If Lawson had once come under his personal notice, then he'd know him again. And once he knew him for what he was, and *what he had been*—Wharton smiled grimly to himself, found that he had overshot the hotel, then retraced his steps.

Just short of the door he stopped again. Some of the mischief—the recognition of Travers, for instance—had already been done. Wharton was sorry about that, in a way. When he had planned for Travers to have dinner at that table, it had been rather as a foil for Lewis than anything else; whatever Travers—always ready to act without overmuch questioning—had thought about it. But one thing Wharton had been careful of; he didn't wish himself recognised. Now, of course, the Travers business had upset all that. His was such an unusual figure and personality that, if Lawson wished, he could trace him back—and therefore Wharton as well—every inch of the way to Frenchman's Rise.

For all that, Wharton was still indisposed to run any risks of personal recognition. Before entering the hotel he put on his spectacles and turned his coat collar well up. The saloon bar happened to be crowded, with only a few minutes to go before "time," and he edged his way unnoticed towards the cloakroom. There, with a pocket comb and a cake of soap, he got his moustache into military shape, with ends like a couple of spikes; then, satisfied with what the glass told him, strolled back to the bar. Sayer—the plain-clothes man who'd done that business with the menu—was in conversation with a chance acquaintance. Wharton hailed him.

"Hallo! You remember me, don't you? Webster?"

Sayer looked hard, then duly recognised. The three retired to a corner with the final round of drinks. Wharton's eyes wandered round the smoky room.

"Your friend's in the lounge," said Sayer. "Or he was five minutes ago."

Wharton made some remark, then felt the pressure of a foot. In the doorway, framed as if posed for a portrait, was Lawson. As he leaned forward, waiting to speak to the barmaid, Wharton saw every line on his face—and found it faintly familiar. In a second or two, the barmaid came over. Lawson said something, turned away, and for the merest moment was seen in profile. Then Wharton finished his drink.

"Just time for one more, gentlemen?"

"Not for me!" said Sayer and shook his head.

"What about you, sir?"

The other shook his head too, and the three of them rose. A final goodnight outside the porch and Wharton was off to the nearest garage. An hour later he was getting into bed at his old room in the "Griffin," Steyvenning.

* * * * * * *

But it was not till he woke the following morning that he found what he wanted—and found it waiting for him, as soon as he stirred to consciousness. That was it! He had been abroad himself at the time, over in France on that Simone Case, and that was how he had lost the thread. But as he lay there he remembered the sensation the affair had caused; the minor, financial crisis that had threatened; the columns in the press—and the pictures. Wharton closed his eyes as he frowned back all those years ago. Three of them, there'd been; Penfold—heavy, sallow, listening to the judge without the batting of an eyelid; Hoggin—short, thick-set, wiping his fingers nervously and going down with a flop when he got his sentence; Lewissohn—Marcus Lewissohn, with that funny little cast in his eye—sneering down at Hoggin as the warders lifted him, and nodding curtly to the judge as his own sentence was dispassionately told him.

Wharton remembered it all. That was where Ballard of the *Record* had first made his name, with those amazingly vital stories of his, that Wharton—old hand as he was even then— had devoured in the Continental editions. And best of all had been that dramatic story of the fourth man—*the man who wasn't there!*

As he sat over his breakfast, Wharton cursed himself for a fool. Everything had been there, stuck under his nose, if he'd only had the sense to see it. Then came a feeling that was not far off complacency. The Case was over. Everything should now be plain and straightforward. As he jotted down side by side with the known facts of Rook's life, the new data which the morning's revelations had brought him, he could see nothing missing. Everything fitted in—everything tangible, that is to say. What failed to fit in was not so much Rook himself as all those queer little actions that Travers had remembered after his visit to Mill House. Motive, of course; well, that was as plain as the back of your hand. As for the rest—Wharton shrugged his shoulders. The man was as mad as they make 'em. And no wonder; stowed away all those years, waiting for disaster, moving off from place to place like a man with a price on his head, and settling down for a restless year or two with no company but his own and that of the woman who almost certainly knew everything.

It was half-past eleven when Church, the auctioneer, dropped in; rather like a decoy rabbit paying a surreptitious vis- it to a ferret. But he was looking like a man whose relatives have at last gone away.

"He came over then?" said Wharton.

"Oh, rather! Lawson came over himself." Wharton grunted. "Nice way for a respectable auctioneer to spend the Sabbath! And what happened exactly?"

"Well, we couldn't do any real business, of course; but he agreed to take the furniture at our valuation—less ten per cent. He's coming over again to-morrow to pay up, and so on. As you suggested, we're going to allow possession, pending the final settlement."

"And when's he moving in?"

"Don't know exactly. May be this week. I left him measuring up the place for additional furniture of his own he's bringing along."

Wharton looked over the top of his spectacles. "You left him there!"

"That's right! He said he'd have to have a good look over the place to see what things of his would fit. He's only going to be there an hour or so."

Wharton nodded. "Nothing special happen while you were there with him? No unusual incident?" Church laughed. "No! I don't think so. He did rather like the piano. We'd put it down as sixty, and when he was looking at it he said it was the only thing we hadn't swindled him over!"

Wharton looked up again. "But it was a perfectly ordinary piano, wasn't it?"

The other waved his hand. "Nothing to it as far as we could see. We shouldn't have got that for it at auction."

"I see," said Wharton, and thought for a moment; then, "What did he say about it exactly?"

"Well, he ran his hand over the wood, as if he were stroking it, and said it was quite an interesting piece!"

"Did he now!" said Wharton. "Do you know, he isn't far out! That piano's been a little gold mine to him. What's more, I wouldn't mind betting that at this very moment he's got it in pieces and having a good look at its guts!"

Church's eyes popped open. "What on earth for?"

"Curiosity! Pure curiosity!" Wharton got to his feet. "Like the monkey who broke the mirror. Well, I must get off back to town. You'll probably see me tomorrow." He held out his hand, eyes twinkling, and with that delightful smile that made you forgive him everything. "In the meanwhile, keep things well under your hat, and—we're extremely grateful to you."

CHAPTER XVI
ODYSSEUS SETS OFF AGAIN

WHEN TRAVERS, rather sleepily, let himself into his flat, somewhere round about midnight on that Saturday, he cast his usual eye round for correspondence and found nothing waiting for him that gave the least promise of excitement—unless it was a stout, quarto envelope, marked—"If away, please forward." He lit the gas fire and, over a nightcap, had a look at it.

It was those sheets of music manuscript which Maine had sent back. The accompanying letter was rather interesting.

DEAR MR. TRAVERS,

I am sending you back the MS. herewith, as I am sure that I can do nothing for you in the matter. The opinion I gave you originally, seems to be absolutely correct—that the notes are a mere, disconnected jumble. In other words, somebody or other has been pulling your leg!

In case you would like to know the lines upon which I tackled the MS., to see if it contained any cryptogram, as you suggested, I would say that I had in mind the "Carnival" music of Schumann. I haven t a Musical Dictionary handy, but you can look it up for yourself in *Groves.*

The idea as exemplified in the "Carnival" music is simply this. Schumann had a friend called Asch. He took those four letters A.S.C.H.—and represented them by notes. S., for example, is in Germany E sharp. These four notes he used for a theme, thus introducing his friend's name into the music. I think you will see what I mean.

Needless to say, I found no such words introduced into the hopeless series of heterogeneous and disconnected notes of the MS., though I went over it very exhaustively.

As for the matter of a fee, which you yourself mentioned, I really must refuse any such thing. But as I have since discovered that I was entertaining a really famous person unawares, perhaps you would be so good as to send me an autographed copy of either "The Economics of a Spendthrift" or "The Stockbrokers' Breviary" (cheap edition, of course!) and I shall be more than grateful for the bargain.

Yours sincerely,

RUPERT MAINE.

Probably Travers' brain was too tired to be functioning well at that particular moment; at any rate he saw nothing in the letter except the very definite news that his own ideas about that manuscript would have to be drastically re-cast. Smiling to himself at something or other that had tickled him in Maine's letter, he took the envelope over to the safe and put the front page with the sheets that had been sent back. With the locking of the safe door, the whole thing seemed dismissed from his mind.

* * * * * * *

The morning brought for Travers that rare and not too pleasant experience of spending a Sunday in town. But for the fact that there was an urgent job of work that had to be done forthwith, he'd probably have remained down in Sussex the previous evening. As it was, by lunch time, he was beginning to get bored with his own company; indeed, after the service meal in his workroom, he saw nothing for the afternoon but a nap in front of the living-room fire. Just before two o'clock he laid his pipe aside and was settling into his special chair, when he fancied he heard music—and coming from Palmer's room, of all places. Then he guessed what it was—that new wireless set he'd inquired about having. Travers pushed the bell.

"That the new wireless set I can hear?" he asked. "Yes, sir!" said Palmer. "I trust it wasn't disturbing you, sir. Would you prefer it turned off?"

"Oh dear no!" said Travers. "It's not worrying me at all. As a matter of fact I'd rather like to hear what it's like. Could you—er—bring it in?"

"With pleasure, sir!" Palmer was really gratified. In a minute he was back with a sturdy looking set, then returned for the loud speaker. Next came a couple of lengths of flex.

"What's all that for?" Travers asked.

Palmer went into details. He was going to plug the set in, there, at the side of the fireplace; the other connections were necessary for extension. He bustled about for three or four minutes, altering this and fixing that, then, "What would you like, sir?"

"Like?" asked Travers. "Oh, I see! What is there?"

"Well, there's Radio-Paris, sir, and—"

"Radio-Paris sounds exciting. Let's have that!" Palmer twiddled some more, blasted strange noises, then got music of sorts to come from nowhere. A little more twiddling—"Radio-Paris, sir!"

Travers listened to the voice. "By Jove! so it is! . . . Er—bring the port over, Palmer, will you, and pour yourself a glass at the same time . . . And have a cigar!"

Palmer moved about the room with as much noise as a ghost. Travers got his own cigar alight; straining all the time to catch the words. A change of programme was evidently being announced, but then, after a minute's silence, came something he could follow clearly—

"Mesdames et messieurs; vous allez entendre un concert organise par la Compagnie DECCA de Paris et de Londres."

There was a pause, *then the faint tinkle of notes on a piano!* But before he could settle again in his chair, the voice—or rather, another—began again—

"Ladies and gentlemen; this afternoon you are going to hear a concert arranged by the DECCA Gramophone Company of Paris and London."

Again the faint tinkle of the piano! Then came another pause; two more announcements as to the actual records to be played, a moment's scratching of a needle, then the sound of a dance band—clear as if the players were at the other side of the room. Palmer coughed.

"Your very good health, sir! . . . Coming through very well, sir!"

"Isn't it!" agreed Travers. "But—er—tell me! You're an expert. What were those twiddly bits on the piano, after the first announcements?"

"Those, sir! It's rather curious you should ask that, sir, because I didn't know till Miss Ursula told me about it, sir, when I happened to hear it one Sunday at Pulvery" . . . and Palmer duly explained. Travers looked at him in a queer sort of way, then all at once hopped up and went over to the safe.

What he was doing there, Palmer couldn't see, but in a couple of minutes he was locking the safe again, and putting into his breast pocket that packet of manuscript.

"Sorry to worry you, Palmer, but get the car round straight away, will you. Oh! and you'd better pack a bag for tonight."

Palmer didn't turn a hair.

"Very good, sir! And when will you be back, sir?"

"Don't know exactly. With tremendous luck I might be back for dinner . . . and I mightn't be in till lunch to-morrow. Still, you're not to wait up."

He picked up the receiver and got through to the Yard. Superintendent Wharton wasn't there, they told him. As far as they knew, he was still somewhere in Sussex. Travers hung up again, then wondered if he dared risk a trunk call. Then he left the receiver where it was.

* * * * * *

It was quite dark when he drew the Isotta up outside the police-station at Steyvenning. The same old sergeant, with the enormously red face, was on duty.

"Superintendent Wharton about, sergeant?" asked Travers.

"No, sir. He left about dinner time. Where've you come from, sir?"

"From town."

"Then you must've passed him on the road, sir."

"Hm!" said Travers. "That's very annoying! . . . I suppose you haven't got a key to Mill House?"

"We haven't, sir. But why not try Mr. Church?"

"Splendid!" said Travers. "But, of course, he doesn't know me. Tell you what, sergeant; if he rings up to inquire, you let him know everything's all right." Church, disturbed in the middle of his tea, was inclined to be a bit off-hand till Travers explained that he really came from Wharton. Then he even fetched his coat and climbed in alongside. This time they went into the house by the front door. One glance round the living-room and Travers had seen enough. And he didn't like it.

"Did you draw up the inventory for this place yourself?" he asked Church.

"Well, I was here all the time it was being done."

"Then, do you remember a rather nice quality Staffordshire figure of a couple of lovers, that stood on the mantelpiece here?"

Church shook his head. He remembered no such figure, and he'd never heard of it. Travers liked things still less. Whoever it was that had got into the house must have taken it, and if so—But that wasn't quite logical. If the burglar had finished with the house, then why had Lawson bought it? He must have had his customers waiting—and those customers could only be those who were responsible for the burglary. And, to complete the circle, if those responsible for the burglary had got what they wanted, then why should they want to buy the house?

It was not till he had got Church to his house again, that anything helpful suggested itself. He made for the police-station once more.

"Get the key all right, sir?"

"Yes, thanks," said Travers. "And, by the way; was anything ever found out about that bag that was taken out of my car that night?"

The sergeant laughed.

"Good lord, yes, sir! We got him almost at once. Chap called Garland took it. A bit of a bad egg. We've had him for poaching once or twice." He lowered his voice. "Between ourselves, sir, I oughtn't to have said he *took* it. His tale was that he found it, and it must have fell out of the car. He got let off with a fine . . . not that anybody believed him."

"What was in the bag exactly?"

The sergeant rummaged in his desk. "Here you are, sir! That's a copy of the list of contents."

But there was no mention of any china figure on that. Travers handed it back abstractedly, and thought again. Why shouldn't Lawson have double-crossed his customers? Why shouldn't he have taken the figure himself, and said nothing about it? But of course—

He turned to the sergeant again.

"Where does this chap Garland live?"

"Right on the corner, sir; where you turn to go to Mill House. Little cottage on the left."

"Is he likely to be in, do you think?"

"He might be having his tea, sir. He's only a young fellow; nineteen I think he gave his age. And he's as crafty as they make 'em!"

Back went Travers again in the direction of Mill House. An elderly man opened the door of the cottage.

"Does your son happen to be in?" asked Travers. "If so, may I see him for a moment?"

Since Travers had been in such a haste to follow up the trail that he had left the police-station with the barest of information, he was lucky to find old Garland in the possession of one son only. He drew him along paternally in the direction of the car.

"I don't want you to be at all alarmed," he said; "but it was my car that that bag fell out of which you were lucky enough to pick up."

"Oh, indeed, sir!" said Garland, perkily enough. "Yes! . . . Tell me now, strictly between ourselves. What happened to that china figure that was in it?"

It was the hesitation that betrayed him.

"That what, sir?"

"That china figure," repeated Travers. "A tree, and two people in front of it, by a seat—all done in china."

"There was nothing of that sort in the bag, sir! I handed the bag over just as it was, sir. You ask at the police-station, sir, and they'll tell you there wasn't nothing in it like that."

"I see!" He nodded his head thoughtfully, heaved a sigh, then took out his note case. In the light of the headlamps, he fingered the wad idly.

"I don't think you understand me, Garland. There's not going to be any trouble for you—even if you did take the figure. You tell me what you did with it, and I'll give you my word that you'll hear no more about it. And I'll reward you in addition for your trouble."

He fingered the notes again. Garland began to speak, stopped short, then blurted it out. There had been a figure, and he'd seen one like it in a shop at Lewes. That was why he'd kept it. And he'd taken it to Lewes and sold it to an antique dealer—for twenty-five shillings. He didn't know the name but the shop was dead plumb opposite Horlick's, the outfitters.

He stuck to his tale in spite of the warning that any lies would be serious. Travers hesitated between a ten shilling note and a pound; then handed over the latter. In a couple of minutes he was back at the police-station again, reporting his contemplated visit to Lewes.

Things went less smoothly after that. The antique shop was found all right, but the proprietor himself was out, and it took best part of an hour to find him. He remembered the purchase, however, though he mentioned no price. And there was no need to phone up Steyvenning to inquire into Travers' credentials, since the figure was no longer in his possession. Only a few days before, he had sold it to a Mrs. Stevens—wife of a Colonel Stevens of Dudgery.

"And where *is* Dudgery?" asked Travers.

"About fifteen miles from here," the other told him. "Which way were you going now, sir?"

"It all depends," said Travers. "Town probably."

"Then it'll be on your way, sir; that is if you're going by Reigate."

"Little place, is it?"

"That's right, sir; only a village."

Travers thanked him and got in the car again. The dashboard clock showed nine o'clock, and the time had gone so quickly that he could hardly believe it. Then he realised he was feeling most sinkingly hungry and something forthwith suggested that half-past nine would be a preposterous time to go calling on an unknown colonel. At that moment, too, the long front of the "Maid-at-Arms" came in sight and he drew the car into the hotel yard.

* * * * * * *

It was just before nine o'clock the following morning when he drew up outside the unpretentious front of Dudgery Hall. The colonel was at breakfast, but he came out to the porch followed by a couple of spaniels. Travers went laboriously over the business and suggested ringing up Steyvenning. The other had a look at the car, then at Travers, then decided it wouldn't be necessary. He was quite a charming old person really, though somewhat obvious. He remembered the figure well enough.

"The fact of the matter is," he said, "it's up in town. You see, it was my daughter who actually bought it. She was married last week and naturally she and her husband are away. My wife is up in town at the moment, getting their new house ready. I rather fancy the figure went there on Friday with the wedding presents—indeed, I'm sure it did."

"Perhaps, sir," said Travers, "you'd be so good as to give me a note for Mrs. Stevens, so that I could call and see her about it."

The colonel rather looked down his nose at that. Mrs. Stevens, Travers gathered, was not too easy to handle—and the colonel was already regretting the airiness with which he had given up what he didn't possess.

"You see, sir," went on Travers, "I'm sure Mrs. Stevens would be only too glad to help by giving up the figure, especially as Tm prepared to pay for it. If I have to report to Scotland Yard that there's any difficulty, they're quite likely to take possession of it as stolen property—and then you'll have nothing, so to speak."

"Hm!" said the other. "I see that. However, I'm going up to town myself to-day—"

"I say!" broke in Travers. "Why not go with me, sir?"

That was why, by twelve-thirty, Travers was dropping the colonel at Highgate. By sheer bad fortune, Mrs. Stevens was out; still, the promise was made that as soon as she came in, which would certainly be before lunch, she should have the matter explained to her. And the figure should certainly be sent round to Mr. Travers' rooms.

As the car swung along past the Pond, Travers had another idea—more humorous, perhaps, than useful. Surely Freddy Burrows was living somewhere close by? Not that it would help matters by calling him that; Fedor Borosov was what he was calling himself since he'd become a really fashionable pianist, and an eccentric into the bargain, though heaven knew he was a queer enough cuss at Halstead!

The telephone box at the end of the road gave him the address, and in five minutes he was ringing the bell. A very dapper footman took his card and left him to cool his heels in the anteroom. As for the austere regard of control that Freddy assumed when Travers was ushered in, that soon had to disappear. Then Travers lugged out that music manuscript and passed over the front page. The look the great man cast over it made Travers imagine for a moment that he was going to be violently sick. Then he stuck it contemptuously in front of him and rattled it over. Then he sat down and played it over, with one or two of those studied eccentricities that helped to pay for the footman. He was even carrying on with a development of his own when Travers pulled him up.

"Well, Freddy; what do you think of it?"

"Well—er—it's—er—I mean, did you write it?"

"Good lord, no! . . . What do you think of the theme?"

"The theme? . . . Oh, yes—the theme. Well, Debussy-ish, you know! Utterly *démodé*!"

"Nothing original about it at all?"

The other shrugged his shoulders with most amazing elaboration. Travers took the sheet back, then held out his hand.

"Thank you, Freddy! See you again some time, I suppose?" and he was outside the door before the bell of ritual could be pushed. The footman panted after him to usher him out at the front.

* * * * * * *

And no sooner did Travers enter the door of his own flat than he knew from Palmer's manner that something had been happening in his absence. Palmer, indeed, had to tell the story in the very act of receiving hat and coat. "Something rather unusual occurred about an hour ago, sir. A man rang you up and said you had some papers for him."

"Papers! What sort of papers?"

"I don't know, sir. He said it was urgent as he had to leave London again to-morrow, sir. Some sort of foreigner he seemed, by his talk, sir. He said it was very confidential and he had to see you personally."

"Did he! And he was a foreigner!"

"Sounded like it to me, sir. A Frenchman, I should say, sir."

"Give any name?"

"No, sir. But he asked my name, sir, and who I was, and said I was to keep what he'd been saying to myself, sir, or there might be serious trouble for me."

Travers laughed. "I see! And did he leave any message?"

"I told him you'd almost certainly be in for lunch, sir; so he said I was sure to ask you to wait till two, as he was going to ring you again."

Travers nodded, then caught a whiff of the lunch. "Do you know, I'm most frightfully hungry!"

"I'll bring lunch in at once, sir." But Palmer still hesitated. "Oh! and something else, sir. Mr. Franklin is back again, sir. He called in only a few minutes ago."

"Really!" said Travers, and his face lit up. "Where is he now, do you know?"

"I should say he's still in his rooms, sir."

Travers thought for a moment, then, "Run along, there's a good fellow, and see if he'll come in to lunch!"

CHAPTER XVII
WHARTON GETS A SHOCK

As TRAVERS SAT there in front of the fire, rubbing his hands and waiting for Franklin to arrive, all at once there occurred to him something that made him shuffle nervously in his chair. That importunate ringer-up had—with the stronger appeal of lunch— been somehow connected with the normal business of Durangos Limited and the financial affairs of which he was the presiding Chancellor. But suppose the caller's anxiety was for that manuscript! Palmer seemed sure he was a foreigner, and for the life of him Travers could recall no foreigner who might be anxious about papers that concerned the ordinary run of business.

Then he dismissed the idea almost as soon as it came. When Rook handed over that manuscript, it had been with the most extravagant and mysterious secrecy—and for reasons of which Travers now thought himself fully aware. And Rook had added that who ever asked for that manuscript would be well-known. That seemed definitely to exclude any foreigner of the type that had rung up Palmer; besides, if the affair were really secret, how should a foreigner even know of the existence of such manu- script—let alone who had it, and the address of the temporary possessor.

In the middle of those ruminations Franklin came in, and just the least bit too confidently. Travers hailed him as if he'd been away for months.

"Hallo! . . . You're looking extraordinarily fit!" Franklin ad- mitted it; said Travers wasn't looking any too bad himself; ut- tered a platitude or two, hesitated on the verge of saying some- thing that promised importance—then blurted it out.

"Rook Case settled yet?"

Travers smiled. "Good lord no!"

"Then there's something most urgent I want to ask you. I'll explain about it later. . . . I suppose you haven't had a man—an Italian—come to see you about that manuscript of Rook's?"

Travers forgot in a flash all the elaborate leg-pulling that had been prepared against his return; indeed he was so startled himself that for a moment or two he couldn't say anything.

"Well—er—nobody *came* exactly . . . but somebody rang up about midday. Who is he? Do you know him?"

"Rang up, did he?" said Franklin, and looked thoughtful. "So he did get here first after all. . . . What did you tell him?"

"I didn't tell him anything. I wasn't here. He told Palmer he'd ring up again for certain, during lunch."

"Then he might ring again at any minute!"

"Well—er—I imagine so; if he was serious."

Franklin scowled. "He was serious enough! The thing is, what are we going to do?" The question seemed addressed to nobody in particular, unless it were himself. Travers waited for something that should at least sound intelligible. Then Franklin appeared to make up his mind.

"Look here now! This is what we'll do! You tell him to come here! . . . Let's see now . . . tell him six o'clock to-night; that'll give time to warn Wharton. If he insists on secrecy, tell him he can have it. Say you'll be here alone—only of course, you won't! Wharton and I will be here."

Palmer's voice came from the dining-room door.

"Lunch is served, sir!"

Travers dismissed him with a wave of the glasses he had just removed.

"Six o'clock he's to come here in secret—only you and Wharton are to be here." He smiled dryly. "Perhaps you'll tell me who he is . . . and what he is!"

Franklin looked at him, then laughed. "That's all right!" he said placatingly, and took him by the arm. "Let's go and eat while we may—and talk at the same time!"

* * * * * * *

It was nearly half an hour later when the bell was heard. Palmer was already at the receiver, and he handed it over with a look that spoke volumes. Travers motioned Franklin to come close.

"Hallo! . . . Yes! I am the man . . . I say, I am the man. . . . Yes, that's right! . . . Oh no! quite impossible! . . . I say, it's impossible! It can't be done! . . . Oh yes; I can see you this evening. At six o'clock. . . . Yes, six o'clock here. You have the address in the telephone book! . . . That's right, only of course I shall expect credentials. . . .*Credentials!* Papers to prove who you are. . . . That's right. And *why* you are coming for the papers. . . . Oh quite alone! Except for my father, of course. . . . Very well then; I shall be unable to see you. . . . He's an invalid—and very deaf. . . . Of course I realise it's very confidential! . . . My dear sir; this is not the first confidential matter I've handled in my life! . . . Yes! . . . At six o'clock then . . . Yes. . . . Good-bye!"

All that took a good five minutes, and as Travers hung up the receiver, he gave a look of humorous annoyance.

"There we are then! Everything as you want it. Get your whiskers ready!"

Franklin grunted. "What was he so anxious about? Secrecy?"

"That's right. . . . And he didn't seem to understand my English."

"He didn't mention any address?"

"Not a word. He was certainly ringing up from a private phone." He settled again to the tail-end of his meal, then stopped and cleared his throat nervously.

"I expect you'll think me remarkably foolish, but it doesn't seem quite—well, playing the game to let this man Rossi come here in confidence—and to have you two here as well. I don't know; somehow it doesn't seem the thing to do."

"Rubbish!" snorted Franklin. "You're too squeamish for a detective. I suppose if you could trap a murderer by telling a lie, you'd still be a super-George Washington! Rossi lied to me; now we lie to him; that's all there is to it. When you've read that diary of mine, you'll know more about it." He stopped, then laid down his napkin. "Hadn't I better ring up Wharton straight away?"

Travers stopped him half-way to the door. "Why did you call Rossi a murderer? Do you mean he's Rook's double? *The one who went up—or came down?*"

"Not exactly," said Franklin. "We might even have to come to that though, before we're through."

He was back again in a couple of minutes.

"What did you tell him?" asked Travers.

"Nothing—except that you'd be coming along to see him on most urgent business in about half an hour. By the way, he said he would have been ringing you up this afternoon himself. I didn't say anything to him, of course, but if you're so genuinely conscientious about having Rossi here, there's no desperate need. I don't suppose he's disguised himself. He's bound to be somewhere in Soho at the moment. You see he must have known it extraordinarily well or he wouldn't have been able to write me that false address—I mean, a real address under false pretences. Wharton's only got to have a few men at the main Soho exits, and he's bound to run into one of 'em. Or we can nab him outside here—if your conscience runs to it."

Travers smiled. "Ah! now you're being bitter with me! . . . Perhaps I'd better read the diary first!"

He pulled up a chair and settled himself in front of the fire. Franklin sat watching him. . . .

"Well, what do you think of it?"

Travers shook his head. "Not very much. I mean, I'd have to read it several times to get hold of everything. All incident and no background makes for indigestion. But this Rossi seems a very objectionable person."

"Objectionable!" said Franklin—and added a description that was much more lurid. "Perhaps you're right!" said Travers. "Tell me; why did he want to keep you there for *four* days? I mean, why not a week—or just enough to give him a clear start?"

"It wasn't the start he wanted," explained Franklin. "He had that all right. What he wanted was just time enough to get *away* from London again before I got here—or had time to telegraph you."

"And who was he? I mean, what is the connection with Rook?"

"Well, if I got the hang of what you told me," said Franklin; "then Rook's wife was Lucia Guardini, and your Mrs. Fletcher was her sister Maria. That's a very real connection."

"It is," agreed Travers. "But it isn't a vital one. It's not such an important connecting link as the man with the squint—the man Lawson I was telling you about."

Franklin thought for a moment. "Well, you know best. You've been more in touch with things than I have. . . . Wharton know anything?"

"That I can't say. As I told you, the last I saw of him was a blob in the dark. He hasn't rung me up since. That call he mentioned to you just now might have been only a polite apology."

Franklin nodded, then gave a quick look.

"And about Rossi. You're agreeable to his coming here?"

"Yes. I think so," said Travers slowly. "I think he's asking for a dose of his own duplicity. That—er—daughter of his—the girl Lucia; she seemed quite a charming type?"

"Yes," said Franklin, and leaned over for a spill to light his pipe. "You'd have thought so if you'd seen her."

"I expect I should," said Travers. He glanced up at the time. "Perhaps I'd better move along to see Wharton. Which reminds me. You'd better go out the back way, hadn't you? If this man Rossi happens to have the front under observation, it might rather queer your pitch. . . . Anything else strike you?"

"I don't know that there was," said Franklin. "Except the manuscript. You'll have to have that handy for Rossi to-night. Did Maine send it back?"

"Last night."

"Find anything?"

Travers shook his head. "Not a thing—except gibberish."

"Might I have a look at it for a moment?"

Travers fetched it from the safe. Franklin took it sheet by sheet and held it to the light.

"This is just an idea I had in the train. There may be something in it, or there may not. I wondered if Rook had used all this rubbish as a camouflage, so that he could use invisible ink."

Travers flushed slightly, and looked the least bit con-fused. Franklin noticed nothing, except that he was fumbling at his glasses.

"Invisible ink! . . . You mean, he wrote between the lines, as it were."

"I mean anywhere," said Franklin. "Just writing—in invisible ink."

"Yes—but what about?"

Franklin looked at him. "What about! You're talking as if there wasn't anything we didn't know. Rook might have written all about himself; who he really was. All about Rossi—and your Mrs. Fletcher—and everything."

"Quite!" Travers nodded thoughtfully. "That's a really good idea. It admits, of course, that you don't accept the explanation Rossi gave you himself."

Franklin positively glared. "Sometimes you're as bad as Wharton. You make me want to blaspheme. Haven't you just read that account of mine? Haven't I said there I don't agree with Rossi? and given reasons?"

Travers smiled feebly. "Sorry! . . . I must have been wool-gathering. And you do realise, don't you, that the problem still remains! What's going to happen, for instance, if Rossi tells me exactly the same tale to-night—and sticks to it? Who's to prove him wrong?"

"Sufficient unto the day"—quoted Franklin, and moved off towards the door. "I shall be in the office all the afternoon, by the way, so let me know what happens with Wharton."

"Right-ho!" said Travers. "I'll ring you the very first thing. . . . And don't forget your whiskers!"

* * * * * * *

Wharton seemed to have just arrived from somewhere. There he was, turning over papers with one hand and holding a sandwich with the other. On the tray stood a pot of tea.

"Awfully sorry to worry you," said Travers, smiling. "Only, as Franklin told you, there's some news that won't keep."

He took it remarkably coolly, Travers thought. If anything, he seemed rather pleased as he finished off the sandwich and pushed aside the tray.

"News that won't keep!"

"That's right!" said Travers. "You know that manuscript old Rook gave me, in trust for somebody? . . . I beg your pardon! Perhaps I'd better begin at the right end. There seems to be an idea that Rook might have used invisible ink—or some device which you know more about than I do. I wonder if you'd let your people have a look at it—straight away."

Wharton smiled archly, as an uncle might.

"Invisible ink—eh?"

He had a look at it himself; smiled again, said there was no harm in trying; scribbled a chit, then pushed the bell. And when that was all settled with, he passed over the cigarettes.

"Take a seat. . . and make yourself comfortable."

"Thanks!" said Travers—and hesitated. "But you haven't heard half the story yet. There's a man—an Italian—calling round at my place to-night to fetch it. The whole story's here. Franklin wrote it—on his way back from Italy. Er—candidly, I think you ought to read it at once!"

That was so unusual of Travers, that Wharton looked quite taken aback. And he drew up another chair, saw Travers seated, then ran his eye over the front page.

"A story, is it? And an Italian coming to your place tonight!" He nodded to himself, then looked round over his glasses. "You don't know his name, I suppose?"

"Oh yes!" said Travers. "It's Rossi. Cesare Rossi."

Wharton let the papers drop. His eyes bulged almost like marbles.

"Cesare Rossi!"

"That's right!" said Travers helpfully. "What do you know about him?"

"My God!" said Wharton. "He asks me what I know about him!" He raised his hands to heaven. "Nothing at all—that's what I know! Only five minutes ago I completed the Case, and on the assumption—"

He strode over to the desk, then stuck a paper under Travers' nose. "Look at that!"

Travers looked.

"Finger prints. . . . Whose are they? Lawson's?"

"They are! And before you entered this room, they proved to me the Case was over—bar arrests. And it mayn't even be barring that!"

"I'm sorry!" said Travers, most abjectly. "But I really don't see—"

"That's all right!" Travers realised that he was being forgiven. "I've merely proved a man to be dead, and you come along and prove he's alive!"

Travers looked startled. "You mean . . . there was something after all in that theory . . . *that one went up and another came down!*"

Wharton shook his head. "I don't think so. . . . I don't know what I *do* mean!" He waved his pipe, contemplated sadly the tobacco that fell on the floor, then shook his head.

"Sorry about that outburst! However—" He sat down heavily. "Let's see what Franklin has to say."

* * * * * * *

It was just after five when Travers got back to St. Martin's Chambers. Palmer reported the arrival of a parcel—by hand.

"Who brought it?" asked Travers.

"A rather elderly gentleman, sir. And he insisted on a receipt—which I gave him, sir. In your name, of course."

Travers nodded—and had a look at it. Then he undid the wrappings. Somehow he couldn't help smiling as he saw that rabbit-faced lover and his insipid, simpering mistress. He even ran his finger along the trickle of blue that was meant to be a brook.

Five minutes later he had locked the figure in the safe, and was in his room preparing for the arrival of Rossi. Palmer was looking at the returned meat-skewer, and wondering what on earth good that had been—except to clear a stopped-up pipe.

CHAPTER XVIII
WHARTON STRIKES

FRANKLIN WAS THE FIRST to arrive; fussing around and trying to conceal the fact that he was feeling remarkably self-conscious. Travers regarded him with genuine awe.

"I say, really! You look positively venerable! Rather fatuous thing to say, but I shouldn't have recognised you!"

Franklin took yet another peep at himself in the glass. He was taking it all extraordinarily seriously.

"There's far too much at stake to run any risk. I think the chair will help. Don't you?"

Travers switched his gaze to the invalid chair.

"Do you know, I never believed you'd do the thing as thoroughly as this."

"Nothing like doing anything thoroughly," was Franklin's sententious remark. "Heard any more from Wharton?"

"Nothing fresh. He said he'd be here well up to time."

"Let anything out?"

Travers shook his head. "When I saw him last, he was trying to register resignation. I rather imagine he's got something up his sleeve."

"Hm!" said Franklin, and looked uneasy. "What did you say he was going to do?"

"He and a man of his—so I gathered—are going to be in that room. I'm to talk to Rossi as I like. I didn't tell him, but I'm using those questions you suggested. Then, as a very last thing, I'm to ask him if he'll swear that he's Cesare Rossi."

"What damn rot!" snapped Franklin. "Of course he's Cesare Rossi!"

Travers blinked. "Of course he is—if you say so. But the word 'swear' is Wharton's cue. That's where he pops in—or out."

Franklin shook his head impatiently. "Doesn't he just love it!"

"You're all rattled," said Travers amusedly. "Let George have his little curtain. He's not stealing your thunder. If Rossi should decide to babble Italian, then you'll get all the limelight."

Franklin grunted again. "Got the manuscript?"

"Wharton's bringing it along. I suggested that matter of invisible ink, which you brought up at lunch. He's rushing a test through."

Franklin got into the chair and tested the wheels.

"Seems all right. . . . By the way; something else I've thought of with regard to that music. Assume Rossi's really entitled to it, and you hand him over the manuscript. Where does *he* come in? What does *he* get out of it? It's no good to *him*! Put yourself in his place. You've come all the way to London. What do you expect to get?"

"Lord knows! Information perhaps, as to the whereabouts of something- Perhaps a map or chart—or a drawing of an invention." He gave a queer sort of smile. "Perhaps money!"

"The very point! Why, for instance, shouldn't two sheets of that paper be stuck together, with—say—banknotes between them?"

"Yes . . . but you held each sheet to the light. There couldn't have been anything. Still, when Wharton comes—Hallo! This rather sounds like him!"

Wharton it was, and a constable in uniform with him. Travers was uncommonly relieved, what with his own private excitement, and Franklin prowling about restlessly. Palmer took the constable over, and Wharton, for the first time, appeared to be aware of Franklin. He winked at Travers.

"Hm! Practising for Christmas?"

"That's right!" Franklin told him. "And what was the idea of the cop? A harlequinade?"

"Not bad!" said Wharton. "Not bad!" He saw the door was closed before he gave his explanation.

"You see, the idea's this. This man Rossi—like all foreigners—will have a tremendous respect for a uniform. If I showed him a plain-clothes man, there'd be nothing to it. If we should decide"—he waved his hand airily—"purely on what he lets out to Mr. Travers here, to exert a little pressure, then our friend in there might come in handy." He fumbled in his inner pocket.

"Here are those papers. Nothing doing—as far as comes within our experience. You'll probably find 'em a bit damp still."

Travers passed them to Franklin, who felt the leaves. There was no need to ask if that double page theory still held water. Travers sorted out the pages and slipped the envelope into the table drawer. Wharton compared times with his watch.

"Anything new, George?" Franklin asked bluntly. "Well—er—not exactly new," said Wharton. "Of course it's been a job collating all the evidence. However—" he made his usual gesture of dismissal—"it's this evening that's going to count. You know the yarn he pitched you, and you'll hear the one he tries on Mr. Travers. Everything set?"

"Everything!" Travers assured him. "The porter's ringing up as soon as he enters, and he'll show him up."

"Good! You know your cue?"

Travers nodded, with no suspicion of a smile, but Wharton must have guessed what he was thinking.

"Is a bit like play acting, isn't it? But do you know what *I* do when I'm inclined to laugh? I think of that old man swinging round and round on his hook at Frenchman's Rise." He hunched his shoulders in the greatcoat, as if he was bound for the Antarctic. "You two carry on. He's due in ten minutes."

It was a domestic picture that was to await Rossi's first inspection. At one side of the blazing fire sat Franklin, huddled in his chair, the newspaper on his knees. Travers was letting a cigarette burn itself away as he lay back in the chair facing him; trying to imagine what it would all be like. Dominating his mind was the wonder if Franklin had made a mistake over the man whom neither himself nor Wharton had seen. If that were so, it would be fantastically horrible. Travers knew that if Claude Rook entered that door, he must shriek!

When the bell was heard, and Palmer popped his head in with a nodded warning, Travers felt his heart begin to race more madly than ever. He fumbled for his glasses, and moistened his lips nervously as he listened. It came—the sound of the lift—the porter's voice—the bell—Palmer—the movement of feet—then the door.

"The gentleman to see you, sir!"

As soon as Travers got to his feet he saw that Franklin, even with the scanty evidence he then possessed, had been right. This man was not Claude Rook. The resemblance was one of type and figure rather than personality. This man was obsequious. He stood there, bending away and smiling with an odious, marionette kind of blandness that made Travers wince.

"Er—come in, won't you? And sit down . . . Let me take your things."

Rossi seemed first to hang on to his coat, then to his hat, making himself disagreeably agreeable all the time, till at last Travers got him seated. There was little noticeably foreign about his dress; a trifle un-English, but not flamboyant. Travers indicated the old gentleman.

"My father . . . whom I told you about. He's very deaf."

The invalid inclined his head. Rossi got to his feet and bowed again. His remark was suitably bellowed.

"It is ver' cold!"

The other pointed to his ears, and smiled. Rossi shrugged his shoulders and sat down again. His English, as Travers was to note, was amazingly good. Years must have gone to the contacts that contributed to the learning of it. It was foreign, of course, in accent and intonation—but fluent to almost an unintelligible rapidity; at least, when he was excited. As for reproducing it; well, Franklin pitied the shorthand writer whom Wharton would have to set to the task. Travers himself reduced it all to something like this.

"You will pardon me if I ask your name," he began himself.

"Cesare Rossi!" It was announced rather than said. "I am Italian!"

Travers nodded. "And the proofs I asked you to bring me, of your identity?"

"Ah!" Rossi hopped up again, like an elderly dancing master about to pirouette, and began pulling papers out of his breast pocket. He exhibited them with a flourish.

"The passport! You see it is me!" and he posed for inspection.

Travers looked—and nodded.

"The—er—certificate—with the photograph, from the Grand Council of Fascisti!—in Rome!"

Travers looked again—and nodded. Rossi produced the next, but was cut short.

"No more, thank you, Mr. Rossi. I'm perfectly satisfied."

Rossi bowed profusely. In the chair the old gentleman was now breathing steadily.

"Now if you wouldn't mind giving me your reasons why I should hand the papers over," said Travers, producing the envelope, "I think we can get this business over in a very few minutes. Do sit down, please! . . . And may I get you a drink? A little whisky, perhaps?"

Rossi settled down with the drink. Every mannerism was that of a man who has prepared a story and must keep to it at all costs. You could see him hesitate, hunt for a phrase, catch it and reel it off with a disarming gesture. Travers sat looking into the fire; detached and judicial. As for the invalid, he was lying back in the chair and sleeping unashamedly.

"You see, Mr. Travers, it was like this. Mr. Rook, I always know him. He was a, what you call, distant relation of mine. We were in England together for years. That I can prove to you if you wish it. He mentioned me to you, perhaps?" He cocked his head on one side, like a sparrow.

Travers looked round to catch the intentness of the gaze.

"By name—no!"

"Well, it does not matter!" A large gesture of indifference and amiability. "After the war we go to Rome, where I take him with me as a partner. We do well—very well. Then there were the troubles; the *Comunisti*—and the fighting; all no good for trade, you understand. Then I begin to see things. I see on which side the bread is buttered. Me—I became Fascist!" He shook his head with the intensity of the remembrance. "Very bad days; very bad. Very much danger. We must walk carefully, so that the grand enemy do not know what we do. I help in all that—and my friend, the Mr. Rook, he help too. I tell him everything. He know everything!" This time, a gesture of pathetic resignation.

"Then we make the discovery! Somebody—a traitor—tell everything. The enemy know everything! Everything is in ruin! Everyone is suspicious! Then I—Cesare Rossi—make up my mind. Face to face I accuse this man, my comrade. At first he deny—then he confess!"

Travers looked round, to see the thrown-out chest and the tilted chin. He nodded, suitably impressed.

"Then what do I do, Mr. Travers? Do I hand him to those who will tear him to pieces? No! I say he is my friend. He has the same blood in his heart as myself. I help him to escape back to England. He say he have no money. Very well, I give him money—his share of the business. Every year I send him money"—he lowered his voice to a whisper—"through a friend! I am to tell him if it is ever possible that he return to Italy. But it is not possible, as you will understand. All this is dangerous for me. Even today it is dangerous—if it is known that I help this man. But I do it. He is my friend!"

A final flourish, then he appeared to become aware of the drink, which he finished at a gulp. He rubbed his hands as if everything was obviously over.

Travers nodded gently. "Your conduct was admirable, Mr. Rossi. As we say—blood is thicker than water. But why exactly did you send this money every year? You say he had the share of the business. What was the money you sent? Charity?"

Rossi, listening with hand over ear, smiled in acquiescence. "That was it! I give him the money for the business. After that I owe him nothing. He tell me—through a friend!—that he want the money. Very well; I send it. Every year I send it!"

Travers appeared satisfied. He paused deliberately, to let the other wonder—as he must be wondering, desperately—just what was known and what was not.

"That was very good of you. But how do you account for this? When he died, he had in the bank *five thousand English pounds*! And the house he lived in was his! And everything in it!"

The other's face coloured. Surprise became blandness. Indignation followed.

"He cheat me, *signore*! As he did before, he deceive me! He take my money—" A sudden pause. His expression changed again. "But, of course, if he take my money, he will wish to give it back. That is why he leave me the papers—is it not?"

His look was anxious. Travers pursed his lips and tapped the envelope.

"What exactly do you expect these papers to be?" Rossi shrugged his shoulders.

"Who knows? Perhaps the money I give him. Perhaps the— what you call—testament, so that I may get the money he leave when he die. Is it not?"

Travers nodded non-committally, then went a step further.

"Just another question or two before I hand over these papers. Will you tell me what Mr. Rook actually *did* in England? What was his trade—or profession—before he went with you to Rome?"

"Ah! His trade?" He frowned, hesitated, stammered something unintelligible, and looked like losing his head completely. Then he sighed. He leaned forward, voice lowered. "That I promise not to tell! It is secret. It is not good that I tell!"

Travers leaned forward too. "You mean—the police might have done something, if they'd known what his business was?"

Rossi's face was all smiles.

"That is so! It is his business—and not mine. I tell him he is very foolish, but he do as he like. I say nothing. He is my friend. If the *polizia* discover, then—" He shrugged again. Then a smile. "That is perhaps why he leave me the papers!"

"Hm!" said Travers. "Perhaps it was . . . You knew, of course, that he was married?"

Rossi's eyes narrowed. His look was as wary as if watching a rattlesnake.

"You say . . . married?"

"You didn't know it?"

"No! I know nothing!" His face brightened. "As I tell you, he is very secretive. He do things and say nothing not to me, his friend. He deceive everybody."

"But you knew his housekeeper!"

"Housekeeper." He pronounced the word as if it were unfamiliar. "I do not understand."

"Never mind!" said Travers, and let it go at that. "Just one thing, and we've finished. Do you, by any chance, know anybody by the name of Lucia?"

The look was apprehensive. He moistened his lips, then nodded. "Lucia! That is a common name. Even my daughter—she is Lucia!"

Travers rose to his feet, holding the envelope. Rossi rose too.

"Signor Rossi, you have convinced me that you are the one to whom these papers should be handed. As a last matter of form, may I ask you the question again. You are Cesare Rossi?"

The smile, this time, was immense and ingratiating. "But of course. I tell you. I show you I am Cesare Rossi! In Italy, everybody know I am Cesare Rossi!"

"That," smiled Travers, "is undoubtedly true. But this is not Italy." He held the envelope tantalisingly just out of the reach of Rossi's hand. "Will you *swear* to me you are Cesare Rossi?"

"But I tell you I am Cesare Rossi!" He lugged out again that fistful of documents. "All these I show you. You see. Here is the passport. And the photograph! Everything you see!" His eagerness was almost desperate. "I know that," said Travers patiently. "All I'm asking you to do is to swear you are Cesare Rossi."

The other shrugged his shoulders.

"Then, if you wish it, *signore*, I will swear. I *am* Cesare Rossi!"

The door opened. Wharton coughed sharply as he came forward.

"So you *are* Cesare Rossi!"

Rossi whipped round. Beside the six foot of Wharton he looked as insignificant a person as one could meet. Then he turned to Travers.

"This man . . . who is he? You tell me it is secret!"

The room was none too warm but Travers saw the perspiration standing on his forehead. He flashed another look at both, then, with a quickness amazing in one of his years, darted for his hat and coat that lay on the chest just inside the door* As he grabbed them, the outer door opened, and there stood Wharton's constable. Franklin's head rolled the other way and his eyes opened. Then, as Rossi stood there, fingering his hat and looking this way and that, Wharton moved over and gripped him by the shoulder.

"Cesare Rossi! I arrest you on a charge of conspiracy with intent to defraud. You are not obliged to say anything in answer to the charge, but whatever you say will be taken down in writing and may be given in evidence."

Wharton got that piece of officialdom reeled off, and waited. Rossi looked scared out of his wits. As he gestured, Wharton held him in what was almost a wriggle. The others watched as you watch a thrush with a snail.

"But I do nothing, *signore*! I come here for some papers! I do nothing—nothing at all! I harm nobody!"

"I'm not talking about what you're doing now," said Wharton magisterially. "Have you ever heard about a thing that used to be called 'refuge'? How, if you committed a crime, you could go to a church—or some place like that—and the law couldn't touch you?"

If Rossi knew, he showed no sign of it.

"Well, that's what used to happen. But as soon as he put his nose outside that church door . . . *they got him!* You went into refuge." He gripped his other shoulder and pulled him round till their faces were almost touching. "You went where the law couldn't touch you . . . nine years ago. Now you've put your nose outside—*and we've got you!*" He stared at him till he cringed away, then nodded over to the constable. "Put 'em on him! Round the arm of that chair!" He watched while it was done, then, "Go into the other room, and wait."

Wharton came over. "You stay there a bit, Rossi, till I've finished!" Then followed a sample of pure Wharton. With extraordinary deliberation he removed his overcoat, folded it and laid it on the chest. Next he got his pipe well alight, pulled out his notebook and adjusted his glasses. Then he waved to Travers from the chair that faced Rossi.

"If you ask me, I think I'll have just a spot." Travers poured it out and squirted the syphon. "Now," said Wharton, "let's gather round and be friendly. I'm going to tell you a story—and I'm going to tell it very slowly so that Mr. Rossi here can follow every word."

He peered at Rossi over his spectacles. Rossi watched, and said nothing.

CHAPTER XIX
ROSSI TALKS

"WE'LL GO BACK about nine years," said Wharton, "and as soon as I open my mouth and say one thing, two people in this room will wonder why they didn't think of it. I refer to the Consolidated Sardinian Investment Corporation and its allied Companies—and what was known as the Penfold crash. I was absent myself most of the time, though I knew a good deal about it; a lot more, 1 might say, than a few of those who took part in it. You remember it, Mr. Travers? . . . I thought somehow you would! Your father will remember it too."

He paused to light his pipe which had already gone out.

"In spite of that, I'd like you to bear with me while I go back and re-traverse the ground. Big financial swindles we're all familiar with. The public have short memories. No sooner do we get one gang of financial jugglers locked up than the public are clamouring to be allowed to hand over their money to the next lot. Perhaps they're like me—not sufficiently conversant with the tricks of the financial trade. I, for instance, can't explain all the details of this particular swindle. The Sardinian Investment Corporation was the parent Company, and it looked pretty good to post-war investors. Dividends on the Ordinary Shares for the two years it lasted, were fifteen and twenty per cent. Then it threw out two off-shoots—Italian Consolidated and the Penfold Investment Trust. Within a day or two of the collapse, all these Companies stood apparently as solid as rocks. Penfold was Managing Director; Hoggin and Lewissohn were Directors, and Chester Ross was Secretary.

"We'll have a look at three of 'em; just a short look—past, present and future. Penfold was the leading spirit. He was a tall, grim-looking man; an Englishman who'd been in the States for some years and had a reputation of sorts on Wall Street, in spite of the shady affair that was responsible for his departure. Hoggin—short and thick-set—was a financial parvenu who began life as a street hawker. He was Penfold's brother- in-law. Lewissohn, clever enough to dodge everything except the law, was an outside broker to begin with, till he joined in with the other two. The fourth man—Ross—was the only first-class brain of the lot. It was a private Company—really himself—that was the germ of the original Sardinian Corporation. Naturally he was an Italian. His name was really Cesare Rossi!"

Rossi gave no sign he had even heard. Wharton's English must in any case have been beyond him. Wharton lighted his pipe for the third time.

"Well, gentlemen, as I was saying; until a few days before the crash, nothing was known. Then rumours got about, principally because of the desperate efforts of Penfold to raise money to stave off the crash. Even then—mind you—they were only rumours. When the crash did come, and the tremendous effect of it was realised, it came like a thunderclap. Still, that's nothing to do with it; the point is that during the early afternoon, Scotland Yard received an anonymous communication, giving fairly full details of how things stood, and saying that Penfold and Hoggin were crossing by the night boat from Harwich, and Lewissohn and Rossi from Southampton to Havre. It was decided to act—other precautions having been taken—and it all proved to be correct. Penfold and Hoggin were arrested at Harwich, and Lewissohn at Southampton; all three with enough cash and securities to keep them in clover for the rest of their lives. *But Rossi wasn't there!* No doubt it was he who wrote the letter. While we were waiting for the other three, he'd calmly crossed from Dover. All we definitely knew was that next day he crossed over the Italian border from Switzerland, accompanied by his little daughter. You see, gentlemen, as I said—Rossi had a first-class brain. Once home he was safe. He knew—among other things—that *Italy does not extradite her nationals!*"

He looked round at them, over his spectacles.

"Yes, but you say, we know Italy has no extradition of her own nationals, hut—she tries them in her own courts! Why wasn't application made, and evidence forwarded from the trial of the other three? Well, all that was done. Only, Rossi was remarkably lucky. The government who received our application was on its last legs. It had enough to do to fight its own battles. And when it ended, it wasn't the end of a government; it was the end of a regime! There were the struggles between the Communist and Fascist parties going on for months. Rossi, as he told us, knowing on which side his bread was buttered, made himself a pretty prominent Fascist in his own district. Then, when everything did seem to be over, and we made a new application two years later, it was talked out and corresponded out till it fizzled out. And there was Rossi, set up for life and safe as houses—so long as he didn't set foot outside his refuge.

"Meanwhile, what had happened in England? Well, when things were finally cleared up, and what we might call the smoke of battle died away, Penfold got eleven years and Hoggin ten. Lewissohn got off with nine. The judge openly in court regretted that the fourth man—Rossi—wasn't lined up with them in the dock. The investors got ninepence in the pound. For three months it was a sensation. Six months later, if you had mentioned the word 'Penfold,' people would have said, 'Penfold? Haven't I heard that name somewhere?' That may have been one reason why the charge against Rossi was allowed to fizzle out. Perhaps Rossi—his countrymen will forgive me the libel—invested some of his money in laying the dust over there."

He knocked out his pipe on the grate, stowed it away in his pocket, then turned full face to Rossi for the first time.

"Eleven years Penfold; ten years Hoggin; nine years Lewissohn. I wonder what Rossi would have got?" He shrugged his shoulders. "Some said twelve years—some ten. Well, that problem will soon be solved. What do you think yourself?" As he asked the question, he got up and moved across to rap at the door. The constable came in at once.

"Nothing to say, Mr. Rossi? Nothing at all . . . before we take you away?" Rossi suddenly came to life. As he tugged at the handcuffs he began to scream; or was it more like a frenzied series of appeals in which nothing was distinguishable but his own name?

"What's he say?" asked Wharton, as the policeman pushed him back in the chair and held his collar. Franklin got out of the chair, took off his wig, and screwed up his face as he skinned off the disguise. As he looked at him the Italian drew back further into the chair.

"He says he isn't *Cesare* Rossi; he's *Carlo* Rossi!"

"Does he!" said Wharton. "Tell him to talk English!" He thrust his chin almost into Rossi's face, and the chair shot back till the constable braced his knee against it. "What's that you say? Didn't I hear you swear you were Cesare Rossi?"

The other began a gesture which the handcuffs checked.

"Take them off him!" snapped Wharton. "Then stand outside that door!"

Rossi rubbed his wrists and shot a look, first at one, then at the other, from under his eyebrows. Wharton nodded over to Franklin.

"Tell him who I am—in his own lingo. And tell him all over again what's waiting for him!" Then a hoarse whisper. "Pile it on!"

Franklin did his best—and levelled old scores in the process. Travers caught a word or two now and again, but Wharton understood nothing. But he kept up a nodding accompaniment. Rossi still seemed to be protesting violently.

"What's wrong with him?" broke in Wharton.

"He insists he's not Cesare Rossi. He swears he's Carlo Rossi!"

"Well, what's he got to grumble at?" asked Wharton curtly. "He came here to collect papers in the name of Cesare Rossi. He's arrested for false pretences. What more does he want?"

Franklin was puzzled. He caught the irony, but he didn't see what Wharton was driving at.

"Yes, but I've told him—and so have you—what he's to expect as *Cesare Rossi*. That's what's putting the fear of God up him. He says he can produce evidence that he's *Carlo*!"

"What sort of evidence?"

"Speak up!" ordered Franklin.

"Antonio Rugati—the Restaurant Rugati; he know me—" began Rossi.

"Where is it—this restaurant?"

"Latimer Street—"

"Shut up!" hollered Wharton. "Mr. Travers, may I ring down to your porter?"

Travers did it for him. In three minutes, two newcomers were entering—Norris and a stenographer. The former had hardly got inside when he was off again, bound for Latimer Street in search of Rugati. The stenographer was told to await instructions.

"Now!" announced Wharton, "we'll see what we *shall* see! Give him the papers, Mr. Travers, and see what he makes of 'em!"

Travers didn't look very happy over it. His speech was rather a spluttering one.

"I'd like you to know, Mr. Rossi, that these papers are perfectly—er—genuine; I mean, they really were given me by Mr. Rook to hand over to—er—somebody. You see, he didn't tell me definitely whom they were for." He indicated the title page. "You do live at a place with—er—Seven Cypresses, don't you!"

There was never a man who looked more genuinely perplexed than Rossi when he'd done fingering those sheets of manuscript paper. And he wasn't acting: Wharton knew that. After the first quick inspection, he looked up as if to speak; then he had another try, then looked up again. It was Travers he appealed to—the one who'd spoken to him as if Carlo Rossi were an equal. That small courtesy seemed to have washed out, for a moment, the memory of the treachery that had lured him into a trap.

"But, *signore*; I know nothing of this! I do not understand."

"Neither do I!" Travers told him. "What I said to you, is correct. These are all the papers I was given by Mr. Rook. If you want me to swear it, I'll do so on anything you like."

Rossi shook his head bewilderedly.

"Take your time!" said Wharton, in a voice that must have struck Rossi as amazingly human. "Have a good look at 'em! See if they're any good to you." He turned his back on the Italian and waved his hand to the chairs. "Let's sit down for a bit and wait for this other chap!"

"If you'll excuse me a moment," said Franklin, "I think I'll slip upstairs and get some of this grease off my face," and off he went. Wharton drew in to the fire, had another spot of whisky and best part of a pipe before he looked at his watch—and Rossi. "Find anything out?"

The Italian shook his head and shrugged his shoulders with a hopeless sort of grimace.

"No, *signore*. To me it is nothing. I do not understand."

Wharton nodded as he took the papers back. He slipped them into the envelope and handed it to Travers. But he couldn't resist a last word.

"Nothing, as you say. Nothing but music paper! *Music!* You've dug a pit and fallen clean in it! That's what the love of money led you into. And you're not the first who's made himself that kind of a fool—and you won't be the last!"

A few moments later, the lift was heard, then Norris's voice in the corridor. Wharton hopped up.

"I'll see this Rugati alone, if you don't mind us making a convenience of your house. You people stay here with Rossi—and don't let him talk."

Rossi still lay back in his chair, done to the world and scared as badly as a man could be. With his handkerchief he kept up a series of moppings. Travers felt sorry for him in a way, and unobtrusively poured him out a drink. Rossi took it with some show of gratitude. Franklin, who'd got back just ahead of Norris, thought that rather unwise.

"I don't think I'd have done that if I'd been you. Give that sort of man an inch and he'll do you down for ten miles."

Travers smiled. "I don't think he'll do Wharton down!"

Franklin grimaced. "Wharton's having the time of his life! He's got hold of a chap who knows nothing about the new rulings on evidence. He'll take out Rossi's liver and slide on it!"

"Wonder how long he'll be?" whispered Travers.

As it happened, he wasn't more than five minutes. When he did come back, Rugati was with him—a typical restaurant proprietor; fattish, oleaginous, and with jet black hair plastered down. His huge moustache straggled all over a purple jowl, and as he fingered nervously the felt hat his damp hands were twirling, he kept his eyes well out of the way of Rossi.

"You sit there, please," said Wharton, then beckoned to the stenographer. "Get ready, Charles! Mr. Franklin, you tell him in Italian the consequences of not keeping to the truth."

Even then, Wharton had to add his own version.

"Now, Rossi, I'm going to ask you to make a statement. Later on, I'm going to ask you some questions. If you want to spare yourself a great deal of trouble, now's your chance." He nodded knowingly as he drew his chair up within a yard. "And if you try to put a lie over on me, God help you! Now then; get on with it!"

Rossi seemed ready enough; the trouble was he didn't know where to begin. After half a dozen false starts, Wharton was getting rather annoyed.

"Catechise him!" suggested Franklin, as much for his own benefit as that of anybody else. Like Travers, he was seeing just enough to make the whole thing inexplicable.

"What relation were you to the man called Rook?" began Wharton, consulting Franklin's manuscript.

"His brother . . . by the father."

"Half-brother, you mean?"

"Yes, *signore*; his half-brother."

"Keep off the '*signore*'!" snapped Wharton, "and keep to the facts. You were his half-brother. Which was the older?"

"I was the older."

"Then when your mother—who was a Guardini—died, and your father married again, this half-brother of yours—Cesare by name—was no relation of the Guardinis."

"That is so."

"What was his wife's name?"

"Lucia. Lucia Guardini."

"And her elder sister was Maria Guardini?"

"That is right, *signore*. That is right!" said Rossi, and grovelled.

That was the way things came out, sentence by sentence. Cesare Rossi—the real Cesare Rossi—had two passions; one for music and the other for money. He was a born financier, as Emilio Guardini certainly knew when he took him into his business and left him a controlling interest at his death. His father was Manuelo Rossi, the pianist, whose name is still remembered by the very, very old; and his mother was Lucy Rowlands—almost the first of that galaxy of concert singers whose names are still reverenced by our grandmothers.

As for the rise of Cesare Rossi to the Secretaryship of the Sardinian Investment Corporation, that seemed to have been one of those inevitable things. Meanwhile Carlo—the elder brother—had expressed a distaste for his grandfather's business, and when it was proposed that he should go to Sardinia and take over certain duties, he ran away to London instead. There he graduated from waiter to the ownership of the restaurant that now bore the name of Rugati. Cesare acknowledged him, but very distantly. St. James's Square, in other words, was careful not to hobnob with Latimer Street, though aware of its existence.

Paris was really the home of Cesare and his wife, before they moved to Beaconcross, where Lucia's child was to be born. As for secrecy, that was obvious. Cesare knew which way the wind was blowing, even if other cheeks than his own were puffing the sails of the Sardinian Corporation. But his plans were matured long beforehand. The existence of that house at Beacon- cross was to be known to none of his colleagues. It was not known that his wife was in England. When the time came to make a quick getaway, the police should have himself to trace—not two or more others who would betray the road by their very existence.

The trouble was that things happened very differently. The crisis was not anticipated till well after the birth of Lucia's baby. When it did come, it came at a terrible time; when that deplorable accident occurred and she was desperately ill. He had never intended to go to Italy himself, in any case. One of the South American States would almost certainly have been his place of refuge! Indeed if he had not been so dangerously uxorious, he would have sent his wife and her sister there to await his arrival. As things turned out, he was in a trap. Once abroad himself, he was there for good. If his wife ultimately followed, she might be traced and his own refuge revealed. If he dared to communicate with her, the correspondence might be opened by the police. But a way had to be found out—and he found it.

"He come to me one night, very secret," was Carlo's version. "He do not tell me why, till I tell him I know; that is, some of it I know. Then it is all arranged. He give me money. I am to go to Italy, and because neither of us go there for years and we are not well-known, I am to shave off my beard and be Cesare. I am to go to the Villa Guardini and stay there. Also he give me a letter from my cousin Maria, which say I am master there. All that is to lure the English police till his wife is better and he can get away himself—somewhere else. So I agree. He is my half-brother. The Signor Rugati is to have the restaurant, where he is head-waiter, and it is him who take the letters."

"A beautiful scheme!—especially for you," said Wharton. "If you were challenged as Cesare, all you had to do was to say you weren't—and prove it. The affair then became merely one of false papers, and that wouldn't take much squaring . . . I suppose he sent you more money, from time to time?"

"A little . . . very little."

"Hm!" He nodded over to the others. "I guess he bled him nearly white! Go on, Rossi. What happened then?"

Nothing did happen—at least to himself—that he'd admit. What happened to Cesare was another story. He remained with his wife till her death, and by this time he probably realised that he'd put himself into the hands of a man who proposed to make good use of the situation. Cesare, of course, was fortunate in one way.

Like Franklin, it was immaterial to him which language he spoke—his father's or his mother's. But there was a new danger threatening. He had to twist and double and throw off the scent those who in a few years would be on his traces. Lewissohn was out first, and he started the hunt. He hunted out the man he thought was Cesare. From him he forced the address of Rugati, though that turned out to be useless since Rugati had no idea of Cesare's whereabouts. All he did betray was that Cesare called each summer. But he swore that when Cesare did come, he had not betrayed him to Lewissohn. If Lewissohn traced Cesare from that next visit to town, Rugati didn't help—and Wharton believed him.

Meanwhile, there was Carlo, safe as a church and flourishing—as Wharton put it—like the green bay tree; and thanks to circumstances which nobody could have foreseen when he took what little risk there was. And there ended the story; at least, it was all that Wharton troubled for the moment to elicit. He sat for quite a good while, thinking things over, before he turned round again to face Rossi.

"That's all you have to say?"

Rossi made a gesture of supreme abnegation.

"Nothing I keep back! Everything I tell you! Everything!"

Wharton turned to Franklin. "Tell him if he doesn't come across, I'll have the handcuffs on him again in a couple of shakes!"

Rossi understood well enough. His shoulders heaved with the immensity of the gesture.

"It is not necessary that you do that. I tell you the truth. Everything I tell you, even when it do me harm!"

Wharton got to his feet and glared. "My God! if the law allowed me to use such language, I'd twist your damn neck!" He paused, then his tone suddenly altered. It became positively genial, though little to the point.

"However—you're his heir, aren't you? His *heir*! You get his money!"

Rossi shot a suspicious look, and no wonder. Wharton was smiling! Rossi smiled too—very warily.

"I am his half-brother. There is nobody else."

"And what about his daughter?" Wharton glared again, then nodded over to Norris. "Get 'em on him—and put him inside!"

That was enough. The story—or most of it—came out with such volubility that Wharton had to put the brake on. Lucia—Cesare's daughter—had shown as a tiny child such an aptitude for music that her father was enraptured. At the time when her mother was expecting another child, her own musical education had begun, and during her mother's absence for what was thought to be merely a few months, it was considered advisable that she should remain in Paris, with friends. It had been Cesare's idea that she should go to the Villa Guardini with her uncle, till such time as he could join them. But what Carlo had told her was that her father was dead, and that he was now to be her father.

"You were a far-seeing man!" said Wharton. "And you sent photos every year—and requests for more money, for her musical education—and other things?" Rossi shrugged ingratiatingly.

"And you told him his daughter was doing marvellously at music? She played the piano marvellously—like himself. And you never answered his questions as to why she didn't write a letter herself; you put him off with excuses—danger and so on! . . . Do you hear? Answer!"

Rossi nodded.

"And you said that if either he or Maria Guardini ever dared to set foot out of England, you'd betray him to the English police? . . . Look me straight in the face! Isn't that what you did?"

Rossi hesitated—looked—then thought better of it. Wharton smiled contemptuously, then turned to the others. He spoke in a sort of aside, as if in some miraculous manner Rossi was no longer able to understand English.

"That's why that old woman sacrificed herself! That's why she stood by Rook and remained in England! I should say he kept him on the end of a string. He'd say that all the time he had the pair of them watched. Perhaps he'd hint that by that time the following year, everything would be cleared up and they might both return to Italy. Then he'd put it off again." He chuckled. "I'll bet he was scared when Lewissohn turned up that time! And

I'll bet Lewissohn made him cough up a nice subscription by way of blackmail. It was he who financed Lewissohn—though he didn't know why!" The thought seemed to please him immensely. Then he sobered up. "However—I'll get it all out of him if I have to twist his scraggy neck!"

He whipped round to Rossi and gave another glare.

"So that's what you wrote!"

Rossi shivered, like a rabbit in front of a stoat; then turned his eyes away.

"That's good enough, Charles!" said Wharton unblushingly. "Put it all down in the form of a statement!" He nodded down at Rossi. "How'll you have it read to you? English, or Italian—or both?"

Franklin repeated, and offered advice. Wharton seemed indifferent till the whole thing was over, then nodded to Norris to take charge.

"Would you mind ringing down to your porter, Mr. Travers, to ask for a taxi to be ready? And if I might use your desk for a minute or two."

They watched while he wrote away—orders for Norris apparently, at least Norris got them. Then Rossi was taken off; chattering and sweating and gesticulating; his voice and Norris's and the constable's sounding like a street fight as they waited for the lift. Travers could catch two words that Rossi kept harping on—*Ambasciata . . . rivolgero! . . . Ambasciata . . . rivolgero!*

"What's that he keeps hollering?" he asked Franklin.

"He says he's going to appeal to the Ambassador," explained Franklin.

"Is he!" grunted Wharton. "Well, I wish him luck!" Then the apologetic cough from the other side of the room reminded him of somebody else who had to be settled with, and he went over to Rugati who was looking as comfortable as if a tarantula were crawling along his spine.

"I take your word for it," said Wharton, "that you knew nothing about why Rossi handed over the restaurant to you. I suppose he made you pay for it . . . through the nose?"

Rugati nodded, most emphatically.

"So I guessed. Well, we know where to find you if we want you!" Out shot his hand, which Rugati took reverently. "Thank you for coming along. Mind you!—not a word to a living soul, or—" A wagging finger hinted the consequences.

CHAPTER XX
DEAD MAN'S MUSIC

WHARTON SAT in an attitude that could reasonably have been described as Johnsonian; entirely surrounded by Travers and Franklin and the table with the tray of sandwiches that Palmer had brought in, and the smaller table with decanter and its own attendant syphon. Five minutes before, he had had to be enticed to remain; now he seemed settled for the rest of the evening, and Travers was just about to take advantage of a moment when he was in the act of finishing a chuckle.

"Tell me, George! When you came in here tonight, did you know exactly what was going to happen? I mean, all about Rossi—and Rook?"

"Well," began Wharton heavily

Franklin laughed. "Come on, George! We're all friends here. No need to temporise!"

"Then . . . I did!" said Wharton. "You won't let me be modest when I want to. I knew dead men don't come to life, though, mind you"—and he swivelled his gaze on Travers—"we all know that *one man may go up and another come down!* . . . I thought that'd amuse you! Still, I've got nothing to boast about. It's the worst show I ever put up in my life. If a man of mine had made such a mess of a job, I'd have had the coat off his back!"

"Nonsense, George!" began Franklin.

Wharton looked at him over the top of his antiquated spectacles.

"Let me tell you a few things. Mind you, I'm not altogether to blame. I wasn't in England when the Penfold crash occurred and I didn't come into personal contact with any of the principals. Also we made the perfectly reasonable mistake of working on a false assumption; that because Rook—I'll call him that or I shall get muddled up with Rossi—because Rook began his—er—hidden life at Beaconcross at a certain time, the causes that led to it must have existed *before* that time. We weren't to know that for once in a lifetime, effect preceded cause. That's why most of our researches gave no result.

"Also, of course, the combination we were looking for was all wrong—or we made it wrong. Penfold shouldn't have been connected with America at all. Rook—whose name of Chester Ross never appeared at all—was really an Italian. The man with the squint, when he did turn up, was a Jew after all. Also you may not know how well Rook had his tracks concealed. Even the address he used in London for communicating with the house agents in Beaconcross, was a dud as far as we were concerned."

Travers passed the plate of sandwiches, and looked over at Franklin.

"Well, we'll overlook it this time, George; but don't let it happen again. We think you've done wonders!"

"Of course he has!" chimed in Franklin. "Only, he's the best grumbler I ever ran up against. He loves it!"

"Wait a minute now!" said Wharton. "Shall I tell you some of the things that stuck out as big as a haystack? He lugged out his notebook, wetted his finger copiously and found the place. "Now then! Take that disguising of Rook. Mr. Travers was right . . . in a sense. It was disguising a disguise. But why did they disguise at all? So as to keep *themselves* out of it! They had to alter the face so that the man shouldn't be identified with Claude Rook of Steyvenning, and they had to alter it so that he shouldn't be recognised as Chester Ross. Chester Ross wasn't all that Mr. Travers so poetically surmised; I mean he wasn't a bishop or a Cabinet Minister. All the same, once we knew he was Chester Ross, then we knew who they were! . . . I submit that we ought to have gathered more from that than we did.

"Then Mr. Travers said Penfold couldn't drive a car very well. We assumed that was due to change of drive. But all of it wasn't. Some of it might have been due to the fact that he hadn't driven a car at all for nine years. And why not? Where had he been? . . .

In jail, of course! As a matter of interest, you might like to know that he'd been out exactly ten days!

"Then something else should have proved the same thing. The man with the squint; why was there such a gap between the visit he paid to Tiverton, and the visit Penfold and Hoggin paid to Mill House? At Tiverton he asked about the piano. He therefore had means of tracing Rook. He must have run him down long before those other two turned up. Then why the gap? Surely *not* that he hadn't his information, but that he was waiting till his customers came out of jail!"

"Dash it all, George!" broke in Franklin. "That wouldn't have been deduction; that'd have been a revelation!"

"Oh no, it wouldn't!—if you'll let me finish. Other things have to be taken into consideration. What about the lack of fingerprints, for instance, at Frenchman's Rise and Mill House? As I pointed out to Mr. Travers; if he or I wanted to commit a crime, we shouldn't wait till gloves were available. There's no record of *us*!"

"Do you know, I can see some things too," said Travers. "Do you remember how he got me to talk about the Stock Exchange, and then showed ignorance that would have disgraced a navvy?" He shook his head slowly. "I couldn't help thinking of something while George was talking. You two won't agree with me, but I'm sorry—in a way—for Rook!"

Franklin nodded over at Wharton.

"What I was telling him this morning, George. He's not a detective; he's a court missionary!"

"Well, he may be right!" Wharton pronounced magisterially. "I haven't got a lot of sympathy for him myself, but I'd rather have him than Rossi."

"Pardon me!" interrupted Travers. "Perhaps you don't understand my point of view. We don't know precisely *why* Rook betrayed the other three. He may have been justified. He may have heard them planning to do the same to him—to make their getaway with the—er—boodle, and leave him to nurse the baby. And something else. We don't know if the money he took himself was other people's or merely represented his private and realised assets, unconnected with the companies with which he was associated."

Wharton was quite tickled with that. He winked over at Franklin.

Mr. Travers, you'd be a most excellent fellow to have alongside one at Judgment Day! . . . However, if your point is that Rossi was the bigger rascal, then I agree. He even got hold of that girl as a hold over Rook—and in expectation of what she'd one day get. And I should say the only reason he allowed her to keep up her music was that he intended to exploit her talents . . . And he was a blackmailer. And he terrorised that poor old woman, so as to continue in possession of that Guardini property . . . By the way, I mustn't forget to ask him where that girl is."

Franklin moved across to the table and began to pour himself another drink.

"I asked him that myself . . . She's in Rome, at the moment . . . You'll have to get the exact address." He changed the subject. "And what's going to happen about the others?"

"You mean ultimately? . . . Well, Lewissohn might get twelve months and he might wriggle clear. The other two'll be lucky to get off with ten years—depends what they're charged with. Rossi ought to get a warm dose too."

"Then what about the daughter?"

"Bit too early to ask that," said Wharton. "That's going to be very involved and it won't be me who handles it. Mind you, I think she ought to get the Guardini property, whatever else she doesn't get."

"And what do you mean by that, George?" asked Travers.

"Well, that five thousand, for instance. The creditors of the Penfold Trusts will get that . . . most likely." Travers laughed. "Most likely, is good, George! If Italian lawyers are like their English brethren, then you and I know who's going to get it. But, didn't I understand you to say that Rossi had bled Rook white?—or words to that effect?"

"That's right!" He smiled tolerantly. "Why?"

"Well, there was that five thousand deposit in the Steyvenning bank, for one thing—"

"Precisely what I said! That was a final, untouchable reserve!"

"I know!" persisted Travers. "But surely we still proved that he had some hundred pound notes. Didn't we agree that the man we disturbed that night—Hoggin probably—was searching for something; something which we now know could only have been money—Rook's share of the swag, shall we say? Isn't that why Lewissohn bought the house—or its contents—as an investment, to re-sell to the other two?"

"Wait a minute!" said Franklin. "There's a fallacy there. Even according to your own argument, they only thought there was a cache; they didn't *know* it!" Wharton grunted approval.

"You take my word for it that Rook had no money left except that reserve. That's why he didn't cut and run again. He couldn't afford to . . . Still, if you insist that he did have some hoard or other, I'll tell you where I think it was."

"I'll buy it!" said Franklin. "Where?"

"In the piano! That's the explanation of all the mysteries during Mr. Travers' visit to Mill House. That's why there was all that talk about music. That's why Rook gave him the manuscript—*Music* manuscript, mark you!—as a continual reminder. That's why most of the music hadn't any sense—any *Musical* sense! so that Mr. Travers might know it had some other sense, I mean a figurative one. The front page was merely a wrapper!"

"Then why the title, containing the address?" Wharton smiled. "Well, not to find Rossi, but to find Rook's daughter—of whom Rossi had written such glowing accounts, as regards her musical progress. *She'd* inherit the piano. *She'd* find the cache—if there was one!"

"Bravo!" said Franklin. "I call that a thundering good explanation, George. It's sheer hard logic!"

Travers took Wharton's glass and poured the General out another tot. He seemed mightily amused.

"When the unholy alliance has finished, I'd like to say something."

"It's your own house!" chuckled Wharton. "We can't very well stop you."

"Well, that's something," said Travers. "But about this theory that's so logical. Let's work it out lucidly—and sanely. Rook is dead, and I discover he wants that manuscript to go to his daughter. I know that because he let it slip when I was with him, the last time I saw him alive. 'She' he began, and then stopped short. And he'd already told me it wasn't for Mrs. Fletcher. Very well then; I know it's for the daughter, and the title page of the manuscript tells me where to find her. I go along, piano and all, and knock at the door. 'Ah! good morning, Miss Rook!' I say. 'I've come from your dearest relative—probably your father—to tell you he's dead. All he left you was this manuscript—and this piano, of which he was very fond. That's all. Thanks very much—and good morning!' . . . Now then; what use is that manuscript to her?"

"A souvenir of her father!" said Wharton at once. "All right! We'll say it was a souvenir. But how on earth is she to know she's to pull all the guts out of that piano? It could only be concealed in the woodwork; I mean to say it couldn't be visible in those places one sees when one removes the front in the ordinary way . . . Then how's she to know? *I* couldn't have told her. There's nothing in the manuscript about it! Now, if that manuscript had been entitled—The Old Piano Leg—there'd have been some sense!"

He looked round at the pair of them. Franklin was trying to look thoughtful. Wharton began to stoke his pipe. Then the General put up the white flag.

"Well, I've always got one suggestion for a man who knocks over my theory. Let him produce a better one himself!"

"Splendid!" said Travers, and pushed the bell. "If you've finished with the food part of it, Palmer can tidy up. Then we'll push this table back and gather round in comfort. Nothing in the way—so to speak!"

* * * * * * *

"Of course," said Travers, "when I said I'd accept your challenge, George, it was implicitly understood that you're both to take me seriously. Tell me! You believed Rook was mad?"

"Didn't *you*?"

"Perhaps I did—right up to last Sunday. Now I know he wasn't. He was scared, warped, nervy; he couldn't be anything else with that load of troubles on his back. But he wasn't insane. He was clinging on to sanity like grim death. Sometimes he almost slipped. He did eccentric things—but he thought he knew why he did them. You'll take my word for that?"

"If you can prove it—yes!"

"Good! Now let's try to see what was in Rook's mind when he wrote to Durangos. Rossi had written him that Lucia was keeping up her English—as he wished. If you question Rossi, I'm sure you'll find that's so. Rook could assume therefore that she knew English as you and I do; the *feeling* of it, that is. He therefore laid his plans accordingly. He wrote to Durangos and asked for a certain kind of man to be sent. I was the one, and I happened to fit in with his ideas of a person who was sufficiently intelligent and trustworthy to be confided in. He thought I had an active brain—and he decided that I was honourable. Very well then Lucia and I were to be complementary. My quickness of mind and her knowledge of music were to operate together. If her English was sufficiently good, she might even function without me; though Rook was doubtful if I could function without *her*. That brings me to the third factor—Mrs. Fletcher . . . Everything clear so far?"

"As mud!" That was Franklin.

"Carry on!" said Wharton laconically.

"Now, what had Rook to expect when his former associates came out of jail? Certainly that if they discovered him, they'd strip him clean of what he possessed; not so much in revenge as to give them some or the comforts they'd been denied for a few years. It was up to Rook therefore, *if he had any money*, to put it where it couldn't be touched—as he did that untouchable reserve which was for Mrs. Fletcher. He'd tell Penfold and Hoggin that he hadn't any money; but he had to anticipate that they'd search the house—and himself. But *there's a point that I think we've missed altogether*. He must have expected the same betrayal; to be handed over to the police! But, once he was in jail, his expiation was over. He had nothing more to fear. And

Mrs. Fletcher had nothing to fear. She could return to Italy. But, you'll say, Rossi might have threatened that if she ever returned to Italy, he'd tell Lucia what her father really was. Well, even accept that. The fact remains that Mrs. Fletcher would have been free to move about in England. She could have come to see me, for instance. Very well then; if Lucia and I were to be the executives, she was to be the custodian!"

"Custodian of what?" asked Wharton.

"George!" said Travers solemnly, "I've got you just where I want you! There have been times when you've found it inexpedient—shall we say?—to divulge too much. That's the position I find myself in at this moment!"

Franklin roared. Wharton himself was almost as pleased.

"Having made that perfectly clear," went on Travers, "I have to add something. Mrs. Fletcher was the custodian; she was his sister-in-law; she was the woman who'd stood by him and saved his sanity. She had to be provided for. Hence what George so aptly called the untouchable reserve; that deposit in her name at the Steyvenning bank. But, knowing what we know now, and what Rook knew then, isn't it inconceivable that he should not have had a second untouchable reserve—*for his own daughter?*"

Franklin swivelled round in his chair. Wharton seemed to be less inattentive.

"After all, his daughter would need money. Her uncle had bled him white—but once Rook was in jail, Rossi's day was over. Maria Guardini would go to Italy, *or if anything happened to her, I should go to Italy*. She would assume charge of her niece. Then would come the enormous cost of the vital part of Lucia's musical education; and there'd have to be enough for a small income in addition. You see, don't you? that there had to be a second untouchable reserve!"

"Hm!" said Wharton. "Perhaps I do." Franklin sat biting his empty pipe. Travers drew up his long legs, sat up in the chair and hooked off his glasses.

"Continuing with Mrs. Fletcher. Why did she return to Mill House? We assumed she came to get news of Rook. Perhaps she did, but there was another reason, and how I know it I'll tell you later. At the same time we might argue out whether she ever slept in that shed, or not. Personally, I think it was a casual tramp who slept there and made the bed. I think she passed that one night out of doors somewhere. The doctor said she must have caught a frightful chill, and she'd been ill for hours. However, she came back and she got what she came for. That brings us at last to the music manuscript, and what was in it."

"Excuse me!" said Franklin, "but didn't I understand you to say that Maine said there was nothing in it?"

"Maine did say so," admitted Travers. "He said so because there was nothing for him to see. He tested the gibberish part, and that was—gibberish. If he'd had the front page—the vital page—even then he mightn't have seen it. Maine thinks in *sounds*, not notes! I tried that out on another expert only this morning. He saw the front page, played it over, commented on it—and saw nothing. He saw sounds—not notes . . . Now we'll come to sheer hard facts!"

"Thank God for that!" said Wharton fervently.

Travers laughed as he went over to the safe. Then, plumb in the centre of the round table he placed the Staffordshire figure.

"There you are, George! That's the centre-piece! That's what Mrs. Fletcher came back for!"

Wharton adjusted his glasses and had a good look at it. Franklin joined him and Travers watched them as they felt all round it and held it to the light for closer inspection.

"A clue, is it?" said Wharton.

"In a way—yes! It was a double insurance. As soon as I got back to town the morning I left Rook, he assumed I should guess what it really was. If anything happened to him, he knew—only, poor devil! he knew wrong—that I should act; provided always that anything had happened to Mrs. Fletcher at the same time. But Rook wasn't mad. He wasn't as eccentric as he seemed. He had to tell me so much and no more. He had to stop short of giving away his secret. He had to and emphasise falsely. He set me childish riddle after childish riddle—and rejoiced to find me answer them. Then at the very last moment—probably even on the recommendation of Mrs. Fletcher—he gave me a final riddle—

and he asked for no answer! That riddle was the manuscript. Shall I tell you the things I ought to have guessed?"

Wharton nodded.

"Well—the address. John guessed that. Then, what did he expressly tell me that tone-poem really was?"

"A theme with variations," said Wharton promptly, much to Travers' surprise.

"Exactly! The theme was the thing—and I didn't see it!"

"And I'm damned if I do either!" added Franklin. "You will, in a moment," Travers assured him. "One last fade-back, and it's all over . . . Recall that night I spent at Mill House, when Rook lacerated my nerves till I nearly shrieked. Do you remember how he harped on that figure? How he bellowed at Mrs. Fletcher, *who wasn't deaf at all*? How he kept mouthing those preposterous clichés—'Deaf to all entreaties,' 'Dead as mutton', and so on? How he hollered that that simpering female there was a baggage, and not a wench? . . . I ought to have seen the method behind that particular madness, but I didn't. . . . And now we come to yesterday afternoon. You're a wireless expert, George. Ever listen in to Radio-Paris on a Sunday, after lunch?"

"You mean the broadcast of records by the Decca Company?"

"That's right!"

"Well, yes . . . I do—if I'm in."

"Remember the piano tinkle after the announcement in each language?"

Wharton shifted uneasily in his seat. "Can't say I do. . . . Oh yes! I remember it."

"Know what it is?"

"Hm! . . . no!"

"I didn't know either," said Travers. "Palmer told me what it was—the notes D.E.C.C.A., played on the piano! If you'll allow me to be elementary—the scale is C.D.E.F.G.A.B.C. Within the bounds of these seven letters for our whole alphabet, we can write any words we like—and represent them by notes. That's what Rook did. His theme was a clue. The rest of the music was rubbish—to accentuate the importance of what wasn't."

He took a couple of sheets of paper from his pocket- book and passed one over to each. "There's the theme—announced first in the bass. We'll look at the treble first."

A D E A D D E A F B A G G A G E

"You see that, don't you? Now look at the same thing—the theme as first announced in the bass."

It doesn't matter two hoots about key or bars. The front page of that music is simply this—A DEAD DEAF BAGGAGE—then a connecting link of two bars, then A DEAD DEAF BAGGAGE. Now do you see it?"

"I see it all right," said Franklin. "But what about it?"

"We'll see that too," said Travers, and like a conjurer producing a rabbit, suddenly produced a hammer from the table drawer. He lifted the figure and balanced the hammer.

"My God! You're not going to break it!" exclaimed Franklin.

"Why not?"

"Isn't it valuable?"

"Ten pounds or so!" He paused as if something had only then struck him. "I say! Suppose I should be wrong! I mean, if I'm right, then George and his friends will have to pay; but if I'm wrong—"

"Pay what?" asked Wharton, not missing a word or a movement.

"The ten pounds!" said Travers. He gave Franklin a whimsical look, then raised the hammer. Before either could say another word, the figure was in a dozen pieces and Travers was letting the ruin fall from his fingers to the floor. With the fragments of earthenware lay scores of what looked like little spills of paper, rolled up tightly as pipe-cleaners. Wharton stared. Franklin drew back his chair as if they'd been scorpions. Travers gave a humorous sigh of relief.

"That's all right then!"

Wharton bent down and without too great a show of enthusiasm, picked one up. He nodded to Travers.

"You're right!"

The three of them got on their hands and knees. In a quarter of an hour the notes lay on the table, spread out in their piles; thirty-eight at a hundred pounds; forty-seven at twenty and thirty-four at ten.

"The second untouchable reserve!" said Wharton, as if accusing it. "And there's eighty pounds too much."

"That was because he had to *fill* the inside of the figure," said Travers. "He had to wedge in those notes till they were packed. He probably used the tens to pack with."

"Some job!" said Franklin. "Fancy winding that lot up and pushing them through that tiny blow-hole." A thought struck him. "But where's the rest?"

"What rest?"

"Well, he put this reserve aside for his daughter; but he had to have some on hand to live on. He couldn't have been stripped to the last cent!"

"Penfold and Hoggin got that," said Wharton. "He might have had it on him, in a belt. That may be why they were so anxious for Lewissohn to buy the house. They wouldn't believe that was all he had. Don't you think so, Mr. Travers?"

"Yes," said Travers. "I think perhaps that is so. But you'll probably get them to tell you that much."

Then, as he groped for his glasses, Travers seemed to become a different person—his own diffident self.

"I say! you people didn't mind my—er—going over all this sort of nonsense and—er—playing the fool—"

Wharton laughed and clapped him on the back.

"My dear fellow! It was most enjoyable! A beautiful piece of work!"

Travers smiled with relief.

"That's all right then! . . . I suppose you'll take that money with you; I mean your people will hold it pending a decision. And about that girl. You having her brought over here?"

"Most decidedly! She'll be our principal witness against Rossi."

"Seems a pity," said Travers reflectively. "You know, George, you ought to be able to keep her out of a garbage heap like this is going to be. . . . If you don't think me abominably rude, you and Franklin talk it over later on and see what can be done."

Wharton nodded graciously, and got to his feet. Travers pushed the bell. Wharton scored his last point.

"I can't help laughing at one thing. You'd have been up a gum-tree if there hadn't been anything inside that figure after all! I know you're one of the capitalist classes, but it'd have cost you a tenner!"

Travers smiled dryly.

"You see, George; the more I associate with you, the more prudent I learn to be. When you make a remark in public, you've generally made sure in private that you're right three times over. Working on that model, I couldn't be wrong."

Wharton chuckled. "And aren't I ever wrong?"

"You wouldn't have been in this case, George!" retorted Travers. "Before I said anything about the contents of that figure, I'd taken the precaution—earlier in the evening—of poking a skewer inside that blowhole. There it was; wedged tightly against something; something that didn't even rattle or rustle when I put my ear to it. However—"

They absolutely roared at that. The sight of Palmer in the background sobered them down. He cast an eye on the piles of paper, and Travers—still smiling—waved his hand.

"You're a student of music, Palmer. Something there might interest you!"

Palmer was puzzled but he came closer and had a look. Then he looked positively awed.

"Music, sir? . . . This is money!"

"Exactly! . . . Music! . . . Notes! . . . Notes of music!"

Palmer nodded deferentially.

"And might I ask what sort of music that would be, sir?"

"Dead man's music!" said Travers . . . and left it, for the moment, at that.

THE END

Lightning Source UK Ltd.
Milton Keynes UK
UKHW020653201218
334319UK00009B/168/P

9 781911 579755